Anna McCormac's heritage is Lakota Sioux and Irish. Raised in Santa Cruz, California, she immigrated to Sydney, Australia, where she practised herbal medicine, focused on antenatal and women's health. As a history enthusiast, Anna suspected that the "Witch craze" era held more than superstition, and began botanical and forensic investigations into the daily lives of people in the 17th century. She currently works as a registered Nurse, holding a Masters in Advanced Clinical Nursing, with a focus on vulnerable populations. Anna spends the rest of her hours working on her next books, and time with her husband and four grown children.

Dedicated to the memory of the senseless murder of countless woman accused of being Witches.

And to my mother, who always said I could.

Anna McCormac

THE BLIGHTED ROAD

A 17th-Century Tale of Plague and Witch-Hunts

AUSTIN MACAULEY PUBLISHERS™

LONDON * CAMBRIDGE * NEW YORK * SHARJAH

A CIP catalogue record for this title is available from the British Library.

ISBN 9781398420809 (Paperback)
ISBN 9781398420823 (ePub e-book)
ISBN 9781398420816 (Audiobook)

www.austinmacauley.com

First Published (2021)
Austin Macauley Publishers Ltd
25 Canada Square
Canary Wharf
London
E14 5LQ

I would like to thank the many authors who have written of life in the 17th century. They gave voice to my characters, and instilled textures, colours and vividness into *The Blighted Road*. I would like to thank Stephen Reid for tirelessly sourcing these elusive titles for me. I would also like to acknowledge and thank the undying encouragement and support of Deb, Nadia and Shannon; and my children, Rebecca, Lauren, India and Kyle for their patience and enthusiasm. And to my soulmate, my husband, Matthew; without him, I could never have found the courage to finish.

London, Summer 1666

The Watchman leaned into the Taylor's red-crossed door, vaguely aware of the lament from within. His presence ensured that plague victims stayed confined, while alerting clean residents that inside this house, death resides. After forty days, the doors would be unbarred and if the inhabitants still lived, then free they were, for a second chance at survival. The Watchman had seen many doors, yet had never seen a breathing family emerge. He sighed and shifted his weight, and was careful to not spoil his uniform on the freshly painted cross.

In the gloom of the eighth toll bell, the Watchman accepted a bribe from the Taylor. Thrusting the coins into the hands of his sentry, the Taylor pushed past, and stumbled down Pudding Lane, desperate to acquire food and medicine for his family. Watching the Taylor's shadow chase him into the darkness, the Watchman was indifferent to the infraction. Tonight, as with guards before, he will abandon his uniform, and with the acquired currency, purchase a ticket of good health. The ticket will allow him to pass through the locked gates, and with a prayer, escape the plague. Counting the silver, the Watchman was unaware of shifting shadows, as three figures ran past.

Hours before, the Anvil Smith, Midwinter, and his family finished the last of their pie. Goody Midwinter was pleased that she had surprised her husband with the meat. Reflecting on her purchase, she had learned that due to the dwindling population, beef was selling at reduced prices. She had then carefully stepped her way back through the slaughter section of London, the gruesome array of blood, rubbish and excrement assaulting her senses.

The good wife had used the last of her milled grains to make a rough crust, and made a mental note to purchase more in the new week. Though the meat was tough and grisly, it was a treat for her family.

Crowded together, the family shared a tiny table and three stools amongst five people, with the pie in the centre. Goodwife Midwinter felt blessed that herself and husband, as well as her two boys and daughter, remained unscathed from the pestilence rampaging through the city.

Each member of the family has their own spoon, though Master Midwinter preferred his favourite knife to other tools. Abigail, the last living daughter, choked slightly on the tough meat. Across the table, she eyed her two brothers suspiciously. The boys usually stood at the table, though tonight they leant against it. They had been notably quiet during dinner, rolling their food around, and now, Abigail believed they feigned fatigue and headaches.

The Smith observed his sons through lowered eyes, and shifted his gaze to his wife. Both were aware of the myriad symptoms announcing the dreaded black plague. "What was the number this week?" the thunderous voice of the Smith contrasted the tinkling of pewter spoons. His wife knew he referred to the Bill of Mortality, a weekly listing of deaths, from each parish.

Clearing her throat of sticky crust, "'Twas over one thousand, husband, a frightful number, up three hundred from last week." Her eyes reflected her worry. "Did you know the Taylor's boy across the way is now down with fever?" A low rumble was the Smith's response, and, "I wondered, as I did see the Searcher leaving the Taylor's house this morning. 'Twas in me forge, and heard a great yell'en, before I saw that woman."

The boys perked up with talk of their neighbour, and understood that the presence of a Searcher at someone's home was grim. A "Searcher" was a citizen bestowed with the power to deem a home infected, thereby forbidding the inhabitants from leaving. Abigail glanced at her mother.

"She was a scrawny polecat, that Searcher, and when the Taylor's lass clung to her skirts, begging to not lock them within, the heartless shrew kicked out until she was free." The Smith shook his head. "Didn't even look back."

"Aye, 'twas on my way back from the market when I saw her hurrying out the door, the Taylor begging that she not report the death to the Examiner." The Smith's wife recounted, then bit her lip, recalling the pitiful incident.

A cloud of worry shadowed the Smith's face as he chewed. Glancing at her boys, Goody Midwinter tried to recall when they were last in the company of the Taylor's son. For the countless time that day, she assessed her children. "John, how are those bites?" She leant towards her son, and pulling up the leg of his trousers, grimaced. "Oh, they look terrible!" The other children, now interested, stretched to see the festering ulcerations. "On the morrow, we will fetch a salve from the Apothecary and pray the plants will clean the sores."

"Yes, Mother, it hurts," John confessed, "an' me skull aches from the pain." Clasping his head, he squeezed with both hands. With a flutter of alarm, Goody Midwinter proclaimed that the boys would skip their evening chores and go immediately to bed.

Turning to Abigail, she told her daughter to hasten her supper, so she could finish her brother's share of work. Excusing themselves from the table, the boys dragged their feet to the narrow staircase leading to their shared sleeping loft. John sent a look of mischief over his shoulder to his fuming sister, while Abigail stared at her mother with disbelief. Shoving a large spoonful of the congealed meat into her mouth, she wondered how her mother can not see their theatrics.

Hours later, Abigail lay in her tiny bed. At the foot of the bed, her cat purred, fat and contented from his last catch. Smiling, she thanked God for sparing his life. Abigail recalled the day when the mayor accused community pets of spreading the plague. All citizens were forced to kill their cats and dogs, and then dispose of them into the evening bonfire. As the smoke from the charred animals gagged Abigail, she pleaded with her father to spare her tabby, pointing out he kept the rats from Mother's food stores. Reluctantly, the Smith agreed, and she promised to keep a vigilant eye on the wandering feline. Now weeks after the extermination, most believed the plague was more proliferate. Certainly, the number of brown rats had increased.

Sleep eluded Abigail due to the endless scurrying of rats in the walls, and the soundlessness of the street below. A new sound of crunching straw beneath her aroused Abigail from a doze. Fearful that rats had raided her bed, Abigail bolted upright. Drawing her breath, she startled from shifting shadows in the room.

Figures stepped into the dim moonlight and Abigail recognised the features of her brothers. Exhaling with relief, "What are ye doing?" she demanded.

"Shhh!" The air moved near her head, and a hand was clasped over her mouth. Elbowing her assailant in the guts, she recognised the grunt as John. Pushing him back with irritation, she strained to see her brothers pulling on boots.

"You are not going outside, are you mad? You know that the curfew falls after midnight. Would you disgrace Father and gamble his reputation to scorn?" she hissed. "You know the neighbours are jealous of our plague-free bodies; their grief souring into cankers. If a bored neighbour is watching as you both dash from our home, come the morrow, a guard will be hammering on our door!"

"Hold yer peace," Thomas, the eldest, insisted. "'Tis long before midnight, and never you mind about the local gawpers, we've not yet been bagged," he whispered harshly. "Go back to yer dreams, Abby, we shall make haste."

Annoyed that an adventure was to be missed, and more so that her brothers would not be caught, Abigail tossed her thin blanket to the side and reached for her outer skirt. Thomas pushed her back onto the bed. "Not this time, Sister, we have a gruesome finding to make, which does not allow for a faint-hearted girl."

Irritated by the insult, she stood up again, and fired her last weapon. "If I cannot go with you, then I will be obliged to awaken Father and alert him to your fooleries. Sure I am, of the yell'en that will come forth from you, after he has switched your behind!"

She could see her brothers exchanging looks, and then Thomas roughly grabbed her arm. "I warn ye we go to the outskirts to see for ourselves if the church is piling the dead in great pits and not in proper burials. The pits will be swarming with rats and the stench will be unholy. Don't be looking to me to catch ye from a swoon." His hands felt unusually hot and Abigail wriggled from the grasp.

Thomas released her, but his hope of not revealing the gruesome truth and of keeping his spying sister off their heels had failed.

The trio tiptoed to the stairwell, and avoiding the broken step, they kept their ears to the rhythmic snoring of their father.

Down another staircase, and through the forge, the eldest yanked the complaining door open. Peering out, the three spied the Watchman up the street at the Taylor's house, who appeared to be distracted by counting coins.

The streets had changed dramatically from a week prior when the boys crept out last. No longer did bawdy laughter spill out into the streets from local taverns, nor the golden light from the gaming rooms warm the darkness. The clattering coaches on the streets and the sounds of merriment were distant memories.

The rattling of pottery and the scraping of moving furniture floated down from a second storey. Babies were heard crying, people were shouting somewhere and there was the sound of muffled sobbing. Rubbish and sewage were heaped near doorways, the muck waiting to be cleared by Rakers, who clearly had not yet arrived.

The three Midwinter youths hurried through a hum of flies swarming near a leaky latrine. They were unaware that soon the sewage would pollute a nearby source of drinking water.

Sobered by the heavy atmosphere dispelling their cheer and adventure, their curiosity nonetheless drove them on through the darkened alleys.

Crossing the town centre, they contemplated their journey around the various wrongdoing watchmen locked in stocks and pillory. Moaning and cursing, the men's transgressions ranged from acceptance of treasures by condemned householders, to illegal escapes. The boys chose to sprint around the captives, with Abigail running hard to keep up.

Rounding a corner, they slowed to catch their breaths, and realised they were now in the wealthy parish of Aldgate. Passing the Pye Tavern, a gentleman's establishment, they looked in at the meagre array of patrons—two drunken men, shouting profanities at one another, while the few others sat in sufferance.

The Midwinter children stopped abruptly. They stood in silence as they gawked down the well-to-do street at the number of Watchmen and red-crossed doors. Typically, Londoners believed the Great Mortality was born from the cesspools of vagrants and gypsies. Plague thriving within the gay homes of gentry was a well-concealed fact. The siblings hurried along and within moments they were on a wider road, leading to the Aldgate Churchyard. The reek of disease and decomposition smothered the sticky night air, with the distant, rhythmic sound of spades shifting the soil.

From their vantage, the siblings could glimpse cartfuls of corpses queuing before the churchyard gates.

Moving closer, Abigail was horrified to see the dead-laden carts were writhing with rats. Unable to tear her eyes from the grisly scene, she watched as they appeared out from the wearers' clothing, swarming at barren flesh.

Bile rising, she diverted her gaze to John's exposed legs. He had not worn leggings out and was slapping at biting fleas.

At the wide gate, the children spied a church Sexton speaking with a bedraggled man.

"But it is our business and duty to venture within and risk hazards," the Sexton explained, and holding the man back continued, "Nay, do not go inside. You must preserve thine self, as you are not called to witness the horror within."

The man muttered words too soft for the three to hear. They watched as the Sexton searched the heavens for patience. Lowering his gaze back to the pleading man, he said,

"'T'will be a sermon to you. Perhaps the last you will ever hear, but go inside if you must." The Sexton gave the man's shoulder a small squeeze, "Go then if you must, in the name of God, and obtain your requested repentance. But harken my words: many a sound man has left behind their sanity inside these walls. May God keep yours."

The man nodded heavily, and the Sexton watched him tread into the churchyard.

At this opportunity, the siblings scrambled over the ivy-covered wall. Careful to not brush a dead-cart, Abigail held her nose and averted her eyes, as she followed her brothers into the churchyard.

Stepping onto the uneven soil, the scene was far worse than what their lively imaginations could have envisioned.

Not simply one mass grave, as speculated, but rather, several cavities had destroyed the once green churchyard. Countless Buriers and Sextons rushed around the pits, trying to complete their endless task of piling bodies one on top of another. Clouds of lyme rose up, tearing the workers' eyes, and their mouths were covered by cloths.

In the far corner, a great mound of dirt, roughly strewn, indicated the original burial pit. Underestimating the magnitude of deaths, the Bishops and Priests had ordained a second and now third pit to accommodate the diseased corpses.

Candles and lanterns were placed around the edge of the great hollows, flickering small shadows at the workers' feet.

Hearts thumping, the three children stared open-mouthed at the void over forty feet long, and nearly as wide.

Thomas inched closer to the side, with Abigail clinging to his nightshirt. Peering into the trench, the faint light from the lanterns illuminated a depth of some twenty feet. Ground water seeped from beneath, explaining why the gravediggers had stopped at this depth.

A few feet away from the muddy bottom, twisted limbs and heads were entwined in unnatural positions, revealing some nine bodies stacked upon one another.

The array of clothing revealed pauper and rich lay forever embraced.

Bodies heaved with seeming life, revealing scores of gluttonous rats, ravaging the deceased.

Nausea flooded Abigail, and for a moment, she buried her face into the back of Thomas.

She should have listened to them and stayed behind.

Nervous horses pulling the dead-carts nickered their discomfort, as their drivers led them rearing to the side of the graves.

The siblings gaped at the bodies wrapped in rugs and linens, frightened and shocked, as surviving family members hoped to confine the disease.

Abigail shuddered when she spotted a small child, purple from plague sores, lying in the pile.

"Close yer eyes, Abby," Thomas whispered, his voice quivering. Motionless with shock, they estimated over a thousand bodies were heaped within just one of the giant pits.

John whispered to them, "'Tis one churchyard, how many more churchyards have pits like these? How many poor wretches ended their days like this?"

A flickering movement caught Abigail's sight, and she watched the bedraggled man, earlier admitted, wandering back and forth along the grave's edge. Muffled by the cloak he wore, the man called for his loved ones, his emotions overwhelmed by calamity.

Grief seemingly consuming his sanity, he suddenly ripped the clothing from his body. Screaming, he threw himself into the burial pit, the bodies elastic beneath him.

Shocked, Abigail took a few steps in the direction of where he had fallen but was halted by her brother.

The Buriers immediately dropped their shovels and rushed to the edge. Assuming he had stumbled and fallen, they stretched their hands out to pull the desperate man from the rotting bodies.

"Leave me!" he bellowed. "Do not touch me, as I am also fouled with plague! Save thyself and hide whilst you can," he cried, pushing himself deeper into the bodies. "I beg thee, abandon me to lie with my family, for I cannot bear to be parted from them!" As he struggled, he slipped further down.

"Pray by the dawn, I will join them in purgatory."

Stunned, the Buriers stepped back, but the Sexton extended his arm, attempting to reach the man.

"Run for the Father," the Sexton yelled. "We need him to give last rites to this poor creature."

"Nay," answered an expressionless voice, "the Priest has been found dead. His body lies shroud near the oak." Stepping back from the pit, the Sexton moved towards the dark bundle that was the Priest.

"No!" he cried, and stumbled to the tree. "God preserve us, we have fallen from Divine Grace!" Collapsing beside the body, the Sexton clutched the Priest's hand, sobbing. "We are being punished for our gluttony, our vanity, our promiscuity."

Stunned, Abigail was startled when John pulled at her arm to leave. She noticed his face was looking fevered, and his breathing was fast. The three swiftly retreated over the wall and back through darkened streets to Pudding Lane.

The next morning, Abigail was roused from a fitful sleep by muffled shouting on the street. Peering out the tiny window, she saw the Taylor's Watchman had abandoned his post.

Two Searchers stood arguing with the still–living occupants, who were bellowing from their room above.

Abigail was concerned for the plight of the Taylor's family, but was too exhausted to make further inquiry.

Pulling her bodice around her chest, she kicked the straw pallet to awaken her brothers. Groaning, Thomas rolled over muttering about his head, but John looking sweaty, did not rouse.

Shrugging, Abigail went downstairs and automatically made her way to the byre where the family cow greeted her with a nudge. After feeding the animals and visiting the Farynor bakery, Abigail arrived back in time for breakfast, their largest meal.

Stepping into the kitchen, she slowed. Her parents were leaning over Thomas, who was hunched over at the table. Appearing hot and out of breath, Abigail assumed he had been assisting his father in the forge.

"What vexes, Thomas?" she asked with vague concern, noticing with disappointment that breakfast was not yet laid out.

"Your brother says a cold wind will not leave his bones," her mother explained uneasily. Eyeing him with disbelief, Abigail now noticed the absence of the other brother.

"And pray, where is John? He is to help me fill the hearth with wood for Father's coking, and I will naught finish that task alone," she stated with irritation. Noticing the expression on her mother's face, she frowned.

"Yer brother cannot rise himself from bed," her father murmured. "The boy did say he was off colour last night and has not roused."

Throwing her hands up with exasperation, Abigail dismissed her parents' strange behaviour. "Those boys get away with everything! Working to the bone I am, and lazy John is still sleeping!" With irritation, Abigail bound up the stairs, eager to kick the straw out from beneath her brother.

But at the top stair, she slowed as she heard laboured breathing from the bed.

Adjusting her eyes to the dimness, Abigail was startled to see John's arms and legs flail as if fighting an assailer, his dark curls stuck to his sweating face. Guilt flooded Abigail, and she yelled for her parents.

By nightfall, both her brothers were tight within the grips of fever. So calm her mother was, applying cool cloths to burning foreheads and whispering nonsense words to them into the night. Abigail ran back and forth with clean water, guilt and fear fuelling her legs.

In the early hours, Abigail awoke from the kitchen chair, heart pounding. Her brothers were crying out in pain and Abigail could hear her parents stumbling above.

Running upstairs, she cried out when she saw the figures on the bed.

Abigail could barely recognise her brothers underneath the purple blotches covering their throats and chests. Incredibly, swellings the size of goose eggs bulged from their armpits. The boys thrashed and cried out in agonised delirium.

Tears stung Abigail's eyes, as she heard her mother sobbing in the dark corner. She could see her tall father explaining to his sons that they'd be fit on the morrow, and to not worry 'bout the chores; they'd all go fishing. Hearing her father speak with such tenderness pained her heart, and Abigail tore her eyes away to not see the fear and pain in his eyes.

Throughout the night, Mother and Father kept a fretful vigil, but as the sun broke through the morning mist, John, always his mother's darling, slipped away from her and into the cold arms of death.

Some hours later, her first born, so cheeky and mischievous, gave a slight smile and closed his eyes.

Abigail stared at Thomas's swollen face. His lips and cheeks were ruby, contrasted by the greyness of his skin. To her eyes he looked alive, but the rising of his chest was still.

Abigail blinked with heaviness. The death of Thomas was not possible. He would mock the reaper and caper out of bed ready for the next adventure, she was sure. Taking his hand, it was hot, not the cold that companioned death. Her disbelief grew.

"Open your eyes, Thomas, you are scaring Mother," she cried. When there was no response, she shook his arm. "Open your eyes, rascal, I know yer a hoaxer!" she yelled and began to tremble.

Strong arms embraced her. "Leave the lad, Abby," her father's voice rasped. "A clever lad, yes, he were, but the plague is a cheating and wily player." Pulling her away, the Smith managed to lead his daughter and sobbing wife downstairs.

The three held one another, and as the wagons carried the boys away to an undisclosed cemetery, mass graves and jumbled bodies haunted Abigail's mind.

She would never let her parents know the horrible truth about where their precious sons' final resting place would be.

Watching the dead-cart turn the corner, Master Midwinter gently untangled himself from his wife and made his way into his forge. Before long, the familiar sound of the rhythmic *"cling-clang"* of his hammer on anvil replaced the silence of the street. Peering through the window, Abigail watched her father, and could not discern sweat from tears.

Hours later, Goody Midwinter still stood in the filthy gutters, watching for her sons to come home. Smoke was now seen escaping from the Taylor's windows as items of bedding, clothing and other chamber fabrics were purified by fire. She distantly heard a dead-cart groan and rattle beneath its load. Distant cursing revealed a stuck wheel in one of the many street holes. A whip cracked, and the exhausted beast trembled with the grim passengers.

Abigail brought tea and food to her mother, but she stood listless, vigilantly waiting for her sons to return. Comforting her mother by her closeness, Abigail noticed the tell-tale beak nosed mask of the Plague Doctor ambling down the street hawking a cure and protection from the plague. She shivered at the sight, as the glass eyes met hers. This was not a strange occurrence, for as of late, Plague Doctors were seen proclaiming such remedies throughout the streets of London.

Abigail's mother stirred and looked to the sound. Not one to fall victim to merchants nor keen in parting with shop tokens, Abigail was shocked when her mother ran towards the Plague Doctor. With a few words, coin was exchanged for small, cloth bundles. Abigail watched from the door of the forge as her mother rushed in and pulled Abigail to their kitchen.

Collapsing into a fit of coughing, her mother struggled to catch her breath. Placing the bundles on the worn table, eyes blazing, she fervently pulled forth their contents. Examining the items, Abigail wondered if indeed her mother had lost her wits. Two bulbs of garlic dropped to the table, followed by a small corked bottle.

Picking up the bottle, she explained, "The doctor tells me that he is a true Physician from the countryside, and has made this medicine himself based on a woman that is wise with earthly healing, and that this remedy will ward the evildoing of the plague away from the user." Removing the cork, she faced her silent girl and instructed that she take a spoonful of the syrup within thrice daily. Taking a spoon from the table, she measured out a dram, and held it before Abigail. Obediently, she opened her mouth and the bitter syrup slid down her throat. Her mother crushed the garlic clove and started rubbing it around Abigail's neck and chest, tears glistening in her eyes.

Searching her mother's face for a trace of sanity, she stood silent, while Mother explained further, "After you have scrubbed ye'self with this bulb, then chew it and swallow it. The medicine in the garlic will protect you, my girl," she said. "Bless you, but you are my last babe, and you must survive. I will pray for your life and for our own." Her eyes filled with more tears, and she grasped Abigail's hand. "Promise that you will repeat this ritual every day."

Mutely, Abigail nodded.

Looking slightly relieved, her mother's shoulders dropped. "Good, and now I will rest, as I am greatly tired and my heart is sick with grief. And remember, Abigail, you must be calm within your soul, as you know terror alone can allow the plague to enter." Abigail nodded again and watched her mother stumble towards her bed.

Time passed in the day and still her mother did not rise. The Smith continued in his forge, not stopping since the morning. After preparing a simple evening meal, Abigail looked in at her mother. Though the day had been hot, Abigail was still not prepared to find her drenched in sweat. She could see her shivering with fever, red hair thrown about the pillow in a halo. Instantly worried, Abigail shook her mother awake.

"Abigail, my girl," she whispered, taking her hand. "I must give you this note." The crumpled parchment fell to the bed. "You must make your way to Wilton, to the house of my younger sister, your Aunt Bess, where once I lived as a girl. She might not be the sweetest of temperament, but Bess is fair, and I beseech you to find her, if by the sake of God, something should come of your father." The last words were lost, as she contorted into a fit of coughing.

Fat tears rolled from her eyes, and the Goodwife turned away so her daughter would not see her blatant fear.

Abigail gasped. Her mother's chemise was speckled with blood from her cough. A sickening dread flooded her body, and Abigail ran to pull her father from the forge. When they returned, the Smith sat and placed his great hand to his wife's forehead. Sodden curls fell away from her neck, exposing purple blotches.

A shadow of dread eclipsed the Smith's face.

"Go fetch cool water and flannel for ye mum." Abigail stood frozen, eyes fixed to the purpling skin. "Curse of hell…now, girl!" he bellowed.

Abigail ran wildly to complete the errand, all the while, tears blinding her way.

Hours later into the heat of the night, Abigail tried to force the strange syrup into the mouth of her mother. Pushing Abigail away with crumbling strength, her mother rasped, that it was "naught to be wasted on her". Abigail's tears were unstoppable, and she felt frustrated and helpless.

Through the night, the purple blotches grew deeper and the frequency of their appearance left Abigail overwrought with fear. She would not believe that her mother was dying. By the eve of the second night, the bubonic tokens showed their ugliness around the milky white middle of its next victim. Weeping sores in the softness under her arms were the cause of pain-filled cries.

Many times Goody Midwinter begged her daughter to leave the room, to not bear witness to her suffering.

Abigail refused, numbly watching from the corner of the room. In between her Mother's bloody coughing fits, Abigail dozed.

Awoken by soft crying, she saw her father tenderly cradling his wife to his chest.

Stumbling to her mother's side, Abigail threw herself across her mother's body. Devastation racked her world, as she was aware of motionlessness beneath. A torrent of tears flooded her eyes, as her mother's stillness was absolute. Time went by as husband and daughter held her.

Eventually, Abigail's arms were untangled by her father, who pulled his daughter away.

With a stifled sob, Master Midwinter lifted his wife, keeping her head tucked under his chin. A perfect curl, which had freed itself, hung over his arm.

The ceiling of the room had never been accommodating to the Smith's height, and he stooped to move through the door. Abigail hastily followed, afraid to be alone. When they made their way into the forge, two haggard guards from the King's army stood waiting. The Smith did not meet their eyes.

"Forge is closed, leave us be." Abigail thought she had never heard her father's voice so soft.

"So it is, and will be from here forth, until the dawning of the 40th day," spoke one soldier, as he painted the dreaded red cross upon the door.

"Master Midwinter, Anvil Smith, ye and all that reside here, are hereby quarantined to your rooms. By the King's decree, it is unlawful for you or any others to go or come forth," the other soldier stated in a practiced monotone. Closing the door behind them, a gaunt guard informed the Master that the wagon would come once the red cloth was hung. His gaze shifted from the Smith's dead wife to Abigail, and there was dread etched into his face. "May God have mercy on your souls."

They startled from the bang as the door was barred from the outside. The Smith slid to the floor of his forge, still holding his wife tight to his chest.

Hours later, the squeaky wheels of a wagon were heard coming down the cobblestones.

"Bring out yer dead," rang a voice filtering down Pudding Lane. The door was unbarred only long enough for Master Midwinter to tenderly add his wife to the wagon. Abigail spied the Plague Doctor standing across the lane staring at them. He dropped his head and shuffled into the shadows.

Abigail did not have the courage to watch as her mother was taken away, so she ran to her mother's wardrobe and buried her face in her mother's folded skirts, breathing in her scent, safe and secure.

Distantly she heard sobbing from her father, and covering her ears, she fell asleep exhausted.

Whether hours or days slipped by, neither was sure, daughter and father locked from the world.

The guard posted was bored and constantly dozing. Abigail noticed that one morning a different man relieved him. She wondered if the day-guard was lying naked in a mass grave now.

Abigail caught the new man watching the window for the inevitable red cloth, indicating that the next inhabitant had passed. She cursed his impatience.

A few days later, the Watchman sighed, as the Midwinter house grew still of voices. Tangled sounds of pain and crying floated down to the street, and he wondered if the Smith or the girl were now dead.

He slapped at the fleas biting his legs and hoped that the suffering would not be long. He was also eager to return home.

Upstairs in the room above the forge, yellow light filtered through the small window. Outside, the sky was dirty and the air drooped with humidity and stillness.

It was the absence of sound which awoke Abigail from a restless sleep. For weeks now, the moaning of dying people and the wailing of the mourners had swiftly replaced the bustling sounds of Pudding Lane. Even these sorrowful sounds had diminished of late.

Today, however, the soundlessness was ominous. Even the morning church bells were mute. Frightened to open her eyes, Abigail strained to hear the breathing of her father. Time was frozen and nothing but a distant creaking dray was heard. The silence was absolute.

Eyes still shut, Abigail sniffed the air, and the stink of plague was suffocating.

Sitting up, she opened her eyes and saw that the figure on the bed lay still. Crying out, Abigail fell to her father's side, and she gasped as his purpling skin made him almost unrecognisable. Panic crashed down on her, muddling her head, and drowning her heart. Abigail struggled to catch her breath in the stifling room as she understood that she was the last living member of her family.

An overwhelming urge to flee from the room, the house, and the memories of where her family died, fuelled Abigail to stumble downstairs.

Once in the kitchen, Abigail pondered where she should go. By law, child or not, she was locked in the confines of the forge for another month. But she would surely die here without food or water. Her mother's last demands replayed in her memory. The thought of leaving her home filled her with dread. How could she possibly travel to Wiltshire? What could she remember of the area? Was there not a famous cathedral somewhere there? The borough of Salisbury was vaguely familiar, and was it not near Wilton? She would need coin, food and a means of travel.

Without looking at her father, she numbly gathered her belongings. Coin was begotten from a tiny space in the floor, concealed by a bowl of turnips. There were a few items of fortune, some copper and two pieces of silver. Abigail tied what clothes she possessed, with oat bread, a handful of apples and a block of her father's favourite cheese. On an afterthought, she quietly went into her father's forge and found his favourite knife—small but very sharp, and concealed that within her bodice. Abigail then dutifully took a spoonful of the syrup, applied and ate the garlic and added the medicines to the bundle.

When the goods were assembled, she soundlessly hung the final red cloth from the window. Escaping the eyes of the guard was important, as Abigail believed he would prefer that she rot inside, rather than give her a chance to escape.

On impulse, Abigail decided that the best solution was to squeeze through the tiny window in the kitchen, which would deposit her into the stables of the Star Inn.

She looked back over her shoulder only once, before dropping onto a mildewy hay pile.

Abigail decided that she would ride her father's draft horse to her aunt's house but was disappointed to discover the stable empty. Her father had mentioned that all available horses were being purchased or stolen for fast departures from London. Clearly, someone had helped themselves to their cow and horse.

Swinging herself over the stable gate, she made her way around the Star Inn. The guard dozed at the door, and with quiet haste, she ran to the end of the street.

Abigail knew the passage to the town gates, which would put her in the direction of Wiltshire. Her father bought iron from a man living just out of the town, a ride she had often companioned. Her father had explained once, that this was the main road leading south, and then west to her mother's family.

Abigail hurried along near the wharves. The wharves carried her deeper into the gaping maw of endless warehouses. There were numerous shipping vessels secured there, some local, and others foreign. A few ships, not so lucky, had run aground, mortally listing upon the rocks off the shore. This spectacle would usually have drawn a crowd, but as Abigail noted, there was no one around to amount to a crowd. Many more ships bobbed forth freely in the harbour, patiently awaiting their missing crews.

It was rumoured that entire crews had succumbed to the Black Death whilst on a voyage, ghost ships navigating their own ways back to land. Abigail shivered at this thought.

Within the warehouses, stored for trade or industry, lay the wares of fibrous hemp, black coal for heating, slick tallow for illumination, and timber for construction. The materials were stockpiled within the cool enclosures or heaped on open quays, awaiting their journeys. How long would they stay waiting to be shifted?

Abigail swiftly passed Lucerne hay, which was stored in giant mounds, now home to many scurrying creatures.

Cobbles paved the streets of the wharves, worn smooth now from years of thick passage. Various sturdy plants, given the opportunity, had pushed through cracks in the stone. Near the entrances of the grain houses, freed seeds had lodged themselves into the non-trampled soil. Before long, there would be more green than stone. These streets, normally crammed with merchants, traders, sailors and unsavoury characters, were devoid of the living. Abigail stayed along the water's edge and noted the surface of the Thymes, once churning with movement, sat idle and moody. Without a breeze, its murky depths swallowed the available light.

The air was unseasonably hot, and the stillness captured the disagreeable but familiar stench of stagnant water and waste. Abigail gagged and gingerly stepped over fallen Londoners, their bodies rotting fast in the heat.

Moments later and Abigail was within the town centre. Remaining residents picked their path through a small drove of cattle, seemingly lost whilst on their way to the slaughterhouse. Citizens were too preoccupied with their own plights to consider capturing the wayward steers.

Everyone plodded along within the centre of the street, decreasing the chances of having contact with 'miasma', the vile vapours of their sick neighbours, lingering near and above condemned homes. Abigail followed their lead and avoided the edges near doorways.

Many people were wearing colourful charms, philtres and amulets in desperate hope of deflecting the malevolent spirit of the plague. Clothing was adorned with knots of magical ribbon, and papers with words or figures to protect themselves. Abigail passed a man muttering "Abracadabra" repeatedly, as he had been instructed by a gypsy who sold him the spell. Stumbling, he staggered on the uneven flint stones, knocking into her. Without comment, the man wiped his brow and veered towards the cooling gloom of a coff-house.

Abigail absently wondered if there were others within.

The air rang from the bellman announcing the dead-carts as they picked their way through the streets. Abigail passed a Watchman nodding to a driver, and unable to lower her gaze, watched the cart stop abruptly, jarring the macabre passengers. Quickly she averted her eyes from the exposed bodies. She could not bear to see her father amongst the piled corpses.

Passing a tanner, she wrinkled her nose at his tanning mixture of dog urine and faeces. Rubbing the nauseating mixture into the raw hides, the tanner smiled a blackened mouth at her offended expression. Abigail frowned at him and wondered why he had survived when her family had not.

She rounded the corner, and a dour display of empty streets and red cloths confronted her. Another turn, and Abigail saw that the churches were boarded shut, as even the clergy had forsaken hope.

Abigail knew she was close to the city gates when she was unable to take another step forward. Drays, horses and masses of people choked the narrow lanes fighting to reach the gates.

The air tingled with fear and desperation.

Abigail climbed a staircase leading to a door where a guard eyed her with contempt. She strained to glimpse the portal at large and could see the main gate was closed. Brandishing weapons, the King's guards fought to keep the frantic crowd from leaving. Abigail was confused, as the gate being the main thorough fare to the outside world, was always open this time of day. Having the advantage of being small and not lumbered down with travelling chests, she was able to squeeze her way to the front of the crowd.

Straining, she heard the words from the gatekeeper. "By decree of the Lord Mayor and Alderman of the City London, upon special considerations, if it shall so please Almighty God, the citizens of London shall remain within the safety of these walls."

"Safety? We are not safe," yelled a woman.

"It don't please me one bit," shouted one man.

"Me neither, let us out!" said another. The rest of the crowd responded with curses, pushing further into the closed gate.

Ignoring the uproar, but positioning himself behind a guard, the gatekeeper continued, "Hark now, with a ticket of fair health acquired from a Physician, thou shall obtain passage through distant gateway. The King wishes to contain plague to this one township, and not spread the scourge across the countryside." Bushy eyebrows peeked above the scroll. "If thee persist through the gates you go, with naught a ticket in hand, then you will cry mercy from the walls of Newgate." This enlightenment was received with more curses and renewed energy from the crowd to push forward. "May Almighty God save thee," he added as an afterthought and quickly dropped back into the safety of the gate cage. Fingering his own fair health ticket, the Mayor's spokesman reflected that he had paid a ransom for his passage, but at least his own escape was assured.

Panic erupted. Abigail, knocked to the ground, battled to pull herself up the wheel of a dray. Crushed between horse and wagon, she clawed at the wooden boards to pull herself free of the mob.

Searching for something to grab onto, her fingers located iron chains within the wagon. Throwing her other arm over, Abigail dragged her body over the side and dropped to the bottom of the cart.

Bolts of fabric fell on top of her, and pulling a sheet of hemp from the bundle, she concealed her presence.

The wagon lurched, and the driver fought his way to the gate.

Abigail knew they were close, when she could hear a man, not the driver, arguing with the gatekeeper.

Within moments, she heard scuffling boots, followed by "a pox on ye all!" and then a thud.

The guards had tired of the man and dragged him unconscious to the stocks to punish him for his bawdy display.

"How's the likes of yer lot hold a ticket?" the gate guard interrogated the driver of the dray Abigail lay concealed in.

"Behold man, see what rewards worthy breeding bears," the driver announced with pomp.

"Worthy breeding, bah! Yer a merchant, and all know the thievery that ye hold as virtuous," he shouted. "A heavy purse will buy anyone a warrant of fair health and a passage from this hell."

Ignoring the insult, the merchant controlled his tone, "Godso, and bless thee for such astute observance. I will endeavour to improve my future actions. Now pray do not delay our passage, as my wife is eager to reunite with her mother."

With one last inspection, the guard called out reluctantly, "Open!"

Steel rang out, as swords were drawn to prevent the surging crowd from escaping.

Abigail's heart pounded. This was her only opportunity to reach the outside and a chance of survival. Holding her breath, the complaining gate was pushed open, and with a shudder, the wagon pulled forward.

Essex, 1650

Orla lay dreaming she is entwined in a spiral dance with a younger Abraham. The swishing of flax and woollen skirts, and the scraping of leather shoes upon flooring, make familiar undertones of sound beneath the merry music. They are engaged in a simple longways dance, with the shaking of hands and the occasional hop. More focused on brushing the flesh of one another, Orla and Abraham forget their counts of six, colliding with the more serious dancers. Hugging her closer and more often than the instructed steps, Abraham's deep brown eyes shine with brazen ardour. Orla's heart pounds with the intensity of his gaze. Glancing over Abraham's shoulder, her eyes lock with the frowning vicar. Turning her face away, wicked mischief infects her laughter as she throws back her head, exposing the softness of her neck. She notices that the couples around her move with the inspiration of the fashionable dances of the day. How graceful and beseeming the local farmers and their goodly wives have transformed, she thinks. Their once listless eyes are replaced by cheeks rouged with vitality and zest. With raised eyebrows, Orla observes that this is not like the usual old-fashioned and dusty dances of the countryside.

The forgotten old guildhall is now alive in her dream, awash in warm candlelight, newly built, and holding as much splendour as could be expected for a stone room with a simple wooden floor.

Another brush of Abraham's fingertips across her wrist jolts her from her thoughts. Falling deeply into the depths of his eyes, Orla contemplates her move to assure that she will steal a kiss from those full lips. With a flush to her cheeks, she raises her face to offer her softness to his searching mouth.

A distant thumping distracts Abraham, and as he turns to look, the dancers begin to fade away. More pounding and Orla was awakened, understanding that someone was rapping the door of her shared cottage.

Poking her head out from beneath the blankets, she inhaled sharply as the icy air bit into her warm cheeks. As the hue of orange from the kitchen fire had dwindled to darkness, she understood it is the new hours of the morning. Before she can drag her leaden legs out of the bed, she heard the grumbling voice of her eldest sister, Alice. "I'll tend to the call, don't bother ye self," she called out into the freezing air.

Sighing, and snuggling closer to her warm husband, Orla vaguely wondered which one of the pregnant women in the area was labouring. Tonight is surely too cold for vulnerable babes to be making their passage.

Orla's thoughts slid to consider the coldest of winters in over twenty years. With much speculation, the country folk still blamed the freakish weather on the darkened afternoon sun, late October.

Though contemporary scientists referred to the transition as an eclipse, the older members stubbornly clung to their superstitions. The gaffers recalled the last time such coldness befell the area, blood had streaked the darkened sky, possessing the cattle and sheep who ran about madly. Later that summer, milk curdled and the cows suffered from quaking tremors, where they fell and died on the spot.

These tales were being retold, causing anxiety and worry, especially in the company of expecting women. Now restless, Orla struggled to get comfortable again.

Superstitious hysteria did not rest easy with midwifes.

Orla contemplated getting out of bed and helping Alice, but fatigue held her still. Recent demands for her and Alice's skills were endless and now extended to neighbouring villages.

There was a dangerous shortage of wise women and Midwives due to the popularity of Puritan ideals. It seemed that every few years, some new church leader was pointing their damning finger at innocent women, accusing them of dealings with Satan. Orla shuddered with distant memories.

One wrong look or an ill-tempered mood on your part, and you could find your neck at the end of a noose. Disease, droughts, floods, mad cattle and sheep, all fed the frenzied delusions of soul-possession.

Orla prayed that the senseless executions would end before all the old wisdom would be lost. Too sleepy to ponder further, Orla hoped that the babe choosing to be born on this frosty night could be taken care of by Alice, without the need of further assistance. As Orla had returned late from a long night and day assisting the Gooding's baby into their arms, she was desperate for respite. The birth had been long and agonising for both mother and midwife.

The soft rattling of jars and bottles alerted Orla that Alice was in need of more than the usual stock they kept prepared in the birthing bag. Alice's loud whisper startled her. "Sister, have ye the draught of lady's mantle, shepherd's bag and nettle within your healing sack?" she inquired. Abraham groaned and shifted to his other side.

"Ai," she answered in a low voice. "Under my skirts in the healing bag, but I do say, the reserves are low. I'll get Mary and young Philippa to help me restock in the morning," Orla added. Curiosity vanquishing her sleep, she sat up. "Is it Goody Appleby or Goody Lagden?" Orla asked.

"Nay," Alice replied. "'tis young Mary Fenner," the worry in her voice noted.

Orla pulled her hands into her thick, woollen sleeping shift. "Bless me, she is far too early to be birthing. Can you not stop the babe from its deliverance, Sister?" Orla asked concerned. "Why, only a fortnight ago, I made a fresh draught of the herbs needed to quiet the restless babe," she added.

"Thank ye, I didst think of the compound, but I believe we are past that point," Alice answered, while wrapping a heavy shawl about her shoulders. "Master Fenner tells me, the babe is already on the way." She sighed loudly. "Now, away with me, and we shall speak in a later hour."

Orla listened to the swift scuffling of Alice's boots on the earthen floor and laid down again, once the door latch clicked into place.

Turning to face her in the darkness, Abraham said in his quiet, rich voice, "'Tis likely, Goody Fenner will lose another babe this cold night, and by God's Mercy, she will have a hope to survive herself." Orla sighed and laid her head onto her husband's chest. Pulling the coarse blankets over her head, the wise woman tried to return to the dream where laughter and dancing could replace the worry and heaviness in her heart.

West of London, 1666

Abigail endured the chaffing of the chains long after the outer walls had disappeared. From where she lay, Abigail could see through the slates in the wagon, and with time, the passing horses and drays eventually thinned so that they shared the fare way with few others.

Cautiously, Abigail lifted her head a bit and ventured to see who else was in the wagon with her. Grimacing as she freed her braids from a tangle of chains, she noted that her hat was lost at the expense of the mob, but at least her wisp was still tied. She lay motionless, straining to hear voices. A shrill voice belonging to a woman and the soft mewing of a baby concluded the number of passengers.

Abigail decided she would stay concealed as long as possible, and when the time arrived, she would try to slip over the side without detection.

Hours dragged by. Abigail, stifled from the heat of the sun and preoccupied with her thirst, was vaguely aware that the baby had not stopped its pathetic crying. She had not lived with a baby in her home, but had heard enough sick ones this passing year to know that the mother was agitated for a reason. Her mind wandered to the disturbing images of abandoned plague babies left in the gutters to die.

At last, the heavy wagon ground to a bumpy stop.

Dislodging her parched tongue from the roof of her mouth, Abigail licked her dry lips and realised how sore her cramped muscles were. Afraid of being discovered, she ignored the urge to stretch her numb limbs. Contemplating her next move, loud anxious voices cut through the muffling of the cloth, which concealed her presence.

"Her head is on fire, Samuel, and now she won't even suckle. She needs a Physician this moment, for God's sake do something!" wailed the woman, her voice fraught with anxiety.

"The nearest town is still an hour's ride, and further yet to reach your mother's cottage," he explained. "I can hardly push the horses harder, as they already tremble with fatigue," came the husband's voice.

"Do not dither, husband, our baby could die while you stare at me like a great stupid ox!" A weak cry emerged from the baby. "Oh my baby, God help us, you are so hot. Shhhh," she cooed. There was a moment of silence, then, "Damnation, you fool, what are you waiting for? Drive!"

A whip cracked, and the horses lunged forward, throwing Abigail deeper into the nest of chains and tools.

The race to the next village was a teeth-jarring experience. When her bruised cheeks could take not another pothole, Abigail managed to turn onto her side and glimpsed a view of the speeding landscape. Nothing looked familiar, and judging by the length of time which had passed, she couldn't remember ever venturing this far from London before. In her new position, she spied a water bag and some apples rolling free from a large hemp sack. Stretching her arms and fingers out, she was able to snare the water bag on two fingertips and rolled the apples her way with her foot.

Luckily, the family in the front was too concerned with not falling out of the racing wagon to notice the movements from behind.

After tying apples into her dirty skirts and sating her dusty thirst, Abigail returned to a prone position and considered what she would do when the wagon finally stopped.

Squat mud cottages with thatched rooftops began to appear in the fields and off the road. Peeking through the wagon's sideboards, she saw the farmhouses beginning to cluster, and squinting, she could see in the distance, a stonewall which fortified the approaching village.

As the wagon clambered and slowed towards the entrance into the village, Abigail could feel her heart pounding in her chest. Though sore and hot, Abigail did not welcome her anticipated escape.

Abigail's mother had said her auntie's home was a few days ride from London, and she knew the time stowed in the merchant's wagon had hardly delivered her out of the shire.

Hopefully, they would continue to the destination further out of the village.

Every length of distance was closer to her awaiting auntie and family.

Frothing and twitching, horses and dray slowed. "Dear God, the gates are locked!" Samuel said with astonishment. Before they could come to a complete stop, he was already yelling out for help. Eyes wide, Abigail noticed that beyond the wall into the village, the streets seemed oddly quiet, considering it was the middle of the week. Abigail felt a shifting in the wagon, and a dusty thump indicated someone had jumped to the ground. She soon discovered it was Samuel, for he began beating the gates and crying out.

"We need help, our babe is in need of your Physician, please, our plight is dire, we have coin to pay, and I swear she is naught with plague fever. Send out your healer, and we shall leave by sunset," his voice rose in urgency. A barking dog was their only answer.

Not able to contain herself further, the mother pleaded, "You must help us! Will you hide within your homes, hugging your own children to your bosom, while mine dies in my arms? God save us, please!"

From an uncertain direction, a contemptuous voice rang out, "The quack is dead from the plague ye's filthy town has spewed forth." A heavy scuffle followed and Abigail could hear the sound of something sliding open. Risking discovery, she sat up a small amount and saw a door at the gate. A small window had opened inward and a haggard face could be seen in its outline.

"Waste not your breath, fore ye will find no pity here. I have water to sell and stale bread, but your beasts and passengers will not be resting here." His voice was gravelly and parched. "Follow the plague road around the village, and ye will find yerself back onto the main southern road, away from us." A distinctive spat could be heard.

"But we need rest and remedy now!" the woman's voice cried. "We are people of means, and I demand attention to my child!"

There was a gurgling cough, and then. "Best make haste to the next borough, lest ye be regretting yer dithering, I won't tell ye again," he threatened, and with a bang, the tiny window was shut. Sinking back into concealment, Abigail knew it was a desperate time, and these people were not going to help, not because their hearts were cold, but because their own grief and fear drove them to self-preservation. Abigail swallowed the lump of her own grief.

"We can reach your mother's cottage by nightfall if we make haste and do not stop for rest," said Samuel, as he climbed back into the driver's seat. "Keep trying to feed the babe, maybe she will suckle if you persist." Worry frayed the edges of his voice.

The woman was sobbing as Samuel urged the tired horses around the stonewall and onto the newly worn plague road.

The road made its way through a series of fields, forcing the horses to a walk. A choking stench of rotting flesh, mingled with the sweetness of the grass, rose through the dray's boards. Holding her nose, Abigail peeked out into the fields, and the mounds of fresh earth explained the smell. Apparently, even fresh earth was no match for the abundant decomposing bodies.

At last the wagon turned, and they were upon the main road again.

Abigail grimly noticed that the baby had ceased crying.

The sun was sinking below the hills, when, as promised, they turned down a lane leading to a small cottage. A heady fragrance of summer blooms filled the cooling air, and tall trees shadowed the last of the day's light.

The horses were pulled up fast, and the brakes complained against the wheels of the dray. Abigail could hear the man jump to the ground, and as the baby and woman made their way down, the door to the cottage was thrown open. There were muffled voices, and then the raspy voice of an older woman was heard directing people to gather items into the house. All were quickly ushered into the cottage, leaving Abigail alone in the darkened wagon. She lay unmoving, knowing that at any given moment, someone would arrive to tend to the horses. She did not wait long. As the horses and wagon were being led into the barn, past the house, Abigail could hear the clatter of thick pots against the stone hearth. She prayed for the life of the baby. Maybe God would make an exception.

The horses were freed from the burden of the merchant's heavy wagon. Abigail could hear them shaking their fatigued bodies, and soon afterwards, the harness fell to the ground in a clatter.

A few more minutes went by, and the footsteps of the stableman disappeared into the house. Blinking to see, she gingerly peeked out from the bolt of flax, and assuring herself that no one else was hidden in the shadows, freed the material further from her body. With shaking legs, she swung them over the side of the wagon and sank to the ground. A movement caught her eye from beneath the wagon. Suddenly, out from beneath the support frame sprang a large creature, and despite its size, it daintily landed on the ground.

The scratching of tiny claws on the gravelly barn floor sent shivers down her spine.

Straining to see in the darkness, the creature's silhouette was recognised in the first light of the moon. Abigail's face contorted with disdain: Rat. The repulsive creature was sitting up on two legs, sniffing the air of its new home. A skin-crawling squeak escaped the little beast, and then a second thud could be heard from beneath the wagon. Out of the darkness, another rat, this one smaller, dashed out the barn door.

It appeared she wasn't the only stowaway.

The sight of the creatures revolted her, as recent memories flooded her thoughts. Not able to bear the thought of the filthy animal scurrying around while she slept, Abigail risked being heard, and threw a neighbouring stone at the remaining rat. Her aim was true, and with a squeak, the indignant rodent bolted into the darkness.

Rummaging through a small chest, she happily discovered some salted fish, cheese and hardened bread. Starving, she shoved the food into her mouth by the fistfuls.

The food was dry in her throat, and she searched blindly for the water bladder. Remembering the strange medicine, and her mother's urgent request, she rummaged around in her bag, and once finding the odd combination, ate the garlic and drank a portion of the black syrup. Grimacing, Abigail washed the taste down with more water, but the bitterness still lingered. Wiping her mouth with a corner of her skirt, she brushed the crumbs from her hands and took inventory of her remaining food. Deciding that her supplies could need some assistance, she felt around in the darkness for the forgotten crates of food in the wagon.

Stuffing some of the food into her bag, but not enough to be missed, Abigail looked around the barn for a suitable place to rest without discovery.

The horses munched their earned grains, watching Abigail without concern. They were too exhausted to care, and the girl had made her way to the opposite side, out of sight and smell.

Making a thick pile of hay, Abigail pulled her knees up to her chest and pulled hay over herself to conceal and warm her body. The exhaustion and anxiety of the day quickly erased painful images and memories from her mind.

Within moments, she was asleep.

The cockerels startled Abigail out of her slumber. She looked around, confused, as she struggled to remember where she was. The light was weak; too early even for the sun.

Memory flooded her mind, and remembrance dropped leaden into her stomach.

Pulling hay from her hair, she stood up and made her way towards the barn door. Nearing the entrance, she distantly heard people crying. Blinking, Abigail looked to the cottage, where orange light still showed from the lanterns.

She knew the baby had died.

Abigail felt alone in the world. All whom she knew were gone. Was she the luckiest person or the most cursed? How could a man of enormous strength, like her father, buckle under the weight of the plague, yet she was left standing? Abigail examined her dirty hands, hardly believing she still lived. Turning to gather her bag, she shook her head in wonder. Abigail would never know that over seven thousand people of London had died that week.

The morning birds began their wakeup calls, reminding Abigail that she couldn't stand there all day. Quickly tying her curls under her wisp, she checked that all belongings were secured in her skirts and bulging bag. Slipping past the cottage, she hastened into the shadows and returned to the main road.

Knowing the desired direction was west, she hurried along with the dawning day to her back.

Essex, 1650

The afternoon sun was starting to burn warmer, and the bumpy texture of the tree branches was a happy sign that spring thaw was on its way. There had been more rain than usual, and everyone shared a smile when the day promised to be bright.

The winter had proven to be a cold and deadly season, and the household of Warner and Bones had kept warm by the increased activity of preparing medicines for the surrounding villagers. Even with their long hours of house calls, administering cups of Elfwort, Coughwort and Iris roots to expectorate phlegm, there still had been many lives lost. The Gaffers could recall only one winter prior in their youth, when the winter had brought such coldness.

Locals were much afflicted with rattling chest distempers, and no amount of mustard or onion plasters, diligently applied, could remedy them all. Breathing sickness invited the deadly lung fever, deteriorating strength with racking spells of coughing.

A new lung distemper had thinned one village of half its residents, not more than a day's ride away. Abraham had read of this terrible illness, and some European scholars associated it with the plague.

Like plague, there was fever and muscle tenderness, but only a violent cough followed, leaving no survivors.

Anyone hearing the stories were compelled to recite extra prayers.

Orla stirred the gooey contents of the large batch of coughing—oxymel, reflecting on her methods of healing. Tasting the black mixture, she grimaced, but knew it to be a worthy batch from its bitterness.

Orla and her sisters, Alice and Mary, knew from experience, that to recognise ill humours early, especially pertaining to the coughing sicknesses, could mean a chance of surviving other distempers.

The key was convincing the simple minds of their neighbours that prevention was the ultimate answer.

Lining up every earthen pot she could find, Orla poured the tarry cough syrup into them, sealing each with beeswax.

She reflected on Alice's simple explanation to the farmers, that as they prepared their land's soil for seed, so they must prepare themselves for the ill winds of winter.

It was genuine concern and interest in the lives of the villagers which won the sisters the trust they needed to make a difference to their minds.

Orla assembled the cooled pots into a basket, which Mary and the last of Mary's children, Philippa, would trade at the market. The village market gathering was an important teaching ground for the wise woman. Everyone gathered to sell and trade foods, wares and services.

Mary and Philippa happily occupied themselves with the preparation of their remedies to be sold at the weekly market. They sold many items, from fashionable herbal tooth powders, to hair washes with goat's milk, to salves and syrups. By far their biggest seller was the 'teas for balanced humours'. Mary simply explained that "to drink a pinch of the herbs each night would keep them in fine fettle". The teas were varied for the seasons many times, in preparation for the forecasted illnesses predicted by the local astrologer, William Bones, who conveniently was an in-law to the sisters.

The teas were made from available herbs growing in the area.

Herbal possets, honeyed syrups, and other items were prepared by the Warner sisters for trade.

The shrewd-minded Alice had nominated Mary to trade their flavourful teas at the weekly markets. Occasionally, if a merchant came through with simples from other regions, Alice or Orla were quick to add them to their shelf.

Chosen for her prettiness and faire tongue, the villagers were softened to Mary's words about their health. The local people were fond of her and all were sympathetic to her husband's recent death.

Mary enjoyed her pastimes taking evening walks with her daughter and little nanny goat by the oak trees. Mary believed a variety of plants fed to the goat made for rich, flavourful and medicinal milk. Sometimes in the warm evenings, she would take Philippa in her arms and laugh and dance with her till the moon rose. Many local people had seen them out together, and some found her behaviour a little queer.

After the syrup was finished, Orla pulled down drying herbs from the ceiling in order to make her popular springtime compound.

She was pleased the orange of the Marigold was deep, and upon examination, the Hoarhound and Priest Crown showed to yield a potentially strong brew. She flavoured the mixture with a hint of Water mint to ensure it would be drunk. It took not only a skilled medicinal hand, but a culinary one as well.

As determined to beat sickness as the sisters were, whole families sometimes were stricken from circumstances beyond the hands of the wise women.

This wintry year alone had kept the church Sexton busy in the chapel graveyard.

Orla frowned, remembering how many folk had simply frozen to death while sleeping.

To prevent this terrible fate, families often slept together in box-beds located near the fireplace, insulated from the freezing outdoors.

She recalled nights so cold, that they brought their cows inside from the Byre to utilise their body heat. Since fresh milk and eggs were pivotal to winter survival, chickens remained inside, and milking was done easily due to a shared wall with the byre. This reminded Orla that she needed to restock the waxy ointment they used to treat blackened noses caused from the frost.

Casting her eyes about the shelves of herbal simples, Orla felt satisfied that her stores to fight plague were once again filled. It had taken two summers to replace all the medicines used when the plague last swept through their sloping valley.

Her stomach clenched remembering the losses, including Mary's son and husband.

Orla recalled that the plague had shared its deadly kiss with all in its path, showing no preference between the old and young. Swiftly, it had whirled to the next village, and months later, communities were obliterated, with only wandering sheep and overgrown fields to remind a passer-by that life once thrived.

Their own village had adopted a few lonely drifters. Souls driven away from homes, haunted by the shadows of their loved ones, they knew they faced madness if they remained.

Orla went to the shelf and removed the sickness journal, a great bundle of recorded papers, loosely bound, recording years of disease, remedies and treatments. This book had been passed from Orla's mother to the sisters, brimming with precious remedies and notes.

Diligent record-keeping noted which herbal simples or Galenical compounds were administered and their dose, and the patients' outcomes were meticulously entered.

Thumbing to a recent entry, Orla read: "3rd of May 1650 Farmer Brooks complaining of great pain from lacerations, self-inflicted with swine pitching fork. Peculiar colour in and around ulcerated wound. Foul stink cometh forth. There is naught a fever, but will be forthcoming if unattended. Instructed to trice daily pour contents of phial (Orla's mingle of Poke root, Wild indigo, Nettle, Figwort) over ulcer. After which apply liniment of bruised leaves of all-heal, ripple grass and soldier's woundwort, which hath cooked without boiling until leaves softened, then stirred into sheep's fat, mixed with powdered colewort. Farmer Brooks advised to not meddle with the ulcer by leeching. Advice to patient, 'Hark ye my words, sir, banish the blundering Barber –Surgeon, and stay thee away from unclean waters.

"May 8: Ulcers are pustulant with look of balanced humours. Putrid stink hath been expelled. Instruct patient to drink dark decoctions of tea at each meal. (Ragwort, rose hips, sorrel and blackberry leaves) Speak with in a twelfth night."

Comparisons were made of individual occupations, family size, age, the amount and quality of food one would have access to and the cyclic changes of the seasons. All these facts painted a distinct picture of a person's overall health, and assisted with the next person. Often at day's end, with cups of tea steaming, the sisters' conversation would turn to the sickness journal, and for hours they would try to decipherer the puzzles and answers it held.

The sisters all agreed that the chance of survival was based on the original health of the person prior to exposure to the illness, especially when the sickness was the plague. There were correlations with the robustness of the patient and their previous health history. Curious observations were discovered that those who lived 'plentifully', seemed to be less resilient to illness than their harder-faring farmers and yeoman brethren.

It was a fact that the rickety bone illness was common in pampered children, gently reared, whereas the sun and dirt-soaked country nippers had sturdier and bigger bones. The sisters knew from their cosmetic trades to ladies and their waiting ladies, that they also suffered an odd assortment of ails, found primarily within their class. Since the ladies were most sinful with vanity, they would use any available ingredients to whiten the skin, including lead. Consequently, after long-term use of these ubiquitous concoctions, repair to the guttered skin from further scarring was essential. Laughingly, it seemed the things they took great effort to avoid, sunshine and fresh air, were the things they might have use for after all.

Though they pondered and spoke often of their speculations of the higher classes and of religious controversies, the sisters would never speak of these things outside their cosy kitchen, especially when the topics bordered on blasphemous.

Like every good Christian of the countryside, they said their daily prayers and occasioned the local church to listen to the enriching words of the Vicar, translating the complex actions of their world into the understandings of God's truth. To the local community, Abraham and the Warner sisters were not overly pious, but maintained enough obedience and humbleness to achieve salvation without regular attendance at church. However, William did not attend any of the church services, much to the disapproval of the local clergy and the village busybodies.

Many a night, after Pip was tucked into her blankets, the three sisters were joined in conversation with the brothers William and Abraham Bones. Both were tall, and the eye fell easily upon their chiselled faces, but here the resemblance ended.

Abraham, the older by three years, had a face free of creases, with exception to those around his eyes. He was generous with his smiles, and around his mouth was a tiny dimple, that endeared him to all he met. His openness and familiarity made him the most popular apothecary for miles. The simple country folk felt at ease knowing that their ailments could be cared for without the lengthy journeys to the general Physician and the huge cost of his fee. Even so, men and women would travel great distances to have medicines administered by Abraham, and to listen to one of his engrossing tales. He always left for his tiny apothecary early in the morning, to ensure that people would not be waiting to be seen. Lock up would not occur before the last person was heard and treated.

William, on the other hand, was handsome in sober, darker ways. His sharp eyes missed nothing, his patients always regarded with intensity. Unlike his brother, rarely was one privileged with a smile.

Yet his brooding darkness only made him more mysterious and attractive to most women who encountered him. To the local people, William's past education and life were an enigma, with never a word in reference to times before he settled locally.

William, rarely seen at the local tavern and never seen at Sunday services, was often discussed in his absence in both establishments.

Where women were gathered, William Bones would eventually enter into the gossip. Though well known in a number of villages, William never engaged in conversation, unless it was within his surgery and with a patient of true injury. However, where he lacked in daily courtesies, he made up in brilliance. William was the only Physician and Surgeon in the entire outer area of Essex. People would travel a day to have their broken bones set or their limbs treated and wrapped from fractures and strains. Silently and methodically, he worked, listening and nodding to the prattles of his patients, never stopping until the last of his patients were attended to. Many a night, he would not bother with the long ride to his home, but would merely curl up on the treatment cot, awaking to the next individual rapping at his door.

Over the last years, William had become more withdrawn from the public, with hair worn long and hat deep, concealing his face. This added mystique and further pondering to William's persona.

However, distance and aloofness had not always loomed over his emotions.

Known only to his brother, William had once been buoyant with youthful aspirations and obtainable goals. Nonetheless, the enticement of a decadent life peppered his behaviour and undertakings, filling his earlier years with unscrupulous actions.

Orla smiled in her musing and reflected that yes, their life was strange at times, but always interesting and fulfilling. They all felt a great satisfaction in their role as trusted healers in the community.

West of London, 1666

The smell of the fresh clover rose heavy on the air as the sun warmed the pastures. It was hard for Abigail to believe that only yesterday she had filled her lungs with air fouled by disease and decay, and today there lingered only sweetness.

Compared to the endless sounds of the London streets, the country stillness hummed within her ears. Abigail filled the air with her own voice, singing ditties in time to her footsteps. The day could almost be enjoyed, if only she could wipe out the vivid images she had left behind in London.

She noticed the mist rising from the fields, disappearing into the air, and was surprised to see faces appearing out of the hay stooks, the morning rousing weary travellers. The hillsides were dotted with the occasional tent of other citizens taken to the open roads for protection from the plague. Abigail observed these other fugitives with interest, but they eyed her with suspicion of infection. Diverting her gaze back to the road, she occupied her mind about the reception she would receive from her auntie.

The sun was bright in her eyes, and beads of sweat rolled off her forehead, when she heard a low rumble and rattling far behind her. Turning, but not breaking step, she could see a great cloud of dust coming down the road. She could just see two black horses, and two more, less visible, pulling a coach. She turned back to the road, but moved to the far edge where the weeds lapped at the dirt and gravel. The coach, finely made, slowed some feet behind her. Resisting the urge to turn and stare, she instead put her head down, and picked up her pace. Harnesses clattering, combined with the clumping of many horseshoes, assaulted the stillness Abigail was enjoying.

"Holla, big boys, slow up there," a voice warm with southern tones called out. Reaching Abigail, the horses slowed to a fast walk. Intrigued, she looked up to a finely pressed metal shade covering the window and a beautifully decorated coach. The iron wheels were padded for comfort to the occupant, and immaculately dressed drivers denoted that the passenger was of unmistakeable wealth. This sight was commonplace in London, but on the open road, the spectacle soured the simple beauty of the surroundings. The horses slowed, their shaggy fetlocks rising and falling to match Abigail's pace.

Peeking out the curtain was the leaden-powdered, white face of a woman whose wig was so big it filled the entire window. Abigail smiled slightly at the comical image, but the occupant returned her smile with a frown. Lips pinched and brows furrowed, she called out in a voice that would put the most relaxed on edge. "Driver, why have we slowed? Surely thou have seen peasant drudgery before." Her tone was impatient, and shrill. "If I am not in Salisbury by the Sabbath, I shall leave you to answer to my uncle." Judging by the exchange of looks the drivers shared, the uncle must have been a foreboding fellow.

"Apologies lady, but we thought the girl might know if the next village was locked or was open to travellers, and if there were an inn we could rest at for the night." He gestured towards Abigail. "The last was closed even to your generous coin," the southerner said with an apologetic inflection. Stretching out the window, the woman's face folded into more lines.

"It is not my desire to dirty my gowns on the floors of some dreary country inn," she called out shrilly. "I have my basket of titbits inside, and plenty of wine. Drive on until I desire a rest from the dreadful jostling. Oh, and do try to control the beasts so that their steps avoid the ruts in the road!" she said with exasperation.

The men gestured to each other, and finally one stated bravely, "Pardon me, lady, but the horses will have to be rested and watered a number of times before we arrive in Salisbury." The velvet curtain did not move from the window, but the voice was penetrating nevertheless.

"Hark, by no means should you disturb me again. I pay thee enough to deliver me to my destination without your excuses for tardiness. The brutes will endure, just as I must."

Abigail kept walking, but returned her gaze to the ground. "Peasant drudgery," that's what the lady had called her. Scrutinising the state of her outer skirt, hatless head and sun burned face, she supposed the assessment was accurate. Abigail was old enough to nurture concerns about her appearance, and in the last few months, had noticed the shy glances from her brothers' friends. She was surprised that, considering her circumstances, she should care how she looked.

"Aahumm," the clearing of the man's throat startled her back from her thoughts. "You, girl, is there somewhere of respect we might be able to stop and rest our horses for a spell?" the southerner shouted above the clattering and clumping.

Abigail, straining to make eye contact with the drivers, shouted above the din, "Sorry, but I am a traveller myself, and know not these parts!" The drivers exchange a baffled look, and before they could question her further, she returned her eyes to the road. Abigail hoped they would leave her to continue her journey in peace.

She was relieved when the driver urged the horses into a fast trot, leaving her eyes watering from the heavy dust. By the time, the cloud had settled the coach and occupants had disappeared.

Abigail had been walking hard, only pausing to drink from her water bag once. The road was entirely devoid of any travellers. Judging from the height of the sun, she knew it had been a length of time since she had left the cottage, and still no one had passed her since the carriage. Sometime later, her hunger could not be ignored, and walking into the pasture, she sat down upon the tall grass to munch some of her father's cheese, and the last of the oatcakes. Looking around, she liked what she saw, or more what she didn't see.

Never spending much time out in the country, Abigail was pleased by the fresh air and the myriad of new smells the soft breeze carried. Having spent her entire life in London, she was accustomed to all the noises of the busy local commerce. She had never noticed the buzzing of bees, which now hovered lazily in the clover, nor the variety of bird song, which filled the air. *Was it always so quiet out here?* she wondered to herself.

It was a pleasant scene, but the air held the knowledge of something more sinister. Abigail's attention was drawn by the sound of distant mooing, which continued to grow louder. Chewing the last of the oatcake, Abigail stood up, and shading her eyes looked at three cows trotting towards her. Upon seeing her, their calling took on an edge of anxiety, but still they made their way towards her. Forgetting her destination for a moment, she curiously walked to meet the cows. It wasn't long before Abigail discovered the cause of their concern.

Swinging painfully from side to side were udders so full of milk, they seemed they could rupture at any moment. Abigail looked closer, and there were distinct red streaks running from each teat, disappearing into their bellies. Abigail was not an expert in the health of cattle, but like most folk, she knew enough to know that these cows had not been milked in days. Their cries were pitiful, and Abigail could see they were in a great amount of pain. They stopped a few paces before her, liquid brown eyes searching hers for relief. Looking around, she did not see anyone around, but did notice a thatched roof in the distant field. Wondering how people could neglect to milk their own cows, Abigail decided to lead the cows back to the barn, where perhaps the farmer or his wife could be found.

It didn't take much convincing the cows, and as they spied the barn, their awkward gait increased. As she neared the farm, apprehension begun to slip into her mind. Where were the people who owned the cows and the pasture? She was edgy, and was startled when she trod on a scarecrow which had fallen to the ground. Covered in dirt, she wondered how long it had been since it fell.

The closer she got to the mud and straw barn, the more she noticed that things seemed wrong. Though early in the afternoon, the farm was eerily quiet. The month was August, soon to be harvest, and still there were overgrown vegetables in the garden, left to seed. Opening the gate to enter the yard, the trio of cows trotted past her, heading towards the milking area.

"Hello, is anyone about?" Abigail called out. Her voice was consumed by the uneasy silence. Latching the gate, she followed the tracks of the cows. Calling out again, she was startled by the answer of a horse pacing in the coral. Noticing that the feed trough was empty and the water was low, she figured he had been locked in there for days. Walking nearer to the horse, she untied the leather knot at the gate, and pushed it open so the horse could find his own food and water. Knowing now that something was amiss, Abigail was torn between staying and seeing if someone needed help, or heeding her instincts and running back to the road.

Thinking that her mother would probably want her to try to help, Abigail cautiously made her way towards the farmhouse. Maybe they were out visiting family, or maybe they were having an afternoon rest from the heat. Despite all her innocent ideas of the occupants' whereabouts, Abigail still trembled with apprehension. Nervously, she stopped before the door of the squat, mud house. Reaching out to knock on the door, her fist fell to her side as the door was already ajar. A recognisable stench was released when she pushed it opened. Gagging, Abigail brought her hand to cover her nose and stepped back, fighting the urge to escape the death which occupied the room. Driven by the need to find food, she pushed herself through the threshold. The room was plain, adorned only with weaved grain husks hanging from each doorway. The table in the centre of the room was piled with an array of outdoor tools, moulding food and bundles of garlic. Her eyes fell to the odd lump on the floor. Looking closer, she could see that on the hearthstones, bundled in a rough hemp blanket, were two children. Her breath caught, as she looked into tiny faces, moulted blue with the early stages of decay. Crying out, Abigail stepped back, tearing her gaze from the dead children. Turning quickly to flee, she was distracted from an object hanging from the rafters and understood this was the children's mother. Her face was bloated, and her tongue bulged from her lips. She seemed unaccustomed to making nooses, as the rope was wrapped around her neck again and again, finished with an exaggerated knot. Barefoot and still in her sleeping dress, Abigail assumed her children had passed in the night, and that her despair had been too much for the dawning light.

Tears streamed from her eyes, and Abigail moved her hand from her nose to cover her eyes, the sight more distressing than the smell. Her search for food now forgotten, Abigail bolted through the door. Fuelled by the grisly scene, Abigail ran from the yard and down the lane, back towards the road. Looking over her shoulder, she hoped that the animals would survive on their own. Slowing past an old yew tree, a great mound of soil caught her eye. She noticed a cross of branches marked the site of beloved husband and father, likely belonging to the family inside.

Abigail jogged for a long distance. Every time her lungs burned and she slowed, she decided she wasn't far enough away from the grim farm. The scene fresh in her mind and the putrid smell clinging to her body fuelled her legs.

Finally, when her chest was heaving and the pain in her sides was unbearable, she allowed herself to slow to a fast walk. Only then did she notice that the sun had begun its long decline into the summer twilight.

Casting her head and eyes about, Abigail wondered where she might rest for the night. Already her wobbly legs were aching from their enormous effort, and her feet slowed with the heaviness of fatigue. Abigail was certain she did not wish to risk another encounter with a dead family, so without effort she decided that her night would be spent outside.

As it was still too early to sleep, she chose to keep walking. She travelled until her legs were ready to collapse beneath her weight. Wearily, she trudged off the dusty road, pushed herself under a fence and made her way into a small grove of trees. It wasn't long before she found a clump of tall bushes growing together and Abigail formed a small nest of padded needles. Taking out her mysterious bottle, she swallowed the last of the bitter drink and chewed a piece of garlic. She tossed the empty bottle into her bag and pulled dried leaves and pine needles over herself. Curling up, her sore muscles quickly twitched into sleep.

London, 1618

June was notoriously a busy month for the arrival of babies. Abraham and his younger brother William were no exception, being born three years and a few days apart.

Torn from the warmth of their mother's womb, their senses were assaulted by the bedlam of the overcrowded ward of St Tomas hospital. Where thousands died each year, the Bones brothers somehow survived. They were fortunate to be born to a family of moderation, with vigorous involvement in the medical world. Their father, a popular Barber-Surgeon near Hyde Park, took pride that his two surviving sons would be by his side to pass on his unique methods of healing.

As their father had been apprenticed in his work and never obtained the prestige of a college of medicine, he was never held in the same esteem as the 'gentlemen' of his vocation. Barber Bones was optimistic of his only sons going to the reputed colleges of medicine, to emerge as academic Surgeons and Physicians. He would often daydream that a son would incur work as a court Physician.

He believed that by exposing them young to the wonders of healing, they would naturally be inclined to follow in and beyond his footsteps.

The Barber's apothecary was a spectacle of peculiar utensils, implements and devices. Trying to keep up with trends, Barber Bones followed the findings of the Italian Physician, Galileo, using contemporary instruments like a pendulum for measuring pulse-rate, a syringe for extracting bladder stones, and a peculiar instrument called the 'thermometer' to measure bodily temperatures. As the citizens of London found it important to keep with the times of the French and Italians, Barber Bones used these tools to attract the fashion-conscious patient.

There were towering, dusty shelves, crammed with an assortment of clay and glass crocks, some of obvious identity, and others containing substances of dubious origin.

Some ingredients, safe under lock, were deemed unidentifiable and left to the vivid imaginations of young minds.

As there was little time for outside friendships, the brothers made the apothecary their playground. As wide-eyed youth, the Bones brothers spent many an hour watching and assisting in the bleeding and leeching of ill patrons.

Though messy and unsightly, they preferred this method to other treatments, namely the red-hot irons. Though usually left to more qualified administrators, Barber Bones would use the irons upon request, if a patient wanted to avoid the outlandish fees of the Physicians. The irons were administered to the soles of the feet, which would char the flesh, the gagging stench lingering in the air for hours. The curdling screams of the patients would leave the boys queasy and quaking in their shoes for days after.

Some techniques he used though, were out-of-date with the ever-changing times.

One in particular was the occasional use of the 'piss-pot' method of diagnosing. Patients would pass water into a bucket, where then the Barber would examine the waste and taste it for tell-tale signs of illness. After the questionable contents were scrutinised, the boys, noses held, were instructed to empty the strong-smelling urine into the streets. This method, recently condemned by the Physicians as 'quackish', was something the boys were not at all interested in partaking, and using the Physicians as examples, persuaded their father that he cease in this distasteful diagnostic method.

Growing older, William and Abraham grew accustomed to the comings and goings of the sick and injured. Their world revolved around various incidents within the day, and conversations focused on the treatment of patients. Endlessly, the brothers would puzzle and speculate over the healing effects of substances like Mercury, a known poison, which when applied to syphilis sores, burns and other skin afflictions, could somehow placate the sickness. They pondered the effects of the capricious assortment of other powdered remedies which had known toxic effects. Some Galenical compounds containing a vast array of dried animal parts, including frog's spawns, Unicorn horns, and blood, fat and bile from miscellaneous animals, were intriguing and more importantly, costly. Barber Bones made no attempt of understanding how or why these agents could hold medicinal properties, only that he held faith in his teachings and the coin these remedies would fetch. When the brothers would ask the exact purposes of the compounds, their father was often vague with unsatisfying explanations.

Most enigmatic, was the use of 'cold deadman's skull'. Keeping only two at a time, their father was secretive of this grisly remedy's effects, and happily for the Bones brothers; it was not for public viewing. They knew that moss growing within the skulls, taken from graves, possessed an infallible healing agent, which once salved, was used for sword wounds. The boys would often speculate which smelled worse, the oozing wound, or the eerie moss.

A patient's condition was determined by different methods. The regarding of one's 'humours' was the first step in determining which treatment was to be administered. There was a series of examinations and questions: "Were the humours in disharmony with the seasons? Was the bile and phlegm black or yellow? Was the humour moist, dry or cold?" The dis-harmonic mixing of humours could metamorphose into life-threatening distempers and sicknesses. Since Barber Bones was not a Physician of educated knowledge, his understanding was shallow but worded correctly to extract the desired fees. Once the dis-harmonic humour was quarried, then the medicaments were administered. Bloodletting, or breathing a vein, followed by cupping with scarification, was a common method of draining off the offensive humour. Emetic purgatives that induced vomiting, diarrhoea, spitting or the use of 'clysters' were carried out, often at the patient's request.

These expensive powders and remedies were given after a lengthy bought of purging. It was a known fact of the time, that excessive blood or phlegm in the body would produce various ill symptoms, ranging from headaches to melancholy.

On a few occasions, stricken patients were carried in, suffering from convulsions and biting of the tongue. Then the help of all available family members was needed. The standard treatment was to remove a good amount of blood from the vein, followed by cupping glasses applied to the shoulders and deep scarification presided over. A strong emetic was administered if the patient could swallow, and if not, then a pitch-like substance was added to the clyster and fed up through the bottom end. Lastly, the hair was shorn close to the scalp, and strong smelling, blister-producing poultices applied all over the top of the head. The patient could be there the entire day and night, tied to the chair, convulsing and howling with pain.

Every day was different, but one could always count on bodily fluids escaping to the flooring, sufficient amounts of moaning, the occasional yelling and the ever-present scurrying rats.

Abraham regarded the ghastly displays of his father's attempt at healing as, at best, cruel. He started to question his father's barbaric acts of pain and by observing the statistics of survivors, believed that most had been better off prior to entering the Barber's surgery. With continuous debates over the authenticity of such remedies like the horn of Unicorn, or the healing powers of skull of a deadman, Abraham started to search for more reliable, time-proven healing modalities. Rebelling, Abraham left London for a time as a young adult and travelled the countryside, observing the healing methods of the wise women and Midwives. Rebellious but not disrespectful, Abraham obediently found his way home upon demand from his father. Displeased by his fanciful thoughts and lack of interest in the prestigious colleges, Barber Bones punished Abraham by casting him into the public hospital sector. Having not a shilling to his name, Abraham was forced to live under the roof of his father, silently swallowing the unsavoury retribution.

St Bartholomew, or more commonly known as 'The House of the Poor' was a hospital where the only prerequisite for admittance was proof of poverty. The first weeks were sobering and humbling for Abraham. There were over 200 beds with constant occupancy. The staffing consisted of three Physicians, two Surgeons and a woman treating infants for scald head, a handful of laywomen and a number of 'helpers', this last category being Abraham's first area of work. A helper would bring broths, porridges and the hospital's brewed beer to the patients unable to get up for themselves, and if needed, would spoon-feed the frail patients. The washing of linen and mopping up of an assortment of somatic fluids was never ending. The only pace at the hospital was a sprint. Sweating, out of breath attendants, were a common sight. Never enough beds meant patients lay upon the floor, crying out for immediate attention, grabbing the legs of those in blue uniforms. Often, there were pile-ups of fallen hospital workers, after sprawling from a patient impeding passage.

Abraham had never imagined such pandemonium and would arrive home at all hours of the night, often too exhausted to put food into his own mouth. The weight fell from his lanky frame with alarming speed. His father watched him closely, but Abraham uttered not a vexing word of his bleak circumstances at St Bart's. Luckily for the young Bones man, not long after his third month, the Physicians and Surgeons learned of his life in the wake of the Barber-Surgeon and quickly recruited his skills to assist in more pressing matters of health.

Since the hospital was the only medical service available to the poor, St Bart's seconded as a teaching hospital.

The hospital was busy, and the next recruits of apprenticing Physicians were postponed. This was advantageous for Abraham, for he was given the opportunity to learn skills privy to the exclusive students of the Physicians' colleges. As with most apprentices, Abraham was thrown into the gory world of amputations and flesh cuttings, observing the details of operations and bone settings with precision. There were common vomiting sicknesses, falls from horses, numerous wounds from fights and a few amputations. All syphilis, gonorrhoea and other venereals were sent to Southwark. The demands were high, with speed more a criterion than finesse. Abraham, always one to accomplish a task with pride, found it unsettling that before he could sew up a wound, or bandage a limb to proficiency, he was sternly instructed to move to the next person.

The results of such hasty, postoperative attention were that Abraham observed many patients fall victim to fever and many were discharged from the hospital only to find themselves in a shallow grave behind St Bartholomew. However disturbing and heartbreaking his work was, Abraham was learning aspects of the body he never dreamed of having exposure to.

Meanwhile, Abraham's more diplomatic brother, William, attended the London College of Surgeons, much to the delight and pride of his father. Though it took every penny to fund his tuition, the Barber-Surgeon was living his dream through his son.

Where Abraham was learning practical, hands-on skills to keep his patients alive, William was engrossed in 'gentlemanly' methods of attending to patients.

William and his fellow students learned the noble and ancient philosophies of the Greeks. They eagerly embraced the thoughts and technique of Galen and proficiently spiced their education with methods discovered in exotic lands during the holy wars. William was an avid learner, and he devoured all contemporary findings and thoughts on the human body. The science of astrology was also an essential part of a healing regime. What days to mix medical compounds and what days to administer them, were very much influenced by the heavens above and their mathematical answers for that day and hour. Failure of a patient's health was often blamed on the blundering of a Physician's astrology. One student in particular, by the name of Nicholas Culpepper, took a passionate interest in this particular school of thought. William was also interested in astrology, and went out of his way to engage in conversation with Nicholas. William found he and Nicholas shared many radical thoughts on science and fundamental issues of healing. William was first in his classes of traditional teachings but craved innovative new healing modalities and philosophies. Nicholas spoke often of travelling abroad with the armies and enhancing his skills from the local healers of the regions, his ambition focused on the available plant medicines of each area. William would listen with growing interest and towards the end of his education, without word to his father, vowed that he would journey to lands such as Italy, where progressive healing methods were a priority in the community and government.

After two years of theory, the students were being prepared to step foot into a hospital and practice their newly found skills on living patients.

Finely educated men from the right schooling would sometimes be sent to practice their skills in the filthy and horrid wards of a church-funded charity hospital, before finally moving onto a more prestigious institution. Hence, they looked to their future classrooms with both anticipation and repugnance.

When William began his apprenticeship at St Bart's, he was at first sceptical but soon deeply impressed by the skills his brother Abraham had achieved in the scant years he had apprenticed there. Even without the title of Physician or Surgeon, he commanded respect that contrasted his youthful façade.

Some of the schooled apprentices were quick to snub his authority. Since he did not share their prestigious titles nor oaths, he was deemed a 'mere Barber' and certainly not to be regarded as peer or colleague. Their opinions mattered not to Abraham, only that they be mindful of sloppy work, especially if tending to one of his charges. Many of the medical students were jealous of his nimbleness with stitching wounds, and setting fractured bones. There was a great difference between bounding and sewing a cadaver, to that of a thrashing and swearing patient. Abraham had the unrivalled title of clean healing in his patients. No convalescing patient succumbed to rot under the watchful care of the concerned young man. William was proud to discover healing philosophies illuminated by his older brother. Abraham, in turn, was very interested in learning all the classical aspects of his new vocation.

Though learning different aspects of healing, the Bones brothers together shared in contemporary and sometimes radical thoughts regarding science, mathematics and astronomy. Many a night, ale in hand, shouting above the din of the local tavern, they discussed the mind-expanding writings of Copernicus and Kepler, and the intriguing writings of Michel de Notre dame, who adopted a Latin name, 'Nostradamus'.

Known for his simple plant remedies, Nostradamus' reputation as a Plague Doctor was widespread. Abraham would often refer to his brief visit to the countryside and the simples used by the wise woman. Nicholas would sometimes join in these conversations, with his interest in healing herbs, and more so, of medicines available to the poor. Often they would converse about the Italian, Galileo Galilei and fantasise of visiting him in his imposed house arrest and engage in conversations about his controversial books.

The Bones brothers, intelligent and tenacious to make the world work for them, both gained respected titles of medicine which would launch them into their vocations, exulting them to a God-like status.

With growing maturity and worldly awareness, they found their father and his colleagues outdated and crude in their dogma.

Their interests lay in many areas, especially if the prospect entailed leaving London.

There was a smouldering heat of revolution, both environmentally and within their souls. With resources available to them by ways of experience and worldly incentive, it was not long before they were packing their chests and leaving the Barber Bones standing, gawping at the closed door.

West of London, 1666

The next few days and nights were thankfully uneventful. Abigail was still surprised that the wide road she travelled was virtually deserted. It was in sharp contrast to her memories of travel with her father, which held images of highways choked with single riders, carriages and merchant wagons, coming and going from London. After days of walking the same thoroughfare, she could distinctly remember each passing person.

The tiny villages which dotted the land were far between when reaching them by foot. The few Abigail had passed through had closed gates, and one held a public sign warning travellers to not pass within, as it was a plague village. Abigail followed the plague road around the village and strained to hear the life coming forth. Most were silent. It was an uneasy sort of silence, the kind which left you feeling alone.

After sometime, Abigail briskly advanced to a quaint sign announcing the next village.

The flowers that bloomed around the base of the oak were bright and cheering.

Abigail's curiosity led her through the main street, and distracted by gnawing hunger, she was hoping to find a Baker and perhaps some curds to place upon the slice. Her mouth was salivating as she anticipated the fresh foods. Within a few moments, she had arrived in the centre of the town. There were two and three-terraced structures surrounding the cobbled centre. Clean washing hung limply on the ropes outside the narrow apartments. In one window, the calico curtains had made their way to the outside of the open window. The terraced houses had a look to them as if the inhabitants had simply left at a moment's notice, leaving doors and windows wide open. A familiar smell, resembling rotting vegetables and turned soil, emanated from the houses. The stink was familiar to the ones Abigail had left behind in London.

There was a wide array of farm animals wandering the streets looking disoriented and lost, and yet not a single face could be seen peering through the windows. In ordinary circumstances, it would have been comical to see cows munching well-kept front gardens and goats consuming fabric bolts, yet not a bubble of mirth could burst through the gloom in the air.

Where were all the people? Maybe they had fled their homes to visit distance relatives such as she was doing, Abigail thought. Perhaps they were wary of passersby travelling with the Black Death as their companion. She well understood their apprehension.

Looking around, she noticed the chickens pecking in the streets, and a few sheep grazing in the common yards around the water pump. Dusty and sweating, Abigail walked to where the town's water source came from.

When she had reached the pump, she realised her great thirst, and after pumping for a moment, the clean water came forth. It was cool, and she bathed her arms and face. Looking up from the dripping water, she startled, as before her a few paces, stood a woman, around her mother's age. "I beg thee pardon," Abigail brushed the hair from her face, "I am a lonely traveller, and I hope you can tell me where I can find food?" The woman was well kept, with a clean underskirt, and her hair tidy, but she gaped at Abigail as if something were not right within herself.

"Grace, is that you, child?" She peered at Abigail. "Come to Mam." The woman opened her arms and smiled. Abigail looked over her shoulder and realised that the woman was speaking to her.

Awkwardly, she replied, "Apologies, Mistress, but I am not 'Grace'. My name is Abigail, and I am on this plague road to visit my—" her words were cut off as the woman stepped forward.

"Don't be a cheeky lass," the woman interrupted. "I knew that you would right yerself. Even when that fool Sexton came to take ye from my arms, and I swore to him that you only slept, that you were not fallen by the plague, not ye, my bright girl, not ye!"

Tears ran down her face, as she stumbled towards Abigail. Fear was mixed with sympathy, but Abigail took a step backwards. The woman was a pace from her, arms open, and Abigail could now see that her tidy dress disguised prominent tokens of plague.

Her bodice was open at the neck, and there was one purpling sore, deeply embedded within her skin. Abigail recoiled and took flight before the woman could reach her. Racing through the end of the town, she noticed flickers of movement around her, understanding that the remaining villagers were hiding. Stumbling through the southern gate, she saw countless shallow graves. The human toll of this pestilence was incomprehensible.

Abigail decided that she would brave a sleep in a barn tonight, as her last few nights on the ground had found her stiff and cold in the morning. Before long, Abigail spied a large barn in a pasture of clover, a lengthy distance from the yeoman's family home. Reaching the barn, she threw the doors open wide and was welcomed by a number of blinking cows. Wrinkling her nose, Abigail quickly discovered that the stable had not been mucked out for numerous days. She jumped out of the way as the cattle pushed passed her, eager to reach the fresh clover. Propping open the heavy doors with stones, she aired the structure, cleared the freshest dung and finally settled down for the night.

The next day was bright, but even though Abigail had slept soundly, she felt sore and tight from walking. As with the day before, she passed few travellers on the road. The buzzing of insects and Abigail's footfalls were the only sound disturbing the silence.

By afternoon, Abigail wondered with frustration, how long she would walk until she saw the signs leading her in the direction of Salisbury? Her food was almost gone, and so she had begun to ration herself to just an evening meal. She was starving and feeling vulnerable.

The August sun was hot through her summer clothes, but her apprehension for the future was cold in her heart. Abigail was shaken out of her daze when she heard a distant clatter coming up the road.

Deciding that she did not wish to be further questioned, she threw herself into the grass to observe the passersby.

When in view, a peddler's wagon swaying and clanging could be seen and heard. Various pots and household needs intended for sale, were haphazardly tied to the outside of the wagon, as if in haste to depart. As the clumping of the big horse neared her hiding place, Abigail could easily see why the dray swaggered along the road. There was no driver, nor any other person guiding the horse. Abigail had seen numerous riderless horses, but not a wayfaring wagon like this. She watched as the horse stopped and started pulling tufts of grass from the earth. It seemed probable that the owners of this wagon had fallen to the plague like so many others of this time. Abigail's next thought was that there was bound to be food found within the wagon. Careful, so as not to frighten the horse, she walked to the back of the wagon, climbed up the high wheels and gingerly peered between the thick hemp cloth.

The familiar stench assaulted her nose and the scene painful, scalded her mind. She released a small scream as the grisly face of the plague stared out through sunken eyes and a swollen purple face. To her chest, the once young mother clutched the tiny body of a baby, the face tender even in death. The sadness of the scene sent a shockwave of grief through Abigail.

Apologising to the corpses, and averting her eyes, Abigail quickly ransacked the wagon, finding some aged vegetables and moulding bread. As she jumped off the wagon, the horse lifted its head from grazing and released a low nicker. Staring at the horse, Abigail spoke out loud, "Of course, ride the horse to Wiltshire!" Slowly Abigail stood up, and making her way towards the horse, she questioned her own intention. When had she ever ridden a horse alone? Living in London, all was accessible without the need of long-distance horse rides, and her father or brothers had always led her. How hard could it be? She argued with herself. Her apprehension of riding the horse was out-weighed by the drive to reach her destination.

Abigail decided the horse would need a friendly name. She considered the people in her life, and because she was so famished, the face of the Baker who always offered her warm buns came to mind. Perkins it is. Naming the horse was far easier than making sense of the complex webbing of harnesses attached to the wagon.

Her father had kept a large draft horse for transporting the heavy metals required for a Smith, and so the patterns of undoing were not unfamiliar, only she had never been faced with the task alone, especially with two older brothers in the house. After a few tries, much sweat and a few curses her mother would not have approved of, Perkins was free from the wagon. Wrapping her hands around the harness, she struggled to get her leg over. Much to her relief, the horse only turned and regarded her with feigned indifference, as she attempted many a time to mount. With one final exertion, Abigail managed to claw her way up onto his back. The lumpy tack was uncomfortable, and she had to double the long reins, but eventually, she found a position between the bony spine and toughened leather harness and settled her weight. Squeezing her legs tight, she tossed the reins, urging the horse to "Gid-up". Snorting and without fanfare, Perkins continued his earlier journey.

England, 1642

As in many families, Abraham and William were split in their political views, with Abraham supporting the overthrowing of a useless king and giving power to the people. But William, as was his father, felt obliged to lay their loyalties with the royal family. William and Abraham parted company in order to show their allegiance to their chosen political sides. Abraham became involved in the revolution between King Charles I and the newly emerging parliament, and soon found himself behind the battle lines of the resulting Civil War. In the long grass as men's blood spilled forth, Abraham perfected his skills at bullet removing, amputations, stitching and wound healing. The fighting took him through Essex, where contrasting the human devastations of war, he was humbled by the land's uncomplicated beauty. His fondness of the region grew, despite the anger and death enfolding the land.

On one campaign, the fighting took his command to a sloping valley, where shadowed by ancient oaks, a stream split the farmland. Arrows whizzing through the air and clouds of powder smoke stinging the eyes, made for tense triage circumstances. Although grim, the cannonballs and shot wounds left holes within the flesh for a quick glance into the mysteries of the human body. Since the church banned autopsies, rarely the opportunity arose to see first-hand the mechanisms of the systems within.

On one particular morning, the sun was making visible the carnage of the night's attack. Abraham himself had only survived by Gods' mercy. Standing up stiff, and with heavy heart, he soon discovered that the majority of the Surgeons were not so blessed. Squatting beside a fallen comrade, whom Abraham had known from his days at St Bart's, he sighed. All this bloodshed and for what benefit? He felt the first rays of sun warming his face, and squinting into the sun, he saw silhouetted shapes in the distance. They carried large woven baskets between them and great bundles of something, tied upon their backs. A handful of lengths before reaching the now standing Abraham, the group split, half turning to make their way to the nearby officer, leaving three others to quickly make the distance to where he stood. Abraham was pleased and relieved that the three facing him would most likely be the healing women of the area—wise women.

This was confirmed by numerous pouches tied to waist belts and the distant rattling of jars and bottles, muffled slightly from hemp bandages. They all wore charms of feathers, shells, oak bark and dried flowers tied with an array of ribbons and leather sinew. They were young and all attractive in their different ways. The eldest was dark and stern, the set of her mouth saying she did not stand for balderdash, but her hazel eyes held sympathy and compassion. Standing in the middle, yellow hair escaping from her ties, Abraham was impressed that a woman, who was heavy with pregnancy, would be out risking her life for the fallen men. Lastly, walking slightly behind the other two, dark braids bouncing at her hips, was a third woman, and Abraham's breath caught. Pointy chin and rounded cheekbones contrasted the classical beauty depicted in contemporary art. With browned face and numerous freckles, she was no courtly beauty. However, her confident grace and clear eyes held uncanny perception for one so young, being unlike any woman he had met in London. The distance shortened, and the women were before Abraham.

"We are the sisters Warner, daughter and granddaughters from a long line of healers and Midwives. We know that you are the only standing Surgeon, and we have come not to gainsay with you in our methods, only to move this rabble out of our fields." The stern one said with crossed arms. "Oh, and if ye wish to make use of that arm in the future, ye best let one of us treat and bind the wound." And she began unloading the bundles from her back. Only now noticing the blood and muted pain, Abraham slid to the ground with an exhaustion which reached his soul.

Crouching down in front of him, the braided girl, who up close looked no older than 18 or 19, handed him some dried fruit, and a cup of cool water. "I am called Orla, my pregnant sister is Mary, and the grumpy one is Alice. Just do as she says, and you won't find need to suffer her temper," and she winked. Without another word, the young woman smoothly and with practised ease, cleaned the wound from the poison of the shot. When Abraham questioned her as to why she did not cauterise the area, she seemed surprised and informed him that the herbal simples she was using would not allow the wound to rot, and to use such an extreme method as cauterising would only weaken him. She finished binding the wound with hemp bandages soaked in a dark and gooey liquid and handed him the contents of a phial with instruction to drink until it was finished. "Sit still until ye are fit and fare to work alongside us," Orla said, and with that, she gathered her leather bags and trudged off to face the field of hollering men.

During the long days that it took to bury the dead and tend to the wounded, Abraham became increasingly interested in all that concerned Orla. When the moment offered him a chance to look up from his work, his eyes would search the horizon for her shape. Without reason, the way she tossed her braids and the way she arched her head when laughing were more interesting than anything Abraham was presently working on. At the brief mealtimes, he would seek her company, and beneath downcast eyes, would steal glimpses of her while feigning interest in his food. He was consumed by her mere existence.

Her information and knowledge of the local plants intrigued Abraham, and her warm laughter and blushing cheeks endeared his heart. Orla, in turn, begged to hear poetry recited in Latin and listened for hours of his experiences in London. Neither could take their eyes from one another.

At the end of the all-too-short week, the company packed up and prepared to move on. Abraham nervously and with a heavy heart, made his way to the roadside to farewell the Warner sisters. Kicking at the gravel and feeling the colour rise to his cheeks, Abraham faced Orla. "Ah, I thank you, I am obliged to thee for tending my arm. It has healed well, and with little pain." Looking away awkwardly, he noticed Mary smiling and stepping away to give them some privacy, but worse, Alice frowning and folding her arms.

Mary, thankfully, pulled Alice around, pointing to some distant plants. "Yes, well, my departure does not dictate that I waste words." Swallowing, Abraham twisted his hands. "Ah, Orla," he blurted out, "it would gladden me to be in your company at a time of your leisure." Noticing the cough from Alice, Abraham blushed and lowered his voice further, "I confess that the sooner you can grant me this pleasure, the lighter my heart will feel, from its burden of your absence." Smiling, Orla searched his handsome face, surprised that such a man of breeding and education could feel sentiment for her, a simple woman.

"Sir, I thank thee kindly for your words. As I know your passing leads you to distant lands, I will wait for word of your return to our village. Mine own heart has indeed found salvation since beholding you in the rising sun." Orla, well aware that her sister's ears would burst from such strain, turned so as to give view of her backside and smiled unsparingly up to Abraham. Overcome by boldness, Abraham took her hand, and brought her fingers to his lips.

"Swear to me now, Orla, that you shall marry not another whilst the war keeps us apart? I swear, woman, you have bewitched my heart!" Eyes blazing with passion, he awaited her answer, aware that Alice had suddenly taken great interest in their conversation.

Still smiling she simply said, "Sir, you carry my heart within your hands," and with that, she placed a tiny cloth tied with a ribbon into his palm.

When the farewells and thanks were finished, Abraham joined the ranks and position, which was fitting, for his station, eyes moist with emotion.

As the wagons got well on the way, preceded by the many scuffling boots, the London healer turned and watched the waving, braided woman get smaller. When they were out of sight, he opened his stained hand to discover what his tiny treasure held. Beneath the folds of the dyed parchment, he beheld a charm made from the heartwood of an oak, artfully carved into a rising sun, and in the centre of the sun, a heart stood out in contrast. If smelled beautifully of lavender and rose, and Abraham breathed deeply of the floral wood. Placing it carefully back within the parchment, he safely placed the parcel within an inner pocket, next to his heart.

They made their way down into the gentle valley, the road hidden by the green hills, twisting their way around the shaded stream, the same one they first came by. Only this time, Abraham didn't notice the beautiful scenery.

For the first time in his life, Abraham's head was filled with notions and dreams not to do with medicines and patients.

1644

William's curiosity and ambitions led him to work as a Physician in the far port of Dover. He was told that if he desired a quick adventure, there were departing ships crossing the channel daily. Wanting to be near the docks where intriguing foreign people would arrive, William took a position as a Physician working in a busy surgery with a combination of healers.

They were thrilled to have a London Physician amongst them, and William had his choice of hours and patients. Located in an unsavoury part of the notoriously rough town meant William's clientele were of mixed and colourful backgrounds. Hearing the strange tales of his patients, who were mostly sailors in the Royal Navy or merchant sailors, fuelled his drive to see these lands for himself. He committed to the surgery and to himself for a specified length of time, so he could save enough coin in order to travel freely. Though William chose to work near the wharves, where there was an assortment of human wreckage to observe, he lived and entertained himself as was becoming of a gentleman of his standing. He would frequent the theatre and became a regular at the Friday night performances. It was here one autumn's eve that he first laid eyes upon Laurel. Delicate and fair, her skin the colour of lilies, her hair fiery ringlets of flames.

The gown she wore was French silk, a deep ocean blue, fitted to give tribute to her exquisite curvature. As one does in crowds, she looked up and for a frozen moment their eyes met, faces and sounds blurred as they recognised the attraction for each other. William had but a brief glimpse, to forget all the other prominent women in his life.

The setting sun of the next evening marked the beginning of their courtship. It was not long into the dark winter, that William approached her father, a notable importer, for Laurel's hand in marriage.

The ceremony was elegant, though without the usual pomp one would presume for such a match. It was William's desire to marry her as soon as was socially acceptable. Even his own family only became aware of the union weeks after the event. William discovered joy within his heart, something he could never remember feeling. Spring followed winter, and soon the days were warm and sweet with new love.

The Atlantic coastal breeze cooled the late summer's day. William had sent a message to Laurel to meet him at their favourite gaming house, and having left work early, was making his way through the crowded streets.

Upon arrival, Laurel stood up, looking flushed and excited. "William," she waved, and motioned him to the corner table near the open window, her lips brushing his cheek. "My husband, on my word, I have news which will put bounce in your step," she exclaimed.

"Matrimony has made my step already so buoyant that I fear I might take flight!" he laughed. "Please seat yourself, as I, too, have sumptuous news, and I implore you to allow me to speak my words, post haste!" Taking her soft hands within his, he sat down across from her.

"Then pray, tell me your news, as you are pert with your words, I expect all soon to be indulging thee with my announcement." Laurel sat back, excitement in her face.

"Without adieu, my Laurel, I depart for Italy in a fortnight!" William explained, but then his smile faded as he noted Laurel's furrowed brow. William hastily embellished. "I have accepted a short time position in Venice, working at the British Naval Hospital. It will give me added opportunity to learn from esteemed Italian Physicians. I will earn more crowns in the scant months there than the entirety of a year in England," he reported with enthusiasm. "When I return, we will have ample coin to purchase a grand home. One your father will truly approve of," he added.

Laurel stood up, her face crimson with the colour only achieved from anger. William never fond of a scene, glanced around to see if anyone was watching.

"Upon my soul, William, how can thee anticipate such a voyage with gaiety without the favouring presence of your wife?" she frowned. "I am vexed that you would consider this journey without me. Am I to stay alone at our cottage, or am I to be nursed by my mother like a child? My desire is to be at your arm," her voice trembling, "now especially I wish not to be far from thee," and she placed her hand on her stomach.

Noticing the gesture, he took hold of her arms. Frowning, William asked, "Especially now? Madam, tell me now, what is your merry announcement?"

Sniffing, a tiny smile escaped from her pretty mouth. Understanding washing over William, he pulled her closer and whispered, "You are with child, my love?" and he hugged her.

"Yes!" she cried, and a river of tears fell from her lovely eyes. Holding Laurel close, William was torn, but knew he must make this journey to prove to her father that he was indeed worthy of his only daughter. William decided that he would not mention that he had hopes of travelling to Florence, and if luck held, he might be able to hear Vincenzo Vivian, a disciple of the famous Galileo, speak. He decided to hold this aspiration in discreet silence, allowing Laurel to believe that his ventures were strictly honourable to his word of work and sleep.

A fortnight later, William was waving to Laurel and her mother from the deck of a Royal Navy frigate. She had agreed, reluctantly, to stay the time under the roof of her parents.

The weeklong journey was uneventful, and William enjoyed the time watching the distant shores, and at night, when the sky was clear, brushing up on his astronomy.

In time, he was at work in Venice, the beauty and flamboyance of the city making London and Dover as dull and grey as coal pitch. William was soon caught up in the exuberance of such a marvellous city, and being a gentleman of means, meant that there were many invitations to events and outings. The warm nights dictated that splendorous parties were often held in grassy and fragrant gardens.

William and his colleagues from the surgery became popular and often included on exclusive invitation lists. As ambassadors to English honour and pride, William found it impossible to refuse the appealing requests.

Absent from his drab navy housing every night, he soon found it a challenge to answer the letters arriving daily from his wife. As his workdays were brimming with a flurry of patients, William's diligent letters to Laurel gradually reduced to an occasion. Her disapproval and irritability were clear in her returning letters. Though abiding to the oaths he swore in the presence of God when he was married, he was not deficient in dance partners, or in his flattery of the young ladies. His love for Laurel never faltering, he justified his coquettish behaviour by lack of liberty during adolescence and his time engrossed in vigorous study. When his allocated time was completed, he was asked to stay another few months. With a wardrobe of fashioned velvet coats, short doublets, billowing linen shirts and silk scarves, William had spent more money on clothes than his entire living allowance for his time at college.

Alarmingly aware that his promised crowns to Laurel had dwindled to a few mere silvers, he accepted the extension.

The pressure was great to save lost income, and so when William began to decline invitations, his friends, both male and female, came to his temporary home and held parties there. As these were less extravagant outings, the wine was courser, the food non-existent and the parties more raucous. It wasn't long after that William found himself one evening entangled in the thick dark hair and milky bosom of a local Venetian woman, known to be vixen in her passion. His friends winking and chuckling, William watched through drunken vision, as they left him alone, face buried in her ample cleavage.

When the morning sun pierced through a thick fog in his head, William turned over, and opening his eyes, he was startled to see the dark-haired wench he remembered arriving at the party, curled up beneath the grey blanket.

Scrutinising her, he knew her by her face, as one of many less desirable women who spent their days in revealing clothing, leaning in nearby doorways. Comprehension hitting his stomach like a fist, he leapt out of his bed, revulsion and regret bringing bile to his mouth. "Get out!" he bellowed in Italian, ripping the blanket from her voluptuous naked body. "Be gone from my sight!" Startling awake, her hair asunder, she sat up and pulling her knees to her chest, started to laugh. It was a mocking laugh, and throwing her head back, William saw that she exposed a neck bruised with bites, probably from his own mouth.

"Ay, 'tis the way with your velvet coat 'gentlemen' she drew the word out. The wine makes ye lust in your pants, outwitting the rules in yer head." Her dialect was thick, and William, struggling to comprehend the insult, was horrified that he was aroused by her blatant nakedness. Laughing again, the dark-haired demon slinked her way towards where William was standing and looked down. "Me thinks ye should heed the words of your master, and not deprive him of what lechery he craves," she finished with a wolfish grin.

Reflecting on that moment for years following, William never knew what came over him. With force, he grabbed the whore's wrist, and twisting her around, William forced her face into the sheets. Pinning her head down and parting her legs with his knee, he thrust himself inside of her, carnal rage pulsing through him. Her cries of pain increased his lust. When the anger had abated, and William's seed was spent, he stood up and begun to get dressed. With his back to her and with chilling calmness, he said, "Go forth with your lewd ways, and never let me see thy vile face again." He heard movement behind him, and after choosing a green silken scarf, he turned to leave and saw that she was gone, door left open to the street.

Things moved fast from that moment. No longer were there parties to attend and laughter to share. William finished his last weeks, and leaving his fortune of clothing in the wardrobe, made leave to return to England.

As the small schooner slowed for the creaking docks, he could make out the small form of Laurel. It was clear, even from where he was, that she was round with pregnancy. He estimated she must be near six months. She did not run to meet him, but walked carefully, and waving, he was favoured with one of her bright smiles.

William was withdrawn and distant in conversation with Laurel. He briefly explained that he had been robbed and that was why he returned with such a small sum of coin. She assumed that his introverted emotions and constant complaint of headaches were from the robbery.

It was in the bedchamber that William's interest in life and in Laurel returned. She was concerned that so much coupling would hurt her baby, but William soothed her worries with soft words and coaxed her body into submission. Weeks flew by, as she prepared their new home for the expected baby.

William had been home for six weeks when one fateful day, while dressing, he noticed something that would change his life forever. Looking closely, eyes squinting to see, William located on his penis, a small, round sore. Probing it with the end of his finger, he felt the sore's firmness and noticed that it was painless.

Quickly, he lifted the palms of his hands up to his eyes, and noticed a faint rash of reddish spots beginning to appear. Dropping the linen undergarment, his knees collapsed and he crumpled to the floor.

Syphilis. The blight of the modern world. Even Shakespeare had cursed the Montague's and Capulets with this pox.

The next month was a blur of anguish and guilt. Laurel soon developed the tell-tale signs of the contagious illness. Looking deep into Laurel's blue eyes one morning, he noticed an irregularity of her pupils. William frowned and smoothed her hair, but each day that went by, her pupils did not maintain symmetry. At first, Laurel was content to have William by her side nursing her through fever, headaches and fatigue. When she would request his opinion of what ailed her, he would go silent and mumble that he was unsure of its origin.

A month later, Laurel was losing her hair and her weight had plummeted. She would spend hours shaking with fever, the 'burnt blood' as it was called, and then sleep for days. To William's great distress, he was plagued by the secondary symptoms of syphilis, developing whitish wart-like sores on various parts of his body. He spent hours seeking salves to ease them. Still, William would divulge nothing to Laurel.

When her pregnancy had reached the eighth month, Laurel said with anxiety to her husband that she had not felt their baby move at any recent time. William withdrew, tormented by guilt and silently cursed himself and Venetian women.

That night, Laurel cried for William to come to her side. When he dashed into the room, Laurel held her hands up, sobbing, as they were covered in blood. Pushing back the woollen blankets, William's breath caught, as blood was rushing forth from her womb. William pulled Laurel to himself and sobbed.

After many long hours, their son was born still. Tiny, with black moulting to his skin. William presumed he had discontinued his life sometime prior to the bloody delivery. William was numb with shock and grief when he sent for Laurel's parents. Arriving in a haste, they were stricken by the loss of their grandson and also the state of their daughter. They had not been told Laurel was so unwell.

With her parents holding Laurel in her bed and the tiny body wrapped in a linen shroud, William proclaimed his diagnosis of Laurel's illness.

Her mother began to weep, and Laurel struggled to breathe. The word hung in the air. Syphilis. No second chances, only a life sentence of physical pain, misery and social humiliation.

Even if Laurel were to leave William, her reputation as a lady of purity and means would be nullified by the stigmata of syphilis. Her future bleak, husbandless, childless, her body decayed painfully every day. Soon enough, she would be physically evident for some to pity but by most, to be avoided, and socially condemned.

Following the silence was the whimpering of Laurel, which quickly crescendoed into screams. Her father, usually self-composed, the picture of English gentry, leapt up and grabbing William by the throat, proceeded to pound his head into the wall. William did not attempt to fight back, and the room spun before William lost consciousness, the last sounds being of mother and daughter piteously sobbing.

William awoke on the floor and could hear Laurel promising that tomorrow she would gather her belongings, and yes, she would be ready by dinner to be collected by the family carriage. There was a low murmur inaudible to William, then the door quietly latched into place. Soft footsteps padded into the room. Not able to face her, William dropped his gaze to the floor. She stood before him, the hem of her night garments still stained from the blood of her labour. "Always know that in my heart, I cherished our love, and never did I question your fidelity. Your selfish lust has murdered three lives today," she spoke softly, her voice laced with bitterness. "I hope she was worthy of your grandeur, William." Then pointing at him, "I blacken your soul with my bitter plight, and I curse you for eternity with self-reproach." As she walked through the door, she turned, and her final words were emotionless, "I despise you, and 100 lifetimes of misery will not redeem what you have stolen from me." William began to quietly sob, still crumpled on the floor. Distantly, he heard Laurel go through the motions of making tea for herself. Feeling numb, William gingerly placed a hand to his throat, knowing the muscles were bruised, and painfully, pulled himself into bed, not caring that he still wore his clothing and shoes of the day.

The weak light coming through the easterly window told William that he had slept through the evening and into the night. He felt the side of the bed Laurel occupied and determined by its coldness that she had not slept next him. Sitting up on one elbow, he strained to hear any signs of morning stirring from the rest of the house. She must have stubbornly slept in the kitchen on one of the chairs, probably clutching her stillborn baby.

Who could blame her, he thought. Slipping out of the blankets, William grimaced at the pain in his throat and neck. He surely deserved the pain and welcomed it. Walking into the kitchen, he stopped short. At his eye level were the small white feet of Laurel. Staring at them, he stepped back, and throwing his head back, his eyes locked with hers. Somehow, death had suspended the anguish and grief she felt in her heart at the moment of her last breath. The pain of her suffering seared his soul.

The betrayal and heartbreak that those lovely eyes held tore his heart from his chest. He fell against the cold wall, sobbing and crying like no other time in his life. His guilt forced his stomach to empty the bile pooling there. Handfuls of his hair fell softly to the floor as he tore at it, attempting to appease his remorse.

Maddened by his sins, he cut his wife down from the rafter, and bundling her carefully in a blanket in the bed, he tucked his dead son with her. He lay down in the bed next to them, and wrapping his arms around his cold family, he cried himself to sleep.

After that, all was a grey haze of shadowy faces of wrath, echoes of sobbing, followed by the inevitable silence, and lastly, a hollowness where the soul once resided. Time was broken only by the darkness and light, which filtered through the window.

Eventually, Abraham arrived at the house. In silence, he packed up the ghostly William and his books and brought him to live with his new wife and her sisters in the countryside out of London.

West of London, 1666

Abigail hadn't known she was asleep until she woke, sprawled on the road. Dazed, but remedied by prospects of losing her mount, she quickly caught up with the horse's meandering gait. Stopping him was a challenge, and feeling weak in arms and legs, she decided that more sleep was needed. Guiding him off the road and towards distant hay stooks, she hobbled Perkins by a stook of his own to munch through the night. Finishing the last of her stale bread, Abigail crawled inside the stook, where the hay was still slightly green and soft. Sleep was swiftly upon her once more.

The next morning dawned gloomy, and the sky was darkening. Perkins was still standing in the same place, though the hay stook had incurred considerable damage. At least one of them had a full belly.

Feeling light-headed and thirsty, Abigail attempted to untangle the harnesses. Frustration got the best of her and she gave up.

Riding along, a fine mist began to fall and soon, both girl and horse were sodden. Though not a cold day, Abigail shivered from wetness and hunger.

Peering through the silvery rain, she saw the signs of an approaching village. Within moments, Abigail was surprised to spot a farmer preparing a field for the winter slumber.

The man turned from his work to stare at the bedraggled girl riding a horse with full harnesses. *Strange times indeed*, he thought.

No sooner had she lost view of the farmer, than she arrived at the gate of a Borough.

A young man with long yellow hair stood in the opening. He watched the approaching rider with interest, as Abigail slowly approached.

Within earshot, she called out. "I need food and water," Abigail pleaded.

The man squared his shoulders. "Just sold the last bread to the travellers before ye. Sorry, ye'll have to ride to the next township." Gesturing beyond the gate, "Follow the plague road around our wall, then through the grove, and ye shall be there by nightfall." His tone was final.

Urging her horse, Abigail pushed past the gatekeeper, struggling to grab the lengthy reins. "I cannot carry on to the next village without food. Allow me to pass through your village. I am travel weary and have coin; even for a crust, I would be grateful," her voice was weak. She kept firm upon the reins and kicked the horse harder.

"Pray, do not fear for my head is cool and my skin free of plague tokens. God has not smitten me with the black death." She pulled her wet bodice out of her skirts and bared her pale middle, to prove that she did not hide weeping sores. Aghast at the girl's indecency, he stepped back from her.

"As soon as I have bread and ale in hand, I will leave these streets, and not look back." Pity and compassion stirred, but afraid for his own people, the gatekeeper hesitated. Releasing a long sigh, he relented.

"For the sake of God, ye may pass. But I won't warrant yer safety, nor are ye to speak my name if anyone ask how ye made it in. Tell them the lichgate was ajar when ye arrived. Do ye follow?" Abigail nodded. Leaving the gate open, the man disappeared into the neighbouring trees outside the gate.

Buoyed by prospects of a meal, she pushed Perkins into a trot and quickly arrived within the confines of the small community.

She rode to the bakery, but quickly discovered it to be devoid of bread and Baker. Glancing about, she spied the community inn, but it had boards across the door, and the familiar red flag was hanging above the entrance.

There were a few folk on the streets, but one glance at the outsider, and they hurried their step away from her. Continuing down the muddy street, she noticed doors opening a crack, and though unable to see faces, she felt as though she was regarded with suspicion. Common for the times, strangers were regarded with hostility as they were blamed for spreading plague.

A once prosperous village making its commerce from travellers was now a ghost town consumed by misfortune.

Before the southerly gate was reached, hissing and cursing were heard behind doors.

Heavy hearted, Abigail hastened Perkins through the village, tears welling as her hopes for food were crushed.

Something hard and sharp contacted the side of her head, the force threatening to unseat her and releasing a cascade of tears. "I only wanted food," she wailed. Another rock fell short of its mark, but startled Perkins to a trot. The next attack came with rocks and the odd rotten vegetable pelting girl and horse. She rode until the village was far behind. Only then was Abigail aware of the blood streaming down her face. Tearing her skirt, she wound the bandage around her head.

Nibbling a rotten carrot, which had tangled in the harness, she continued down the highway, hoping she was near to her destination.

Essex, 1650

The August sun burned hot, and Orla was absently slapping at biting bugs, as she hurried to gather the Ragwort she had found growing between two pastures. She still needed to prepare the comfrey she would be using to infuse in bees wax for her birthing bag and wanted to return home before it got too dark to see her work properly. Picking the Ragwort, Orla mused over what garments she would dye, as the flowers would yield a bright yellow which held well in woollen fabric. A bright outer dress for Philippa would bring a smile to her face, and if the dye held in cotton, she would surprise Abraham with lemon-coloured undergarments, giggling at the thought. The wise-woman filled her large basket with extra herb, as the juice from the herb was also a cooling wash for eyes, soothing for burns and healing to skin ulcers.

After a short time, Orla stood, and wiping her brow, shouldered her basket with the prized herb. Noting the position of the sun, she decided she would have enough time to walk back under the shade of the trees near the stream.

Humming to herself, she came to where the River Colne met with the hot valley. She noticed that Farmer Wenden, for the first time in her memory, had planted rye in the pasture he usually kept for grazing. She frowned and stopped when she discovered that the edges of the river had become a dry bed of rocks and buzzing insects. Months earlier, the river had threatened to overflow. Orla noticed that the mud around the banks was still damp, so it must not have been so long ago that the water had dried out. The summer had been hot and dry indeed. Climbing back up the incline, she walked the edge of the rye field, tall grass tickling her legs where she had tied her skirts. The cool shade was a welcoming refuge from the fiery sun.

Orla was happy that Farmer Wenden's rye was looking so healthy, as he sold his grains directly to the village Baker, where many of the local people could acquire different textured and tasting breads to the ones they made for their daily meals. As with most country people, Orla knew how to recognise a healthy crop of grain. As a wise woman, it was second nature for her to observe all plant life. Letting her mind wonder to the future rye breads, she licked her lips in hungry anticipation.

Walking along, her sharp eyes caught a colour in the rye, contrasting the maturing green-gold of the grain. Squinting, she looked for the source of the distraction. Inching her way into the grain, she stopped when she came to the anomaly. On the head of the rye kernel, shaped like the rest of the grain, stood a purple mass exuding out of the ears. At first glance, it could be mistaken as a discolouration, but upon closer examination, the objects were larger and different in texture to the neighbouring grain. Looking around, Orla discovered that most of the crop contained the odd dark shapes. Picking the purple mass from the rye, she brought the surprisingly light object to her nose. Breathing deep of its fragrance, she wrinkled her nose in distaste. It was the foul smell which tickled her memory.

A good length of time had passed since she had been so close to this offensive odour. She knew it was more than an odd generation of grain, though she could not remember ever seeing the rye with this dark colour growing in it. As a wise woman, there were few plants around her region she did not know, whether it was for healing, beauty or bane.

Therefore, to find a plant of unknown origin was both surprising and intriguing. Orla was excited about her find, and carefully plucked the purple plant from the grain, marvelling at how it took the shape of the rye kernel it grew upon.

She keenly wondered if this was the only crop it grew on and if it took the shape of other grains. She tied her outer skirt up a small amount, so that the delicate plant was handled carefully. Orla decided she would bring back the other members of her family to examine her strange find and made a note to check the other grains in the area to see if they, too, held the strange plant.

The next morning promised another hot day, so Orla, her sisters and Abraham arrived early to the rye paddock. As William had many patients to see, he did not go with the group; however, he took interest in what Orla had found, remarking as he departed that he would search through some of his books for any explanation of a plant found growing on other crops or plants.

Alice, as always, had marched ahead of the group and was the first to pluck out a specimen of her own. Squeezing it between her fingers, she sniffed at it carefully. "Tis the stink of spoiled vegetables, and yay, I do know this plant," she mused.

"I believe this is the simple which will bring forth the babe when lodged in the womb. And it will also stop the womb blood from draining, so that it will not take the life with it. I have only ever seen it dried, and it is not abundant, but I would recognise that odour anywhere. If this be the same plant, then deadly it is in the hands of a fool." She looked to each of them.

Abraham was scrutinising his purple specimen in the sunlight, when he looked up to see Mary bringing her piece to her mouth.

"Stop," he yelled, and leaping forward, knocked the purple plant from her hand. Everyone stared at his uncharacteristic outburst, and Mary's hand held in mid-air from the surprise slap.

Frowning at Abraham she said, "What worries thee, Brother? You more than most know that the passage to understanding herbs is to take the study within one's mouth. Truly, it seemed the correct thing to do. Surely only dried is it lethal?" Orla moved closer to her husband and sister, as this was indeed peculiar behaviour for Abraham. She was interested in finding out if his vast memory recalled a potentially lethal plant.

Abraham turned to Alice. "You said yourself you recognised the smell of the plant, and its uses. You also know that this plant is deadly in unexperienced hands. We all know that many plants become potent when dried and aged; however, my feeling is that this plant is deadly from its birth."

His look told the women that he was serious, and they stepped closer to hear his verdict. "Before I announce my finding, one that might be incorrect," he hurried, "I believe we should walk along the river bed crops, and see if there are other plants like this one."

They all agreed and headed off down the riverbank.

Sometime later, the group came to a halt as they discovered that the next field of rye, as far as they could see, also had the shadow of the mysterious plant growing beside the normal grain.

"Perhaps," Mary said with her melodic voice, "this is the colour of the grain at different times. As we have blue eyes, and Abraham has brown, maybe so the grain changes colour too." Orla and little Pip nodded, remembering that many plants with the same use, sometimes varied in colour and shape. Alice stood staring at the field, furrows of wrinkles deepening in her brow.

"A good thought Mary, but I believe this occurrence to be more sinister," Alice replied, not taking her eyes from the rye.

"I have to agree with her," Abraham concluded from behind the group. "But alas, patients await, so let us go our ways, and consider in silence and discuss after the night-time sup."

Later on that evening, after William had arrived home, early for once, the adults sat around the table, while Philippa sat near the last embers from the evening's supper, sewing a wedding gown for her corn doll.

Coarse, sweet lemon cake was a treat after their evening stew, and everyone gathered to sit and discuss the day's findings.

The aroma of fennel tea filled the air, and sipping at its sweetness, Abraham said, "How now, William, did the day grace you with some idle time, to have a search through your book?"

Startled, William drew himself back from wherever he had been and sat more alert. "Indeed, my day was fare, with scant few sufferers stepping over my threshold. Pray, with the position of Jupiter and Saturn, I am expecting some intriguing souls and perhaps some chaos to come through the door of my apothecary in soon time," he answered with introspection.

The sisters glanced at one another and wondered at William's cryptic prediction. He was exceedingly accurate with his astrology, and often graced them with enough insight to prepare compounds in advance for dawning sicknesses. As a Surgeon and Physician, he was also a keen astrologer. Though requested often by gentry with coin a plenty to predict events, William usually declined, preferring to keep his astrological insight a quiet affair. Clearing his voice from what seemed lack of use, William launched into his report.

"At a quiet hour, I searched the shelves of the books I acquired from past colleagues and some from travel. The nature of this dark, odorous plant thriving upon a consumable grain, encouraged me to search through food plants and to re-consider Galenic philosophies on medicinal foods."

Alice rolled her eyes at Orla, and she suppressed a giggle, interpreting her look of 'For a man who is usually absent of words, he can be long-winded when he chooses!' Abraham, catching the interaction shook his head slightly, but William distracted with his thoughts, missed the exchange, and continued.

"Through faith and troth, I found some fascinating writings in reference to tiny living things, they called 'fungus' namely ones which grow in whey to sour into cheese, and those which rise our breads that can be found growing on food

78

crops. In one certain volume, there was reference to a purple object, a 'fungus' which grew on certain grains, and was used to cure headaches. However, it noted with great attention that to administer more than a weight of a few scruples would be folly to the life of the individual," William reported.

Alice nodded her head and added, "I tell thee, this is the same plant!"

William flashed a look at her, and continued, "I was compelled to search my apothecary, and when I was not enlightened, I closed the doors early and headed to Abraham's." Glancing up at Abraham, he asked, "I hope thee is not angry that I would search through your stores?" A wave of Abraham's hand said that the action was trivial, and to continue with his story. "'Twas the rarity of the plant, of which the few pages spoke, which led to insight into the identity. Ignoring the simples and compounds in the front room, I went directly to the dusty jars Abraham keeps, for God knows what reasons," rolling his eyes, "and I began searching through them. And so, under a cloud of dust, on the top shelf, I found a jar, which contained a dried purple lump. Freeing the cork from the jar, I gagged from the gaseous air which filled my nose. I then recalled reading that this simple would have the odour more like a poisonous mushroom than of a dried plant. Rubbing the aged dust from the label, I was pleased to discover that it was the same mentioned within my book—Ergot." William looked pleased with himself.

"Aye, 'tis the name!" Alice exclaimed, thumping the table.

Abraham scratched his head, "'Ergot', the name does not toll within my memory, yet once I must have acquired it."

"Forsooth! Ergot, yes," Alice said with excitement. "As I said, Midwives will sometimes use this curious plant to encourage the greater movements of labour, and if the mother is dangerously losing blood, the birthing woman will risk the use of the herb, instead of watching her bleed to her death. Though this simple is rarely seen in trade or with merchants."

Orla and Mary nodded their heads with affirmation of what they too had recalled. They knew that this medicine was hard to find, sometimes years going by without any being discovered, so they were not accustomed to keeping it in their own apothecaries and had grown used to working in its absence.

"So, this is a happy find, to replenish our stores with for future use," Mary added.

"With certainty, I do encourage all to harvest and dry it," Abraham said, smiling at her, "but I am still troubled that such a deadly plant would choose to grow upon the grain which our bread will come from. And the cows which we drink our milk from, how often will they consume the grain when the farmer has turned his eye?" Abraham raised his eyebrows. "How can we know if the poison is not blighting the milk? How do we know that the bane will not pass into our bodies through the milk and bread?" he questioned, reflecting the dangers of using botanical pharmacopoeias—a fine line was often walked between healing and poisoning.

"Your fears are in vain, Abraham; after the cutting, milling, grinding and baking in a hot fire, surely the bane could not still live?" Orla stated.

Turning to her, "How then, my wife, can you prepare medicines which involve boiling with great heat, and then use with worthy results?" he questioned. "What if this ergot becomes stronger from the heat of the Baker's fire? What if entire villages are sent to their grave simply from their supper's bread?" he gestured.

Orla thought Abraham was being overly dramatic, but allowed him to continue. "What if the family cow was to consume this grain and then passed the poison through the milk?" he repeated. "Whole communities could fall sick from their humble bread and milk!" His agitation was apparent, and the speculations were concerning.

Setting her tea down, Alice looked at Abraham, breaking the silence, "'T'would be a curse more terrible than the plague if whole families have to fear their bread and curds." Alice was visibly shaken. "For the sake of God, Abraham," and her voice dropped to a loud whisper, "I pray thee hold thy tongue of this fanciful talk of blighted bread! Ye know the hysteria of a frightened Puritan." She gestured in the direction of the Puritan Reverend's house. "All we need is one sick child or one dead cow, and ye will have the lynching crowds at our door!" she exclaimed.

Mary had been writing the notes and conversation within the healing book, and at Alice's last words, stopped and closed the cover. Hissing at Alice, Mary stood up, "Hold thy tongue," and gestured over to where Pip was still sitting. "She does not need wicked thoughts within her head of innocence." Going to where Philippa sat, Mary sat down and stroked her long hair, kissing the back of her head. Humming to herself, and lost in her sewing, the contented girl was oblivious to the seriousness of the conversation.

Abraham, head in hands, softly said, "We will not speak of this openly, but I beseech you all, do not trade or use any rye breads or grains this season, until we learn more of the effects of this mysterious plant." Lifting his head, "I have uneasy feelings about this, and I do not wish to prove my suspicions from the demise of my own family. Do we all agree?" He looked to each face, and all agreed.

William stood up to take his leave. Looking surprised, as it was early by his standard, Abraham said to his brother, "Shall I walk with you to your home?" As it was a usual nightly ritual for the Bones brothers, all present were taken aback when William announced he would take a short ride and would see himself to his small dwelling later in the evening. Struggling with the latch, his swollen joints aggravated by the syphilis, he fumbled it open and slipped out the oaken door.

Wiltshire, 1666

Another day of swaying and jarring passed, before Abigail reached a sign pointing in the dusty direction of Wiltshire.

The sprouting grass down the narrow road made Abigail wonder when the last traveller had passed this way. Instructed by her mother that her childhood home was the first off the King's Highway, Abigail knew that her journey was almost at an end.

Imagining that soon she would be bundled into a large hug and fussed with over her ordeal, Abigail's eyes blurred with relief. Forcing Perkins into a rolling trot, it wasn't long before tiny farmhouses cropped up in green fields. Carefully searching the fields for movement, she saw only grazing sheep and cattle.

Praying that her auntie had not fallen to the same fate as other villagers, she urged Perkins faster down the road.

As she passed the third quiet house, her stomach clenched with apprehension.

At the fourth, she spotted a woman raking Lucerne into bales.

"Hello," called out Abigail, forcing a smile.

The woman stopped working and stared at her, her brow slightly creased.

When the woman did not move, Abigail assumed her hearing was poor and urged Perkins towards the fence.

"Please, I am looking for the home of Bess Cottle. She is my mother's sister." When the woman only stared, she added, "Not a young woman and would have hair like mine." Pointing to her own red-matted hair, she nodded.

Eyeing her as if pox-riddled, the woman gestured towards the road. "Across the way, not long on yer horse. If ye get to town, too far you've gone." She hastily finished and turned back to her work.

Surprised by the woman's abruptness, Abigail thanked her and turned Perkins back down the road.

Excitement replaced exhaustion, as she turned down the grassy path, leading at last, to her new family.

She noticed that her auntie held a large tithe, perhaps two acres, and in the distance was a low mud house. Abigail noted with uneasiness that the crops had not been harvested, and that some of the land was fallow. She couldn't see or hear animals fenced in the yard. Not even a hen ran to greet her.

By the time she had reached the house, her anticipation was replaced with worry.

Clambering off Perkins and looking around, Abigail called out, "Hello? Auntie Bess?"

"Who are ye?" called a voice similar to her mother's. Startled, but relieved, Abigail smiled and turned towards the source.

"'Tis I, Auntie, Abigail Midwinter, your sister's daughter from London," she answered, but the smile quickly wilted.

Auntie Bess stood with only her undergarments on, and these looked as if they had never been washed.

Her hair, once cascading curls, had turned to ropes. Underneath the smeared filth, Abigail could recognise a younger version of her mother.

A movement from Auntie's legs caught her eye. From behind Bess's shift emerged two young children.

Abigail gasped. Skin covered bones, and thin matted hair stuck to their heads made their foreheads look larger than normal. Inside the sunken sockets, their eyes were glazed.

Judging by the array of discarded animal bones and the lack of any four-legged presence, they had eaten their only means of ongoing survival.

"Margaret's whelp?" Bess suddenly seemed to recognise Abigail. "Yer, I can see ye have her ways when she was a lass." Abigail was about to smile when she continued. "Full of herself, and too good for humble folks—let that great ox-smith take her away to London."

Taken aback by her vehemence, but determined to tell her story, Abigail pressed on. "Auntie Bess, Mother, and…" she stumbled on the words, "and my family have died in the plague." It was the first time Abigail had uttered the words, and they choked her.

Backing away from Abigail, shadows passed over Bess. In a monotone she replied, "Me husband is months dead from the lung fever, and all the babes but the two standing, are in the grave." She pointed a withered finger to the distant churchyard. Her face then hardened, and she faced Abigail.

"We don't welcome yer filthy London plague, so methinks ye'd best carry on yer way." Bess stated with edge in her tone. Pulling her skeleton children closer, they backed towards the door of the house.

As her aunt's words hung heavy in the air, Abigail swooned with comprehension.

"You don't understand, Aunt; our family is dead, and your sister's last words were that I find you," she stammered.

"And what? Mother ye, with two starving babes of my own? Nay, yer mam turned her back on us when she married that Smith. Why should I sacrifice what scarce food I have on a plague-ridden whelp? Curse you, girl! Be gone, before ye spread plague to my clean family!" She flailed her arms menacingly.

The world was darkening, and Abigail struggled to breathe. Panic stricken, she opened her arms to reach Bess. "No, you can't make me leave, I naught have anywhere to go!" she cried. "I beg thee, Aunty, I am strong, I will find food for all of us. I am not fouled by plague tokens and am naught with fever." She placed her hand to her head for emphasis. "Auntie, there is only us left in this world, you can't turn me away!" Abigail fell to her knees, pleading.

A piercing pain shot through her head, and as Abigail sat up, she glimpsed her aunt swinging a thick stick. She was too slow, and her head was nearly knocked off, as Abigail fell to the ground. Struggling to stand before the next blow, Abigail managed to find her feet, and through blood and haze, stumbled towards Perkins. Pulling herself up, Abigail urged the horse into a trot, and looking over her shoulder, she glimpsed her aunt standing near the house, blankly staring into the distance.

It was the last time Abigail would ever see another kinsfolk.

Essex, 1650

The rye grain dried and predictably, the grain turned golden yellow, which signalled to the farmer that it was time to be cut. Abraham watched with growing apprehension, and spent his free time looking through volumes of books for any information supporting his suspicion. On one such day between seeing his patients, Abraham had the inclination to go and search through the records kept by the local church of health and food crops over the years. After persuading the suspicious Rector that his queries were in order to better his efforts as a 'servant of God', the Rector reluctantly allowed Abraham into the archives. Abraham searched and read many a dry document on the mundane tax collections of the community, the birth of babies, the death of the old. After hours and weeks spent hunched over in the tiny, airless room, Abraham had almost forgotten why he had come to the old church. His mind wondering, his thoughts lingered on his brother.

Though William kept his face well hidden from the public and his family, Abraham knew he was suffering the ravages of syphilis. Abraham knew his brother's eyesight was failing, and that his mind sometimes would take misdirections of conversation. But these could be concealed. Not so easily hidden were the ball-like nodules Abraham had spied on occasion growing forth from his brother's forehead, and lately was certain the red inflamed skin on his brother's cheek was another lesion. William vehemently denied Abraham's gentle diagnosis, and Abraham offered various salves from the wild pansy to clean the wound and other simples to numb the pain, all of which William refused.

Of late, William had increasingly taken to 'rides' after supper, and on some evenings would not return home. More peculiar were the mornings William did not leave his small thatched house. Something was distracting him, so much so, he was putting his family and work second.

The sisters joked that perhaps there was a woman involved, and when Alice bluntly inquired one afternoon, William turned crimson, answered defensively and avoided the entire family for a week.

Abraham decided to not mention William's sudden absences, nor his worsening health. Orla had laughingly suggested that perhaps indeed his heart had been stolen, and that would explain his odd behaviour and sudden departures. Abraham had not found amusement in her speculations, and with a shudder had recalled the haunted eyes of his brother after Laurel's tragic death. The family was never told of the entire tragic story; they might have their suspicions of syphilis, but no one had yet to ask. For William to have a lover meant that by new theories, he would infect his lover and she too would share his fatal path. Nevertheless, Orla was rarely incorrect about the 'goings and doings' of folk. So lately, Abraham had searched William's eyes and mannerisms for the sparkles of love. But what he found left him uneasy, as he saw only guarded shadows and an increasing restlessness.

It was early autumn when Orla came running to find Abraham squinting over some old parchments. He startled, and the papers fell from the low table. "By God, woman, you scared the life from me! You are in the house of the frowning Friar, by all means, do not arouse him! Whatever are you doing here?" he exclaimed, voice quieting as he saw the worry in her face.

"You must come immediately, the children at the Dowsett's home have not stopped vomiting for three night falls," she said with haste. "I applied the pit of an onion and roasted nutmeg to the stomach, and even spoonfuls of Wormwood, salt and lemon has not relieved them. Mary, too, has tried every remedy, and Alice is hours away, helping with the birth of the Muggelsten twins. I know not what to do," she finished, twisting her hands.

Standing up, Abraham questioned, "Vomiting? There is many a sickness children bring forth into their bodies, why would you be in a state over such a common display of excessive humours?" He waved dismissively, already bending to collect the fallen papers.

"Their pupils are huge, Abraham, and the children are thrashing and fitting as if their souls were possessed," she whispered loudly, "and their feet look as if a rot has set in!" Orla was outwardly distressed.

"Make haste, my husband, as I fear the children will not live to see the next nightfall. The parents are convinced that the Devil inhabits their soul, and they begged me to collect the Puritan Reverend."

Still bent down, Abraham stopped. "Serious that does sound." Tossing the papers upon the table, Abraham hurried through the door. Taking her hand as they ran down the stairs of the church, he stopped and said with concern, "Pray, what do you believe I can do that you and your sisters cannot? This is work where your herbals triumph. How can my crude methods measure to those likened to what your family have known for generations?"

Orla, touched by his humbleness, found a weak smile for him. "My love, can you not think of what would cause this? The colour of the ejected fluids is brown and black, like that of one poisoned. But, if this is so, then, God save us, what is the villain of this poison? Please, Abraham, go there now, I will do as the parents beseech and fetch the Reverend," Orla said as she turned to make way in the easterly direction of his home.

"Orla," Abraham called out, "be wary. You know the Reverend does not hold us in regard. Your thoughts and practices breed fear and condemnation in his soul." He then added, "Do not dally. Bear your tidings, and make haste to our home." Smiling tenderly, but with concern, "*Carus Amor*, I do not want you near that man for any length of time." Orla nodded, softened by his Latin. She prayed she would not have to endure Reverend Cardell's dark looks for very long, always glaring, forever accusing. How his daughter, Faith, could endure his unrelenting rigidity, Orla would never know.

Thinking of the family as she hurried along, she recalled his daughter was less convinced of her father's preaching than he demanded. It was rumoured that he bore a formidable temper, unusual for Puritans, whom made practice to shield emotion and practice temperance. She recalled that the young woman was often in open conflict with her father. Faintly smiling, Orla cheered the poor girl.

After a short time, Orla could make out the low roof of the cottage through the thinning leaves of the autumn trees. Pushing the loose hair back under her straw hat and unconsciously tidying her skirts, she released her held breath and took long strides up the path leading to the door. As she approached the front garden, she heard raised voices, seemingly engaged in an argument.

Feeling uncomfortable with the prospect of interrupting and facing an already angry Reverend, Orla slowed. As she entered the garden, she could hear banging inside the cottage. Stopping in her tracks, Orla could hear the voices clearly. She recognised the booming deep timbres of Reverend Cardell, "Do not defy God or me with your unholy disobedience! Wherefore doth goes in the night hours?" Silence and then, "Do not take me as a fool with blind eyes and deafened ears. Darkness abounds in thee, I can see, and the reasons, I pray to our Holy Father, shall be revealed." More silence, and a soft muttering, then, "I know not what salacious habits thee partakes in when you slink out the door, but if I catch you again, I will send thee forth from this house! Come now, upon thy knees and pray that God will redeem your tainted soul from your sins!" There was a scuffling, and like a flash, Faith came bolting from the house.

Blonde hair loose, not bound as was deemed proper, brown, plain dress billowing, she looked like a freed animal. Eyes wide, she ran past Orla, her bare feet oblivious to the gravel and sharp sticks which littered the ground. Disappearing into the trees, Orla was left alone in the garden.

Looking up, she locked eyes with the crimson face of the Puritan leader who had made his way to his small porch. Casting his arms out in an exaggerated welcome, he said with sarcasm, "Goodwife Bones, the Lord truly graces me today with thy visit." Orla was sure he was suffering just seeing her. "Hast thou not enough potions and enchantments to concoct that you must bide your time with me?" Struggling with her composure, Orla quickly informed him of the grave state of the children. Rolling his eyes at her prognosis, Orla pushed the point of urgency, stating the family required him for prayers. Before she could retreat, he retorted, "I shall go thither but I warn you, woman, do not think of casting your indecent spells and charms in the presence of myself, the voice of the Lord. If I suspect that your dealings with the devil is the cause of their bewitchment, then I will submit your unholy name to the Witch-hunter of the region." Slowly retreating, Orla shuddered at his open threat and his eyes full of hate. As he advanced down the step towards her, his look was dangerous. "God will have vengeance upon those who lay snares of evil for his innocent lambs. Retribution will come, aye, and not just to you, Witch, but to your whole accursed family! Now begone!" he raved.

Blood drained from her face, as the Puritan openly named Orla a Witch. Holding her tongue of all she thought of his delusional fanaticism, Orla concentrated on humming a loud tune to drown out the condemnation that he and his God threatened. She did not take the short path home, which led through the adjoining land, but instead hurried in the direction of where she knew the road was populated.

A few sad days later, Orla and her family joined the community to grieve the loss of the young Dowsett children. Staring at the small mounds, the air pungent with disturbed earth, Orla still could not believe the day's earlier events.

The Warners and Bones had done all they could, and William was finally persuaded to leech and bleed the youngsters. The treatment had shown to have no effect, leaving William a black eye from the thrashing of the oldest child. Even the prayerful ravings of the Reverend had not calmed their tortured souls. They died hours apart, both sweat-drenched and with the black rot in their legs. The community was shocked and horrified by the swiftness of the mysterious illness. No one could understand how or why this sickness worked, much to the remorse of the healers. Reverend Cardell took the opportunity to point out the failings of 'the Witch sisters' and openly condemned William for his brutish methods.

The death of children was a tragic but common occurrence, but to lose them to such a violent fate left the villagers unsettled.

Three weeks later, the full moon eclipsed the night sky, leaving all in a chilling darkness, which lingered well into the warmth of the next day. It was later that week that two widows and one gaffer fell to the same ravages as the children. Whether by grace of God, or the fact that they were already frail, they died soon after the vomiting and diarrhoea had begun and were spared but just a few uncontrollable twitches. William spent hours pacing outside his house, muttering to himself alternative cures for the stricken, until stumbling with exhaustion, he was led by Abraham to his bed.

In the same month, Alice attended births which were born still. One was but six months in the womb, the other was ready for the world. Both mothers had blamed Alice for her neglect in knowing that they would be born dead.

Alice was the best Midwife for miles, and she knew that their death was a misfortune. Nevertheless, Alice was uncommonly silent and withdrawn. Orla knew that the pregnant women had been healthy prior to the stillbirths and had no insight herself into the mystery. The lives of babies were fragile both before and after birth, but to lose two in one week was a bad omen for the superstitious.

Wreaths of garlic began appearing on doors, charms were being worn, and outside the church on the Lord's Day, the sound of prayers and psalms filled the air.

There was an odd mix of country traditional methods to ward off devilry, combined with Christian prayers and confessions. The community was single minded in its will to lift the heavy blanket of darkness from over their village.

The Puritan Reverend, once an outcast for his extreme religious viewpoints, was now drawing a larger crowd. He gathered his flock with promises of salvation, but only through steadfast prayers and dedicating their lives to serving God.

The spectacle of more villagers donning black and brown clothing, and their usual seats now empty in the Church of England, made for unsettled nerves in the remaining community.

Within a month of the death of the children, two more people died. Both similar in age, both started with vomiting and slurred speech, then thrashing, delirium, strange visions and a swift death. They complained of severe stomach pains, all with sensations of falling. The most astonishing was the extreme pain caused from a burning sensation in their limbs, which was followed by their turning purple. Those afflicted described the feeling as if they were being burned alive. The Warners and Bones spent endless hours administering pain relief remedies and tried in vain to save those afflicted.

People were growing more superstitious, and rumours of Witches conjuring black magic were rampant. Some tale-tellers were saying that the burning was caused from the cruelty of a Witch holding effigies in the likeness of people over a burning fire.

The villagers became increasingly paranoid and scrutinised the actions of their neighbours, noting any odd behaviour within their daily lives. Even the most level-headed were suspecting wickedness for the disturbances in the weather and for their everyday misfortunes.

Abraham and William worked tirelessly trying to discover the cause of the mysterious illness.

William's health was deteriorating before the eyes of Abraham. He watched with concern, knowing syphilis was destroying his brother's body and his mind. But William was behaving in other strange ways—different symptoms than those related to syphilis.

The local people were beginning to panic that they were in the throes of another plague-like epidemic. Some speculated that this was a sister to the Black Plague, with a different face, but the same ominous outcome. Abraham could see very few similarities, only that both took their victims swiftly and painfully.

William found reference in an ancient volume to the strange jerking and twitching people suffered with this illness, referred to as 'St Vitus Dance'. The named revealed that these convulsions, this 'dance', were symptoms of a more sinister origin. William and Abraham discussed how they had seen the St Vitus dance in other fevered illnesses.

The population of the shire queued at the apothecary doors, eager to be bled or leeched. Pots of syrups to rid of foul humours sold out within weeks. The Warner sisters were up to all hours preparing tonics, collecting the roots and barks of autumn plants and making charms for the inconsolable crowds of superstitious people.

Abraham found himself, before the morning sun, back at the church's archives, trying to find answers.

One day, after hours of straining his eyes to read damaged parchment, Abraham noticed some papers dated October 1632. Having methodically read daily records, he decided to jump twenty years prior. These records noted the exceptionally cold winter, and how the frozen churchyard now held many lost lives. The mention of increased rainfall, causing spring floods, and then the hotter-than-normal summer caught his attention.

The records recounted that many people had died from plague, and there were an above average number of late miscarriages and stillbirths. Where specific deaths were meticulously mentioned, one particular entry 'death unknown' kept appearing.

"Have we not ourselves barely survived a freezing winter and a searing summer?" Abraham questioned out loud. "Could the strange weather somehow play a role in this?" Abraham sat back on the chair and tried to recall the seasons past.

Reading further, the archives proved to be enlightening. The account soon began to list the high number of deaths in the last month, and interestingly, the deaths were said to be 'queer and violent, the church suspecting demonic possession'.

Abraham read the sentence twice, and continued. There was reference to a 'righteous man of God' who had evidence to prove that the deaths were caused by the work of Witches. As there were no other explanations, they gathered any women who seemed likely to be consorting with the Devil. There was a chilling list of 'accused Witches', all who confessed to having engaged in 'carnal rites with Satan', and then continued to possess the souls of the innocent. The guilty were then sentenced to hanging as their crimes of sin against the church were also seen as treason to the Crown. Being illegal for family to bury those accused as Witches, their bodies were buried in a mass grave, without marker, nor rites to prepare for their passing into the next world.

Rubbing the goose bumps on his arms, Abraham was doubtful that these wretched souls had confessed, but, in fact, had been coerced to say anything to save their own family. Abraham reflected with dread the abhorrent persecution of thousands of innocent women.

Reading the next line, he let the papers fall from his hands. The archive stated: 'The ghastly afflicted souls were thrashing about, and the vomit they expelled foul smelling. The poor wretches' possession absolute as they raved of seeing spectres and wild colours. Witches were the only answer and the sole perpetrators of possessing the innocent. Confessions were obtained by trained Witch Hunters and Confessors. Trials and sentencing carried out by the Church and Crown.'

The symptoms of the possessed matched those of the present-day people. The implications of this information in the hands of Reverend Cardell could mean the deaths of innocent people, most likely people within his own home.

Cardell should never look at these findings. Peering carefully out the heavy doors of the archives, Abraham listened carefully for the footfalls of the Vicar. Eyes tilted upwards and muttering, "Forgive me Father," Abraham rolled the relevant parchments into his riding cloak and dashed out into the waning sunlight.

Finishing off the rest of the mutton and onion stew, Philippa reached for the last chunk of coarse bread. Abraham was staring at the bread, and as Pip removed it from the clay plate, he caught her wrist.

Startled, she dropped the bread. "Apologies, Uncle, I did not know you wanted the bread," she said, blushing.

Blinking and dropping her arm, Abraham hastily said, "Oh, my dear, I am obtuse, forgive me, of course this is your piece, but tell me, was this the bread you and your mother made this day?"

Looking at Mary, he raised his eyebrows for emphasis. A puzzled expression flashed across her face. "Why, yes, Uncle, Mum and I make the bread every second morning."

Abraham took a breath and turned his body. "And tell me, Mary, where didst you acquire this grain; is this not rye?"

All looked to Mary, knowing the promise of rye-free breads was what Abraham questioned.

Smiling, Mary patted his hand reassuringly. "Ease yourself, the rye was traded to me from Goodwife Basnett, from her own fields in Wivenhoe. As a matter of fact, the other day I was to learn that those rye grains of Farmer Wenden's were sent to a Baker in Colchester and London," she stated. They all exchanged a look.

If indeed the rye was blighted with ergot, and sent to Colchester, then that could imply the entire borough could be poisoned.

Abraham looked at William. "Brother, have thee heard any recent news from Colchester or even London, and how fairs the health of the citizens?"

Inward with his thoughts, William seemed to answer from a distant place. "Indeed, there is another outbreak of plague, only in the last month."

The two stared at one another, calculating the time travel of grain to Colchester and London, the milling and the baking.

Letting out a breath, Orla asked aloud, "Bless me, so whom then tithes the small land we saw on the outer rim of the stream?" She added, "As you recall, that pasture had the ergot growing on the rye, as well as Wenden's." They looked to one another for the answer, concentrating on the landholder's name.

"Where does the town Baker acquire his grain?" William asked cautiously.

A shiver ran through them all, and Abraham answered, "The lowest bidder of course. If there was a reduction on the grain due to a poor crop, then that would be the Baker's choice, as he guards his coin well." They were all silent with the implications.

"Abraham, ye still believe that the ergot could rot those who eat the grain?" Alice frowned. Abraham rubbed his temples as he often did in thought.

Putting his hands down he said, "I can only speculate. It is curious though that the church records make mention of the extreme winter weather, and then the sickness of the people came about the same season as ours: freezing winter and a hot summer. I searched the last twenty years for other weather references, but there was none to match our last seasons to the deadly ones prior." Exhaling, he continued, "Strange as well is that the height of plague seems to correlate with these weather patterns and this unexplainable sickness, or 'possessions' and Witch trials, as the church records state."

All sat in contemplation of these sobering findings. After a while, Orla spoke up, "Husband, could consuming poisoned grain weaken the body to make plague stronger within?" Orla queried. "Perchance the increase of plague is from poisoned food—from the blighted grain? How can that be?" She shook her head in confusion over the parallels.

Abraham took her hand. "Excellent question, my wife," and his smile showed his pride. "I, too, have pondered such correlations. 'Tis why I have weakened my eyes, searching the church records for any ties between virulent plague years and the growth of ergot. Having combined my notes and findings of ergot with William, there was a sobering hypothesis. I read of ergot in early years, but then naught a mention of, and even then, found only in rare years, with no growing cycle nor prediction of growth mentioned." He raised his eyebrows. "I would guess that when ergot grew in the couch grass, it was collected and dried by the wise women. But after weeks of reading through the archives, there is naught a mention of ergot in food crops." He inhaled. "Therefore, my thoughts about blighted grain are mere speculation until I find solid proof. Perhaps if Baker Reid is using the rye from the far field, then we should question him if this is the grain he has been using since the first illness broke out?" he questioned.

"And then what brother?" Alice queried

He looked Orla in the eyes. "One of us shall have to consume the rye bread and observe our body's response," he said slowly.

"That is folly!" Mary exclaimed. "The last thing we need is to have one of us succumb to this frightening affliction!"

"Don't be mad!" chimed Alice. "The village people are eyeing us, dark with suspicions already! Must we give them another reason to cry 'Witch'?"

"How else can we be sure?" Abraham replied to Alice. "Have we not spent our lives in service to the fettle of others? We are familiar with the language of this affliction, to recognise if the partaker is being poisoned. If so, then we shall purge the noxious postulant from the body and restore it with herbal compounds."

"No Abraham!" Orla exclaimed. "You will not sacrifice yourself!"

"Enough!" startled, all eyes fell on William. Standing, William announced, "Settle it, I will. I shall ride to the Baker's house and petition an answer from him. He will divulge to me, as I hold the astrological fate of his life over the next year." He let slip a wry smile.

Taking his cloak off the wooden peg, William reached for the door.

"Ride with care, Brother, the sky is moonless," Mary added.

Without turning, he said, "Shadows can sometimes be illuminating," and disappeared into the darkness.

Hours later, in the blackened night, a small knock was heard on William's door. Opening it, a young woman fell into his arms and he kissed her passionately.

"Mine beautiful angel," William said, and wrapped her in his arms, bringing her inside.

Abraham had retired to bed, and Orla was contemplating her second butter biscuit when a thin rapping on the door surprised her.

"Godso, can we never have peace," breathed Alice as she flung the door open.

Expecting to see an agitated husband, the sisters were surprised to see the Puritan Reverend's daughter.

Small twigs and dried leaves clung to her disarrayed hair. Judging by the amount of mud soaking her hems, she had ventured through the pasture to arrive at their home. It was not the smoothest passage but certainly the most discreet.

Mary the first to respond, opened her arms to greet the girl. "What ails you, child, at this darkened hour?" She asked in her gentle manner. "Please, come hither and join us for tea."

Looking like a creature of the wilds, she cast her eyes around the room, seemingly searching for the fastest escape.

"Are ye coming in or not, lass? My tea is chilled by the night air chased in at your heels," grumbled Alice.

The girl struggled with an inner conflict, and with much effort, managed to pass the threshold.

Retrieving the milking stool from beneath the table, Mary patted it with encouragement.

"Faith, that is your given name? Would you take a tea to steady those trembles you are suffering from?" Mary asked sweetly.

Faith wondered if the Witch could see into her soul and quickly pulled her shaking hands into her sleeves.

"Mistress if you believe it will benefit, then yes, thank you," she said warily.

"Aye, child, the seeds come forth from the Anise flower, easing melancholy and soothing the soul."

She reached for the heavy kettle hanging over the glowing embers.

Looking around the cosy room, Faith observed with interest the assortment of drying plants and flowers suspended from the low beams. Layers of flaxen sheets tied in the corners held drying flowers, berries and roots. Jars, earthen bowls and jugs were crammed into every available space.

The room smelled pleasantly of spring blossoms and tilled earth.

Abruptly, she was aware that the other hags were staring at her, so she settled her gaze to the centre of the worn table.

The sisters noted a slight quaking to her hands, and her eyes darted around like a caged animal, but other than the usual untidiness of the girl, nothing seemed out of normal.

"As thee are not suffering from any noticeable maladies, pray do tell, what ails thee," Orla asked with thin patience.

Accepting the tea, and pleased that the taste was surprisingly sweet, she looked to each woman.

"I believe I am with child," she blurted out, "and as you know, unwed."

Orla choked on her tea, and Mary dropped a plate.

"Oh! But ye are a babe," exclaimed Mary, and reached to put her arm around Faith.

"Bless me, how many years old are ye, lass?" Alice asked frowning.

"'T'will be 16 when the leaves change," she answered.

The sisters looked to each other concerned. Faith's visit was worrying and potentially dangerous.

"Are ye certain, lass, that a babe grows within ye, and does the man who did this to ye know?" Alice asked bluntly. Faith appeared to grow anxious from the last question and began fidgeting.

"When didst your bleeding come last," interrupted Orla, hoping the girl was being paranoid and that she was merely a week or so late.

"'Tis been two moons and the third waxes," the answer was a definitive diagnosis for the experienced Midwives, and again they glanced at one another, pleading the next to ask the dreaded question.

Keeping her face impassive, Orla queried, "Faith, you have told us thou art 2–3 months with child. Pray, what is the purpose of your visit?" The last words were whispered.

Looking the sisters in the eye, so they would know she was serious, "I beg of thee, Wise women, to give me the plants which will cleanse this sin from my womb."

Alice rose and placed a small log on the embers.

Unflinching, Orla's gaze did not waver. "We are sorry for your journey out, but we cannot help you, lass. The Almighty Lord hath blessed you with His gift, and we will not mock His judgment," Orla spoke firmly, suddenly on guard.

Why was the Reverend's daughter pregnant, and demanding for a compound, which would surely see her in perdition? Suspicious that this was some devious scheme by Reverend Cardell to condemn the sisters, Orla readied herself for the next trap.

Faith now sat straight, and without a hint of earlier recklessness, proclaimed, "The Lord, Mistress," looking at Orla, "has been mocked by this conception from the gravest of all blasphemy."

Echoing her father's tone, Orla shivered.

Placing a hand over Faith's, Mary gently said, "If you speak of pregnancy out of the marriage bed, then sure I am, that repenting prayers can redeem your shadowed heart."

"Only the flames of damnation can scour my soul," Faith whispered with fervour.

"Alas, ye are sounding like yer sire," Alice said with open exasperation.

A strange look came over Faith. "Perchance the words are uttered from his evil spawn writhing inside me."

The sisters stopped breathing with her shocking confession.

The fire snapped, and Orla jumped. "God preserve us," whispered Alice. "You say, that as God is your witness, thine own father hath…molested you?"

Faith nodded her head once. "And now, will ye choose the simples from yer shelves to restore my innocence?" The question was demanding to Orla's experienced ears.

Sharing a glance with Alice, Orla knew her sister had relented by a slight twitch of her eyebrow.

"You understand that your request could hold grievous consequences for our name and lives?" Orla asked, struggling to keep her voice emotionless.

Like a cloud passing over the sun, Faith's face darkened. "Aye, I know the peril I bring into your home once those simples are relinquished. But, ye must believe me that I have naught another choice!" Her voice rose. "God's eyes do not look upon me with such suspicion. Do you believe I will return with my father, and his companioned Witch hunter and cry bewitchment?" she asked laughingly.

Orla paled.

She was not aware that the Reverend kept company with a Witch hunter. And the sisters shared a surprised and worried look.

Alice leaped from her chair and roughly seized the girl's arm, pulling Faith's shocked face inches from her own. "Beckon the Witch hunter, the Devil himself, to our home, and I swear, girl, ye will not awaken from yer herbal draught," she rasped dangerously.

Pulling herself free, Faith again was the wild creature, ready to bolt from the room.

Faith was convinced she could see false concern in their eyes, and these sisters, these…Witches could inflict terrible things on an innocent soul.

Her father was right about one thing in his sermons…they were damned.

Orla, blocked the exit from her retreat. "Leave her be, Alice," she sighed, "'Tis only a turn of words these days." Addressing the girl, Orla continued,

"Do ye know the Hawthorn growing behind Sullivan's orchard?". Faith nodded.

"Meet on the morrow at the sun's height, and I will instruct you on administering the simples."

Faintly smiling, Faith reached for the door's latch, but before she could open the door, Orla placed herb-stained fingers over hers.

"Remember, lass, if thee betrays the house of Warner, then as God is my witness, I will curse thine soul."

Her voice was threatening.

A grim look fell across her face, and Faith fled to the safety of the darkness.

Orla grimaced at the tartness of the Hawthorn berries, noting their abnormal powdery texture, as the berries should be juicy.

It had been a dry season to shrivel the inside, but their skins still held the properties required.

Picking leaves and fruit, as the herbs worked best together, she reviewed her instructions given to the Reverend's daughter.

"Boil up this herb first with covered lid," pointing to the yellowish root, "Then after pounding the posset," gesturing to the small cloth bag, "add the herbs to the pot with the yellow root. Cover the mixture again and let it gently boil down till it's dark in colour and pungent in the air." She spoke slowly so the girl understood.

"Drink two drams, five times through the day and next," Orla instructed. "Your insides will feel as if poisoned, but that is God's wrath, punishing you, for going against His will," Orla's face was impassive.

"Make water from soaked barley and Watermint and drink often so as to fortify the body during the poisoning." Orla punctuated the word in order for the girl to understand the gravity of her deed. She also carefully observed the girl for signs of unnerving, after her descriptions of the side effects, but Faith only stood with her head down.

Though listening carefully, Orla noticed that Faith was flushed and her pupils looked odd. She noticed a tremor in Faith's hands. These were not usual symptoms of pregnancy.

"Are you ill, lass? You don't look sound," Orla asked, brows furrowed.

"'Tis a hot day, Mistress, and my head is swooning, but I am well fit to drink the brew," she answered.

"Make sure that you are strong, as the plants are merciless to weakness," Orla advised concerned.

"Yea, Mistress." She waved impatiently and reached for the posset.

Grabbing her hands, Orla noticed they felt clammy. "If the blood does not lighten in a half day, then you send for me," Orla warned. "You are strong, but your life could bleed forth if you are blind to the warnings." Releasing her hand, Faith then snatched the parcel, and without another word, disappeared into the trees.

With a bag full of Hawthorn, Orla reflected on the girl's health. Was she affected from an ill wind, or was she simply nervous around the Wise woman? Orla felt uneasy, and beseeching God, Orla begged forgiveness and promised to endeavour to bring forth more of His precious creations into the world alive and healthy.

Wiltshire, 1666

Abigail draped herself over the horse's neck and clung to the mane for her life. She didn't know how long she had ridden; only that the autumn's day was hot like the summer. She watched the ground in a blur of brown and yellow and was lulled by the breathing of the great animal.

Fear and the smell of blood had powered the mare down the road and through a field.

In the distance were treetops, and as they neared the grove, Perkins could smell fresh water.

Going down a steep incline, Abigail almost slid over the top of her horse. Finally sitting up, her head swam with colours, and for a moment, veiled shadows narrowed her vision. Rubbing the darkness from her eyesight, she was thankful for the coolness of the shade offered by the trees.

"I should let you lead from now on," Abigail said appreciatively as she slipped off the horse and gingerly walked to the creek.

Numbed from the pain and the shock of her abandonment, Abigail didn't notice that she was being watched.

Cupping her hands, she brought cool water to her sunburned face and cracked lips. Tentatively, she leaned down to wash some of the caked blood from her face and head.

A kicked stone froze her. Heart thumping, she found the knife in her bodice and concealing it, sat up, and turned to see Perkins' lead held by a man.

"Ye won't be needing this nag anymore, will ye, wench," a voice from behind startled her.

Stumbling to her feet, she backed into the creek frightened.

"I need the horse to carry me to Salisbury," Abigail tried to sound important.

"Well, the nags no good fer ye, as you be travelling the opposite way to Salisbury." He laughed loudly.

"Forget the talk," the one nearest said. "We're taking the horse, and it 'twill fetch enough coin fer ale." He grinned, and Abigail felt sick.

Leading Perkins up the embankment, Abigail made a last effort to grab the reins.

"She's mine!" Abigail yelled, and clawed at the man holding her lead.

Slapping her hard in the face, she fell backwards down the hill.

"Vexing little bitch, aren't ye?"

Afraid for her life, she ran into the creek.

Though sharp rocks were cutting into her feet, Abigail managed to keep her balance on the slippery creek bed.

She was running so fast, Abigail was sure she was out of sight when something hard hit her from behind, knocking her face first into the creek.

White lights blinked in her eyes, and as the pain grew monstrous, the white was replaced by dark.

Essex, 1650

Hook, thread, pull, the rhythmic monotony of the spinning wheel was lulling Orla to sleep.

Weaving was Orla's least favourite chore, but since trading the linseed/wool blend for a skin bleaching salve, she was eager to create a new underskirt for Alice. She contemplated the needlework for the hem with tiny blue bells, knowing they were her sister's favourite flower.

Orla was enjoying the quiet of the gentle breeze drying the hanging herbs when galloping hooves alerted her that someone was arriving with haste. Standing up, she recognised her husband in a cloud of dust, dismounting.

"Husband, what vexes thee, to leave the apothecary so early?" she asked.

Tight lipped, Abraham responded, "'Tis the Reverend's daughter, she has fallen from the same illness as the others. She is vomiting black bile and thrashes about as if afflicted from the St Vitus dance," his voice was tinged with concern.

Guilt and nausea swept over Orla.

"Dear Lord, 'tis not the sinister sickness of the others, but the simples I administered to expel her wayward pregnancy," she confessed.

Looking surprised, Abraham grabbed her arms, "Forsooth! Why did you not inform me of this folly, Orla? You know the dangers of using herbs such as these. Is your mind unhinged, woman? The Puritan zealot's own child?" He gaped at her incredulously.

"We could all hang with his allegations!" Abraham was shaking, and Orla knew with sickened dread that he was right. If the Reverend discovered that Orla had willingly administered the herbs to bleed the womb, then her entire family could suffer.

"Have you been to see her yet?" asked Orla, breaking free of his grip.

"Nay, your sisters saw me on the road coming home early, and hastened that I come here to retrieve you, as you were the last to see the girl." He looked at her with growing anxiety.

"According to Alice, a passing milkmaid heard the Reverend shouting prayers of exorcism and ranting words of possession. All the while the girl inside moaning and crying out. The maid, concerned, found Alice in town and thought she could help the girl, but Alice was reluctant to attend the Cardell house alone. I saw Mary, and she is on her way too."

Orla felt cold dread prickle her skin.

"Let me collect my bag."

Within a few minutes, they were at Reverend Cardell's cottage.

Delirious wailing could be heard from inside, then the Reverend's voice, "And the Devil shalt be cast forth from yer tainted soul!"

Alice and Mary were outside waiting, looking worried.

"God save us, the man is possessed himself," Alice stormed. "We can't get near the girl, but we saw her from the threshold."

Taking Orla's hands, "As God is my witness, I have never seen such a sight, sister. Not in all my years."

Orla could see fear in her eyes.

Pulling at her sleeves, Alice began pacing. Orla, anxiety growing, said, "I must have given her too much of the roots, this year they seemed a powerful harvest. Is she bleeding?"

"I cannot tell," answered Alice.

Orla remembered how Faith looked just a few days back. "The girl looked as if her humours were out of balance when she met me for the herbal compounds. Her pupils were large, and she trembled. Sister, do you think the herbs hath caused further imbalance?" Orla asked.

Alice looked surprised with this news. "Imbalanced humours would not agree with those remedies, true Sister, we must get inside and assess for ourselves. If Faith bleeds in excess, then I will administer the Lady's mantle," Alice began rummaging in her bag.

Orla watched Abraham carrying his treatment bag and push through the crowd of people, gathering in the yard. He went up the step onto the porch. Determined to see their patient, the sisters followed close behind.

"Sir," Abraham's voice cut through the Reverend's prayers as he stepped through the doorway.

Surprised, he noted that Faith was bound. "Untie the girl and allow me to examine her, as she is in obvious need of care."

Orla looked into the sparsely furnished room, noticing only a plank table and two tree stumps for chairs. They certainly followed the Puritan tradition of simplicity. Orla spied Faith and her breath caught.

Lying on the dirt floor was Faith tied at the shoulder and arms. Her legs were pulled up and Orla could see a pool of dark blood. Her concern grew as she saw that Faith's feet and hands were purple in colour. A decay, like frostbite, had set in, and Orla desperately wondered how this had occurred.

She whispered to Alice and pointed at Faith, "'Tis the same purple rot we hath seen on the village children." Pulling Mary into the conversation, "Godso, could this be the 'Holy Fire' poisoning Abraham hath discussed?" The sisters were worried.

Faith's face was contorted in agony, her mouth frothing.

Cardell caught sight of Orla and advanced on her, signalling that he wanted her to go.

"Satan ravages my daughter, your kind is not welcomed; your heathen medicine is only a hindrance!" He eyed them with distrust. "Perchance she is under a bewitching spell, which hath made her mind manic and her body quake?". Eyes glinted with accusation at Orla.

The Reverend then squatted down beside Faith's head, and grabbing a fistful of hair, brought his face inches from hers and shouted, "Confess your lust, daughter of Eve—I know you were born of sin, unclean temptress to Adam, and now," he gestured to her prone body, "God hath forsaken you! Confess now, that these so-called Wise women hath possessed you, making thee Satan's servant like themselves!" The spittle of his rant ran from his chin.

Orla was shocked and sickened by his outburst. How could any father speak to his child like this, especially one who was clearly so unwell.

Orla regained her wits, and the healers started preparing their remedies. Thinking out loud, Orla said, "For Faith, add Knotgrass to the Lady's mantle to stop her bleeding." Nodding, Mary assembled the compound.

"Alice, didst you bring the Woundwort and Velvet flower?"

"Aye, 'twas lucky they still bloomed," she replied.

"Good," Orla answered, without looking up from her medicine bag, "bruise them and add Yarrow flowers, and the rest of my Toadflax." She handed bundles of herbs to Alice. "Afterwards, as you know, apply them deep into Faith's womb."

Cardell tried to block the Wise women from their work.

"Get a hold of thyself, sir!" Abraham's deep voice boomed, and he placed his hand on Cardell's shoulder. "Your child is ill and must be attended."

When Cardell did not move, Abraham pushed him away and kneeled at her side. Disgusted by her treatment, he untied Faith and examined the colour of her frothy phlegm. Looking up at Orla, he said, "Her body is befoul with black bile and fire blood."

Reading the concern in her expression, Abraham hastened to reassure her, "Nay Orla, 'tis not your herbal simples. Fair to say, her body is consumed by some other pernicious substance."

Realisation dawned on his face.

Abraham looked down at Faith. "Child, our desire is to save you," he said softly. "Tell me, have thou been eating bread made from the grain of rye?" Faith moaned and thrashed, but did not answer.

The sisters looked to one another, their suspicions now confirmed.

Cardell was standing just behind Abraham and was listening intently to the conversation.

"What sort of nonsense is this?" exclaimed the Reverend. "Of course she has eaten rye, as our bread and meal come from this humble grain. What folly is afoot?" he asked distrustingly.

Without answering Cardell, Abraham continued with his quiet questioning of Faith, all the while noticing a crowd gathering at the door.

Many were unconcerned for the strange girl and her erratic behaviour, but they desired to witness the confrontation between the popular Reverend and the Physician. Good gossip was in the making.

Out of the faces, Orla recognized William, pushing his way to reach the door, and she did a double take. Orla had never seen him looking so unkept. His hat had fallen, exposing his usually hidden face. Orla gasped. The once chiselled face was now alight with angry sores, some deeply ulcerated at his forehead. Rolling his sleeves up, William unknowing exposed further syphilitic lesions.

Without seeing Orla, William pushed her aside, Orla flinching at the hot, clammy touch.

Abraham, spotting William, stood up and stopped in his tracks, also shocked by the extent of William's ulcers. Abraham recalled that he had not seen William in the light for many weeks now. His syphilis was well into the tertiary stage, and Abraham was heartbroken for his brother's plight. But right now, he needed to collaborate with William on Faith's prognosis and took a step closer to him.

But rather than speaking to Abraham, William's face was contorted with anguish.

"Faith!" he shouted and fell to the girl's prone side.

"O' my darling, my little bird, what misery has fallen on thee?" he cried, bringing her pale hand to his lips. Faith quieted slightly, his words seemingly soothing her, though her body convulsed in a sudden seizure.

The Reverend instantly went silent from his rantings, as did the room. The stillness amplified the fair words falling from William's tongue.

Cardell regained his composure first and turned to William. "How now did you address my daughter in that familiar tone?" his voice was dangerous.

Without hearing Cardell, William tenderly wiped the mess from Faith's mouth and tried to calm her trembling. His mutterings were loud enough for the room to hear, and all stood shocked,

"All will be well, my angel, my love, my Laurel." William's voice was honey-sweet.

Orla's breath drew in loudly, and Abraham's medicine bag dropped with a heavy clatter.

Abraham squatted down by William, and said quietly, "Brother, this is Faith, the Reverend's daughter. This child is not your wife, Laurel; remember, William, she has been gone many years." He shared a look with Orla. "William," he continued, "I know that your head is filled with ill winds and muddled by unbalanced humours, which cloud your clarity, but do not confuse this moment with the past."

Abraham, knowing the syphilis was devouring his brother's sanity, and concerned by the size of William's newly revealed lesions, was eager to remove him from the damning eyes of the townsfolk.

"Nay, Brother," William cried out, face glistening with sweat. "I hath returned Laurel to mine arms with the magic plant Orla hath plucked from the grain." The brothers locked eyes, and Abraham shook his head to try and silent William, noting the widened dark pupils.

"Magic?" echoed the Reverend, and he crossed himself stepping back. "What evil unfolds before me?"

Abraham motioned Orla over to Faith.

"Goodwife, assist her," he ordered.

Moving towards the flailing girl, the Reverend suddenly lashed out, "Not you, Witch! Get thee away from my child." His face twisted. "This is your evil work, is it not? This child, tormented from the death of her mother, always has been a challenge. Now, her soul is possessed by the likes of your tainted medicine that you disguised in a morning tea. I did see her drinking the tainted brew this very morning. And now, the Surgeon proclaims he acquired a bewitched plant from thee! What justice, woman, do you have here?" his voice rang out accusingly.

Tears welled up in Orla's eyes as she feared for the lives of Faith and herself.

Shielding the girl, Orla bent down to treat her. Faith looked up with wild eyes, pupils large. Startling Orla, Faith wailed, in what seemed a lucid moment, and then pointed at Orla. "Witch! Witch! She threatened to curse my soul, and now this Witch hath poison me to taketh my babe! All of them!" And a ragged finger pointed at the shocked looks of the Warner sisters. Orla stunned, stood up and backed away from her.

The crowd at the door backed away, repeating the dreaded word: "Witch."

Their minds were racing; Was this the reason for all the deaths and illness? That the healers were, in fact, servants of Satan?

"No!" cried Orla, stepping towards the faces of her community. "These are the delusional words of a sick young woman and her deranged father," she pleaded. "Can't you see that the Reverend's religious tyranny has afflicted his own daughter?"

Stunned by the blasphemy of their beloved Reverend, the crowd silenced, and a palpable anger could be felt in the air.

"No, Orla, hush," quietly said Abraham, and he moved closer to her side. Hearing his voice cleared her furious head enough to see their fear was taking a dangerous turn and growing more menacing.

Recalling her latest outburst, Orla's stomach turned.

Only now did she notice that the crowd was a sea of black and brown flax— the colour of the Protestant 'Separatist'.

Orla suddenly recalled that the pew seats of the local Church of England had become empty, compared to the increasing numbers of these religious reformists at their place of worship.

Her mind clouded with the frightening implications of their fanaticism.

Orla noticed that Abraham had successfully managed to push the people out of the doorway and addressed them, "Do not fear, goodly people." Abraham's voice was pitched to reach everyone milling around, "'Tis not the Devil's play, but merely the unfortunate poisoning from blighted grain." He struggled to place hope within his voice.

"Only Satan can command blight," came a voice from the side.

Abraham gently replied, "Nay, good neighbour, 'tis God's resolution if our crops fail or thrive, as well, God's will to call His children back to heaven."

Orla listened to Abraham as she tried to settle Faith's thrashing about. She knew Abraham as a man of science, knew he struggled with godly notions.

His words were clearly to placate the extreme convictions of the Puritans.

Abraham stepped back from the door and pulled William back from Faith.

"Do not assume to preach the holy teachings of our Almighty Lord!" boomed a voice.

The Reverend attempted to regain control of the argument and advanced on Abraham.

Pointing at his medical books opened to anatomical illustrations, "You, Master Bones, a heathen with your obscene books depicting God's children in repulsive detail, that only He should know." And pushed past Abraham to be seen in the door.

"You," pointing at Abraham, "with your evil words of blighted grain...Pray tell," and Cardell paused for emphasis, "how would thee know such a curse hath fallen if you were not consorting with Lucifer yourself?" Shrugging dramatically, Cardell inclined his head to the growing crowd.

Their mood was growing dark, like summer storm clouds, and their agitation was clearly seen.

Orla became increasingly concerned for Abraham as accusations shifted from her to him.

"Goodly citizens," Abraham pleaded, again pushing past Cardell, "I beg thee listen to the words of the man who hath comforted you in your sickliest hours, attended your wounds and upholds an oath dedicated to healing." Glancing back at Orla, he motioned her to try and calm Faith.

The townspeople stilled, curious to listen.

A gentle breeze moved through his hair, and his words rang out. "The rye that grows in our very fields has a sickness growing in its heads, called ergot, a poisonous fungus born from putrefying wet grain which is causing the terrible deaths of our people." Gesturing to the inside of the house, "Alas, I believe that this poor, young woman, Faith, struggles in the throes of ergot poisoning."

Murmurs of unease rustled the air.

"I be a farmer, and I've not seen this," came a voice from the back.

"I ask you this Master Farmer, how hath your animals?" Abraham questioned. "For those whose land neighbours the rye." His voice rose to reach the people in the back. "Have thee noticed odd behaviour in your oxen? Curdled milk from your cows?"

"Aye, I have," answered one.

"Yes, and hath any of you noticed a purple blackness on the ears of your animals such as a frostbite? For I believe, all beasts can fall ill from the ergot poisoning too," Abraham reported gravely.

The crowd stirred, and some began speaking to those standing next to them.

Another farmer called, "Me heifer and her calf stumbled about for days, and then, as God is me witness, she turned on her babe, mad she was, killing it she did." Pausing, the crowd held their breath.

"On the second day, she dropped to the ground, quaking and frothing before she died. Vexed to the guts I were."

The crowd looked apprehensive and Abraham hurried on.

"I know your confusion, good farmer. The fungus sickens the strong grain. Except for its purple colour, the diseased grain disguises itself as the shape of the normal rye head. Beast and man know not that the poison of the fungus resides within." And Abraham added, trying to deflect Cardell's outburst of magic grain, "'Twas, Orla, my goodwife who, with her keen eyes, spotted the strange fungus living amongst the healthy rye."

The villagers were engrossed in what he said, so Abraham hastily continued, "It is the observation of myself and family of healers that after the grain was harvested, that mysterious deaths cursed our village.

"We hath all visited the homes of many sick people with common feelings of a crawling skin and odd tingling in the fingers. And how many of you have suffered the falling sickness of late, I pray thee? All of these strange and ill humours I doth believe are from the ingestion of the poisoned grain."

Orla glanced at the Reverend and was surprised he listened. Faith tossed and thrashed, her hands held tight to a seemingly agonising headache.

Alice and Mary were meanwhile mixing remedies to administer to Faith.

Abraham continued, "Through countless nights, we strained our sight in old books and tested our memories in an effort to comprehend the signs displayed by the ailing and dying. Since that first faithful day, when one of our neighbours fell ill, the five of us have worked all hours to discover the origin. The Wise women have recalled their family teachings, and William with his scholarly education, has shed light on this terrible sickness."

Glancing at William, Abraham noticed with alarm that his brother was swooning from another syphilitic fever. Sweating profusely, coupled with his ever-increasing tremble, he looked horribly unwell.

Abraham hoped no one else had noticed and continued his explanation before another outburst from Cardell.

"Reading back through the church archives, I noted accounts of similar patterns to our current weather. Freezing winter, warm spring, and then, according to the deaths and births columns, increased miscarriages, stillbirths, and..." Abraham looked at Faith, "...convulsing and ravings. The ergot poisoning can bring delusional sickness such as seeing spectres and altered lights, burning limbs, purpling skin, and...sadly, death." Abraham regarded the crowd with a pleading expression, "I believe my research hath found that certain conditions of climate promote the growth of a fungus which can blight grain. I can't yet say if other grains are affected, as we have only studied the rye. However, the Wisewomen have found ergot in Couch grass, a common herb, and found it to be medicinal. This poisoning from ergot, which I strongly believe is linked to the illness mentioned in the church records as 'Holy Fire', is named for the burning pain it causes and is an unholy curse upon mankind." The villagers were again talking quickly to each other, trying to recall past weather patterns. Some were animated, some stood stony-faced. Abraham spoke louder to carry over the voices.

"Goodly people, please, allow me to finish! 'Tis my understanding that when seasons are harsh, with specific conditions, this fungus grows upon the grain and the poison thrives, and all those who consume it, from beast to man, fall ill.

"Not even the heat of the ovens' fire can destroy the deadliness from the blighted grain. This fungus holds some medicinal properties, but only in small measures, and in moderate quantities is deadly. This means that our suppers' bread could prove to bring sickness."

A collective gasp shattered the air like breaking glass.

The Warner sisters looked at one another, as Abraham had not yet confirmed his findings to them. To the sisters, it made sense. Many plants were poisonous, and a few were deadly. It was their business to know which plants gave life, and the ones which took life.

The crowd was buzzing with Abraham's observations.

"Nay, Brother, this blessed plant can bring forth a new way of seeing the world." Abraham froze as William stumbled towards him.

Grabbing his arm, Abraham struggled to keep William from nearing the startled crowd.

"Sit thee down, you are unsound, your ravings will be the end of us!" Abraham whispered harshly.

"Take your hands from me!" William shouted. The crowd silenced, as they had never seen the brothers wrapped in conflict.

"You know only that the plant brings sickness, but in small doses, it can show you the world in different colours, different details and even faces can change." He pointed to Faith.

"After our meeting that night, I visited the Baker Reid, and he confirmed he does use the rye from a small field off Farmer Wenden's land."

"And what of it, Bones?" came the voice of Farmer Wenden, swiftly growing tired of talk of his grain being poisonous.

William, seemingly unaware of the interruption, continued, "After careful deliberation, I decided that ingestion of the ergot fungus would be appropriate penitence for my prior sins." He hung his head, and eyes still cast down, he continued

"Faith convinced me that she, too, must participate—guilty she is of her mother's death birthing her, and forever tainted in the eyes of her father, she also sought penitence." People stood again in shock at hearing this disclosure.

"We picked the ergot rye and made it into bread to test if the oven heat would transform the properties. And then we ate the bread. Little pieces at first, and then more until the world changed in colour and distorted shapes appeared. With small amounts, the world became a more beautiful place, but if we were greedy, then vomiting and convulsions were our punishment." Looking at Abraham with a feverish gleam, William continued, "I am without doubt, Brother, you were correct in your speculation. The hallucinations, the convulsions and the gangrene—'tis the ergot which is afflicting the people."

Noting Abraham's look of disbelief, William added, "I beseech you, how could we know if we did not test the bread?"

"Dear God," Abraham whispered, and anxiously looked towards the girl and the Wise women.

Orla regarded Faith, and now understood why the girl had looked so ill and acted so strange in the fields. She had been suffering the malice and bane of the ergot.

"Brother," William laughed strangely, "when I fed the ergot to Faith and myself, she did change! 'Twas extraordinary. Yes, she was ill, but afterwards, her mind was open to the suggestion that she hath been my lost Laurel, and behold, her face, her ways, her grace, all transformed!" He exclaimed, and turning, gestured towards Faith.

"You see, Abraham, Laurel lies here before us. After the fits hath vanished, then forever she shall be mine." William again fell to her side.

Those that could hear, stood muted, struggling to understand the strange words of their Surgeon. Despite their fondness of the healers, delusions, hallucinations, convulsions, all sounded like satanic possession to them.

"William, you are deranged from your illness. This child is not Laurel, and you have poisoned her with the ergot!" Orla cried out.

Cardell pushed his way onto the porch and shrieked, "'Tis the work of witchcraft and Devil play, these healers belie you with faire words, all the whiles possessing the souls of children by poisoning their daily bread! Does thou hear the villainous words from the Bones quack?

"These confessions of unearthly visions and demonic faces appearing before him..." pointing at William, "This creature's soul is indeed possessed!" The Reverend's hands reached for the heavens and intoned, "O' Lord, as your humble shepherd, I doth hear your celestial revelations. Give me the strength to guide my flock from these shadows and back into your Heavenly light. Lord, we beseech you!"

"Blessed God," some of the crowd responded.

Cardell looked back down to stare at William, his face gaunt. "Our Lord, in His Almighty wisdom, hath revealed to me that the Surgeon Bones consorts with the Archfiend himself and hath bewitched the soul of my child." The crowd gasped with the accusation, and their mood noticeably darkened.

"'Tis not possession, you small-minded fool!" Abraham yelled at Cardell. "My brother's mind is deranged from syphilis. His tongue is not his own, his words are slave to the sickness, made worse from the poisoning of the blighted grain."

Orla exchanged a look with Alice, as they had suspected such a malady devoured the soul of William, but his diagnosis had not been spoken of.

112

The gathered people recoiled, as they were fearful of catching the miasma from William.

"You lie!" shouted William, rushing towards Abraham. "How can thee speak with such venom? You know me to be of clean body and sound mind." Aware that William's secret was now public, Abraham tried to diffuse the shock.

"William, thou hast no need for shame. Thousands are stricken with this dreadful malady, their bodies and minds laid waste," he said gently.

"Do not play the fool, Abraham! 'Twas my fault Laurel and our babe died because of my sinful actions. I could not control my beastly urges, and Laurel took her life! My babe, my son. O' brother, your eyes were not cursed by the sight of his tiny body." William clawed at his face. "Perfect, my son was to behold, but only he did not breathe. My sickness, worse than the pox, killed them. I murdered them both!" And suddenly, William doubled up in pain and began to vomit black bile.

Orla was startled to see William collapse and knew the poison was killing him.

Abraham and Mary rushed over, trying to rouse him. Attempts at spooning mouthfuls of remedy into his mouth were impossible as William was unresponsive.

Orla could hear the crowd roar with William's last words. "Murdered his wife and babe? What sort of demon would participate in such evil?" they were asking.

Orla could feel the energy of the crowd, electric like a summer's storm.

Sure now that Faith was dying from the poisoned bread, she joined Alice and motioned Mary back over. "Make haste, Mary, let us try the oxymel syrup of Watermint and Devil's bit for William and for Faith."

Orla could not believe the chaotic circus unfolding before her.

Abraham was again arguing with the Reverend, and Orla went to Williams side, trying to rouse him. "William, William!" Orla shook him, and he finally came around. "You must tell me, did you know Faith was with child when you fed her the ergot?" she pleaded for an answer.

His brows furrowed his confusion, answering her question before his words did.

"She is with child?" he implored. "We have a baby again?" He looked stunned. "How do you know this, Sister?"

"Again?" Orla questioned, then remembering his first wife, looked at him with dread. Avoiding the question, she continued,

"William, the ergot would have poisoned her and the babe. I beg thee, did you know?" Orla was perplexed as Faith had accused her father, the Reverend, of raping her and making her pregnant.

"No, no, she didn't tell me! I would not have allowed her to eat the ergot if I knew! Lovers we have been each night since midsummer, but we followed the cycles of the moon. She should not be with child!" Orla could hear hysteria building in his voice. "Again I beseech you, Orla, how did thee know Faith was with child?" Orla watched Alice frantically adding more herbal compresses to abate Faith's bleeding. But her womb bled unchecked.

Mary spooned the dark oxymel into Faith's mouth and asked, "Why does she bleed like this when ye said the ergot stopped the mother from bleeding during birth?"

"God, yer daft, girl," Alice snapped. "Ye can't feed a woman, new with child, poison and expect the womb to hold. We know not how much she has eaten either." Mary blushed, and went silent and Orla frowned at Alice for her sharp tongue.

Glancing over, Orla saw Cardell staring at her, and pushing past Abraham, he pounced on the Wise women.

"With my own ears, I heard you speak of pregnancy. Perchance you speak of my daughter?" Cardell blared at Faith. "As God is our witness, are these abhorrent tidings true?"

"Cease yer yelling, you witless fool!" Alice demanded and blurted, "If you'd kept your beastly hands off her innocence, then still intact her sanity and maidenhood would be!"

The room ringing with commotion, stilled with the outburst.

Orla came alongside Alice to explain the newest development that Faith was likely pregnant from William. Orla's eyes met Abraham, and he stared at her with disbelief.

"The girl came to us, begging for help," Orla hurried. Abraham's face was grim, and he subtlety shook his head.

"Pray, help from what?" Reverend Cardell growled.

"From yer evil lechery," Mary retorted, and turning to the people in the cramped room, she explained. "The Reverends' own child came to us for herbal simples to expel the pregnancy. Faith hath accused her father of incestuous acts.

114

"How could we refuse when she confessed that the abomination of his lust grew in her womb?" Mary asked the gathered people.

Searching the faces within the room, and from outside, Orla saw with horror, disbelief and anger directed towards them.

Eyes crazed, the Reverend took a step towards Orla. "Incest? What vomit do you spew forth, woman? No doubt, from the mouth of a serpent, wherewith you learned these lies." He looked disgusted at their allegation.

Orla stared at Cardell, his words and eyes full of truth.

Sudden images of William and Faith flooded her.

Faith's words came rushing back. It was not her father who had raped her.

Kneeling at his daughter's head, Cardell buried his hands in her hair. "Only a creature bound for the bowels of hell would stand before God's Shepherd and proclaim such blasphemy," he shouted, banging Faith's head into the floorboards. "Mendacious demon, I will flagellate the scourge from your soul with my own hands!"

Faith screamed, while Mary tried to pry Cardell's fingers from his daughter's hair.

"Take your fouled hands off my love!" Pushing Cardell hard, William fell a top the Reverend and slapped him.

"Dear God!" cried a woman in the crowd. Three men rushed forward and dragged William off Reverend Cardell. Brushing himself off, the Reverend stood, and narrowing his eyes, pointed at William's ulcers. "This creature, this trusted healer is riddled and plagued with sores, syphilis sores if mine eyes do not deceive. Filthy and vile!" Cardell looked mortified.

Rounding on Orla, he pointed and said, "Perchance, Witch, you shield the brother of your husband? Aye? So be this the truth." Cardell's smile was dark. "You and your Witch sisters knew that the Surgeon had tainted my daughter with his accursed pox. When you discovered his damned seed sprouting within her innocence, you schemed to destroy the blight from her violated womb, in the guise of a morning brew, is this not true?" he accused

"'Tis not true!" Orla shouted above the commotion. "William only now realised that Faith carried his child." Orla pleaded to the gathered villagers. "I beg thee, you must know the pleas for help from Faith, rang true to our hearts."

Alarm turned to panic, as the allegations were thrown.

One man yelled out: "Ye hath possessed the child with ye Witch craft!"

"Murderers! The lot of them!"

"They are all Witches!" someone else yelled.

The sisters felt ill and trembled from the allegations as they continued to administer medicines to Faith, though she was clearly failing.

"Confine your judgement, I beseech you!" Abraham shouted above the din. "The truth shall be revealed, and righteousness shall prevail."

"Indeed, I promise there shall be revelations," an icy voice cut through the bedlam.

All eyes turned towards the speaker in the doorway.

"Who in hell is that?" a rough voice rang out.

A handsome man, tall in height, rich clothing adorned his slim body. Fine linen collar and sleeves accented the gilded buttons on his leather doublet. "Our saviour," Cardell proclaimed.

His boots extended far above his knees, the fine leather artistry accentuated in intricate designs at the top.

The common folk had never seen such finery.

"Sir your timing is impeccable." The Reverend rushed to the doorway, and met the man on the porch.

"I do not tarry when grave warrants such as these from thine parish are made. Such wicked accusation of witchcraft can destroy the sturdy foundations of a thriving community such as this." He smiled a wolf's grin and privileged the Reverend by extending his hand.

Noting the filth beneath the Puritan's fingernails, the man quickly withdrew his hand, attempting to conceal his disgust. He thought to himself that if he were going to obtain the silver crowns he desired, then he would have to exhibit some esteem to yet another religious fanatical.

With a broad grin, the Reverend used the voice he commanded within his church. "This be the honourable and renowned Mathew Crashaw. Profoundly knowledgeable in His Majesty's law, and," he paused looking at Orla, "a formidable Witch hunter," Cardell sneered, pleased with himself.

"The Witch hunter has arrived upon my request to investigate the unholy events which hath been darkly unfolding in our shire. Children dying of a rot, babes born still, possessed people, Satan hath made his home in our village." He surveyed the mob to assure they had all heard his words.

The air thundered with commotion. People inside rushed outdoors, excited that a genuine Witch hunter had arrived. Fearful of condemnation, Abraham hurried to Orla's side as she stumbled with shock.

William feebly lifted Faith and pushed his way outside with her, limp in his arms.

"Stop the quack!" shouted the Reverend. "He is taking Faith!"

Lucid, but gaunt and pale, William called, "She is in need of urgent treatments, and I make haste to my apothecary where I have the tools to treat her."

"Thou art going nowhere with my daughter! Halt him, I command it!" bellowed the Reverend.

The townspeople shuffled uneasily. William was a respected Physician and obviously not himself at present, but he had proven his competency years before Reverend Cardell had arrived.

"I said stop him!" the commanding voice of the Puritan compelled some to obey.

Two farmers stepped forward and tried to impede William's progress.

"Do not cause my delay, this girl will surely die without treatments!" William's voice rose to near panic.

Abraham was holding Orla, as she looked near a swoon.

"*Meus Dilectus,*" he whispered in Latin, "do not crumble beneath the terrors of your past. Fear and hysteria are abundant, and your strength is necessary." Abraham struggled with his own composure.

"Yes, husband, I know, but a Witch hunter has arrived, my nightmares relived!" Orla cried

Brushing a tear from her cheek, he could see haunting memories in her eyes.

"Make haste, beloved, and gather your sisters outside. We must regain the trust of our people, before their wits are lost in Cardell's hate-filled tempest."

With sinking heart, Orla spied her sisters already being harassed by the Witch hunter. In the small room, Alice's voice carried, abusing the man. "Forsooth! Ye art too wrapt and shrined in thine own wondrous glory to see these people are ill!" she mocked. "Return yer vain words and showy boots to London, and leave us to our business of healing."

Before the man could retaliate, Orla swiftly stepped between them and pushed her sisters out the door.

As Orla passed, Crashaw seized her by the arm.

"God so, thou art a fetching wench." His eyes pierced her soul and feeling her tremble, he smiled.

"But yer bewitching beauty shall not taint my wits," he loudly whispered.

With a movement of air, Crashaw was suddenly thrown against the wall. A wink of steel and scuffling boots, and Abraham held his dagger to the Witch hunter's throat.

"Dare to speak to my wife again, and I shalt slice the muscles from your throat, and not in the tidy style of the churgeoun, but as a haphazard butcher," Abraham growled.

Orla stood stunned. She had never witnessed her husband raise a weapon.

The Witch hunters' grin froze.

"Wife?" he jeered. "Thou art openly confessing that ye exercised conjugal rights with this creature, an accused Witch?"

"My wife is no Witch," Abraham hissed, "and our matrimonial activities are not your concern *impurus, salax canis.*"

Orla knew enough of Latin to know the Witch hunter had just been insulted.

Abraham withdrew the blade from Crashaw's neck, red drops of blood staining his silk scarf.

A sneer now replaced the grin. "You will regret that, sir." Crashaw threatened and quickly adjusted his scarf and collar.

Abraham pulled Orla out the door and hugged her, but stopped dead at the mayhem before them.

Groups of women stood screaming at Alice, blaming her of purposely fouling their births and killing their babies. Ridiculously, she was being blamed for the falling of a goodwife's pudding!

Alice was desperately trying to reach Mary, who was being harried by a mob, accusing her of midnight visits with demons, riding her goat and dancing at Witches' Sabbaths. "Is that goat yer familiar?" one voice was heard, asking Mary.

"How else can ye stay so fair to the eye, whence ye should be a hag by now," a man shouted. "I've seen ye by me own eyes eating the hearts of dead babes to keep ye faire!" Mary paled and swooned, overwhelmed by the hateful accusations.

"Yer old eyes are blind, John, as little Mary never ventures from home after nightfall!" Alice shouted across the heads.

"Is that so, crone? As God is mine witness, I hath seen that Witch on moonlit nights near the oak behind the cemetery," John shouted back.

Alice knew Mary enjoyed her evening strolls, but would not admit this to the mob.

William was struggling to free himself from numerous dirty hands, while Faith hung listlessly over the Puritan's shoulder. He broke free and hurried Faith back into their house.

"Dear God, save us," Orla implored, and ran down the step to catch Mary in a faint. The poor lass was of a delicate constitution, forever the weakest of the sisters. Orla pushed a Yeoman hard, who was berating Alice for hexing his limp manhood.

Abraham joined William, attempting to free his brother of the big Smith who restrained him.

William tried to stop the Puritan, and as he lunged for Faith, the Smith swung his mighty fist, colliding with William's jaw. As Abraham tried to intercept the punch, he was knocked down by the Baker, screaming that his talk of blighted bread was ruining his trade. Farmer Wenden, Yeoman of the questionable rye, joined the attack.

Abraham was able to stumble to his feet, but did not get the chance to argue his point, as he caught sight of Crashaw sauntering onto the low porch and perching himself above the crowd.

Clapping his hands loudly, he proclaimed, "Goodly citizens." His voice carried above the chaos. "People, in but a short time, I hath seen and harkened the discords of wicked folly." He purposely looked over at Abraham.

"Hath not I told thee that evil runs rampant in this town?" bellowed Reverend Cardell as he positioned himself near the Witch hunter. Abraham noted that Faith was not with him, and presumed she was back inside the cottage.

Crashaw smiled at the Reverend like a parent of a spoiled child. "Indeed, these passing moments have been very illuminating. 'Tis clear to me that social order and restraint are demanded forthwith." He nodded to Cardell and to the people gathered below.

"As my father before me, appointed by King Charles, I now continue his legacy to maintain secular justice within his Majesty's countryside. This means, goodly people, that the proceedings of alleged witchcraft and trespassing against property will commence, and I will see that justice prevails and malevolent workings are abolished."

Some people clapped, some stood silent.

The Witch hunter regarded the crowd, calculating the degree of superstition and blood thirst etched on the faces. Crashaw would draw from their fears and greed to achieve his ultimate outcome: to fatten his purse and satiate his lust for torture.

His father, a renowned Witch hunter, had made a good life for himself and family, living off the superstitions of a witch-crazed world. A hard and cruel man his father had been, but he taught young Matthew the art of reading and writing, and the finer skills of manipulation and torture.

Though the Crown no longer funded Witch hunters, it also turned a blind eye to existing Witch hunters who arguably brought order to disorderly communities. If the Witch hunter and his employees profited from the deed, then it was their business. News was scarce outside of London, and literacy was low.

The simple people of the countryside did not know that Witch hunting was becoming unpopular. And that Witch hunters did not actually work for the King anymore, but still they used the guise of 'Crown law' to command law and collect their fee.

Crashaw peered into the dirty, gullible faces of the common people. He recognised the same, burning fervour witnessed in every town he travelled and sighed. *How pathetic and predictable these simple-minded fools are, but rich they will make me,* he thought.

Mesmerised by the Witch hunter's words and hawkish scrutiny, the crowd stilled.

"Master Donne, please step forward," Crashaw called.

Heads turned to spot the unknown person.

From the back, a well-fed man in fine, but soiled clothing, gnawed a piece of wheat grass. With a glare, he observed them with condemning eyes. Many could not hold his chilly stare and looked away uneasily.

Swaggering around the perimeter of the group, he stopped a few feet behind the Warner sisters.

Smiling, Crashaw inclined his head. "My collaborator and premier witness for the Crown, Master Donne, Witch confessor." Donne bowed with exaggerated sincerity, and noticing Orla, simpered past her, grinning, displaying a blackened void where teeth once were.

With seeming fondness, Crashaw grinned at Donne. "Have thee gathered the jailers?" he questioned.

"Aye," Donne replied, now turning his attention and leer to Mary. He licked his lips with an oily tongue. Mary whimpered and hid within Alice's arms. The Confessor laughed.

Crashaw continued, "Excellent. Pray, goodly men, reveal thy selves to me."

Five men stepped out from the crowd. Two of the jailers looked sheepish and were residents of their village. Orla frowned as she had just delivered to one jailer a healthy baby son. The other three were not recognised and must have been brought in from neighbouring townships.

Selection was never random.

One of the Witch confessor's jobs was to carefully appoint jailers who were chosen for their biased viewpoints of the accused and were offered a substantial amount of coin for their loyalty and assistance to the matters of the Crown.

Each man positioned themselves near the brothers and the Warner sisters. Orla noticed the jailers from her village kept their eyes downcast. Not knowing that their pockets were heavy with coin, Orla wondered what these men could possibly have against them?

"I demand you explain thyself!" Abraham's tone commanded attention. "Pray tell, why are these jailers eyeing us as if we were villains?" he gestured.

"What forked tongue has tasted power, and now art drunk from its intoxication?" Abraham turned and questioned Reverend Cardell.

"God's truth, 'tis your lunacy that this once tranquil village is now mad with antiquated superstitions!" he spat at Cardell.

Gesturing to the crowd, "Hath your ears not harkened my words, goodly citizens, or are they filled with loud misguidance of this zealous fool?" Abraham's face was crimson and he was oblivious of the growing discontent.

"'Tis the ergot I say, which has poisoned our people, taken our children, maddened our animals, and the ergot which sours your minds." He hurried to explain.

"*Ignis sacer*, or Holy Fire, this plant is named. 'Fire' from the burning pain, 'Holy' as the toxin is likened to God's curse," Abraham clarified.

"History books, written by the Romans, report of entire villages being accursed from accidental ingestion of this poison—this malignant growth upon their grains. The people were afflicted by terrible visions and pain, before going mad, and their hands and feet turned black with rot, swiftly killing them," he described.

The crowd looked at one another puzzled and concerned. This was a tale they had not heard of before.

"What evil folly is this?" bellowed the Reverend, as he pushed through the crowd. "These tales thou art spewing are stories of possessed souls, wretched and tortured by demons, not from ingestion of their daily bread." He implored with the gathered people. The Reverend's words made more sense to the simple people, as he had of recent been preaching the danger of demons at his sermons.

Superstitions were a part of life, and easier to accept than Roman history and the mystery of science.

Abraham, noting the confusion on the faces of the crowd, raised his voice and was determined to not be interrupted again by Cardell.

"I beseech you, goodly citizens, for those of you eating the rye, I beg thee to stop and recall your health. Have you been purging yellow bile?" he questioned.

"Does your body tremble without a chill? Do your eyes beguile your mind?" Raising his fingers to his forehead, "I ask you to recall, have you seen flickering lights and spectres within the shadows? Do you feel as if your mind is not your own?" He searched the faces of the people and noted some frowning with consideration.

"If you have answered yes, then most likely you are being poisoned by blighted grain."

Abraham had dreaded this moment of revealing his suspicion to the common people, for fear of condemnation, for fear of retribution.

"I swear," and his voiced wavered, "'tis the truthful word of your Physician and neighbour whereby I offer this information. I mean no harm but am trying to prevent any more deaths."

Abraham's face pleaded with his people, as they shifted their weight uneasily, casting back their memories to recall ill health.

Hollow clapping broke the heavy silence.

The Witch Hunter Crashaw made his way to Abraham. "And this is how, innocent citizens, you have been manipulated. By the compelling, bewitching words of your so-named Physician." The crowd looked at one another, and Crashaw continued, "Do not believe that Witches only come in the guise of women, for here stands before thee one in the flesh, a demon-male, a Magician. Who else but a servant of Lucifer could know of such heresy? Lived and worked this land for generations you have, and yet this man knows secrets of the very grain you eat and entwines it with malevolence."

Crashaw pointed at Abraham, "Behold, a hellion, a Heretic who hath betrayed your trust, defiled God and taken your coins for tainted remedies to cure you of madness and illness he has actually caused. Cast your eyes on the Heretic, the slave of Satan, Abraham Bones."

Some people gasped, and Abraham heard Orla cry out, "Lies!"

Abraham was stunned for a moment, but quickly regained his composure, as he registered anger and betrayal in the eyes of the gathered villagers.

"My people!" Abraham shouted over the din, "those of my community, we have laughed together, shared food and drink together, we have cried and comforted one another. And now our village is being torn asunder by a terrible poison, and we are all victims of a senseless 'Witch Craze', delivered to you by servants of Matthew Hopkins, the Witch finder general.

"These mongrel dogs, Crashaw and Donne, are criminals, thriving on the coin of the highest bidder, carrion birds drawn by the decay of human morale, fear and paranoia. To succumb to these swindlers, these villains, is to relinquish coin from your hard work, and your good souls given to the real devils!" He pointed at Crashaw, "There walks the wickedness of the world, not I nor your healers present." This further promoted confusion and growing anxiety in the townspeople.

Crashaw, who was adept at reading people, could see the group wavering on the Physician's words. Wise words they were, and he knew he needed to gain the upper hand.

So Crashaw smiled at Abraham, and cast his well-practiced look of pity in response to Abraham's accusations.

Luckily for Crashaw, distraction came, as out of the crowd, Baker Reid rushed at Abraham, pushing him hard to the ground. Abraham nimbly jumped back up and stood stony-faced as the Baker shouted at him. Orla held her breath as she was aware of the crowd's escalating discontentment.

It was time for Crashaw to make his move, otherwise he could lose the momentum of the craze.

"Master Donne," his voice carried over the loud raucous, "I weary of standing before these accursed souls, you and your jailers remove the Warners and Bones to the guildhall where we shall conduct our interrogations forthwith...oh, and arrange a chair and ale for myself." The Witch confessor nodded his head and snapped his fingers to a bystander.

As one seething mass, the crowd ignited. They shepherded the newly accused Bones and Warners together, roughly pulling arms and hair, and tearing clothes in the rush to drive them to the guildhall. There were a few voices of protest and mercy from people who would not believe that their healers could be doing the workings of Satan. Their pleas were lost in the bloodthirsty cries of the vengeful mob. The villagers wanted answers to the bizarre illness and deaths of their families and neighbours. Their fears and grief needed to be vindicated, and the Witch hunter had convinced them the answers lay with the Bones and Warner family.

Orla's world slowed as the pandemonium around her raged. Each face which swam past was distorted either in fear or anger.

She was pushed and pulled like a rag doll caught between two children. Terrible memories threatened to drown Orla, as images flooded her. She saw through the dappled light of the leaves, her mother hanging from a tree. Defiled and betrayed. She remembered the cruel laugh of the Witch hunter all those years ago, who in a day, had destroyed her family and left herself and sisters motherless. The memories flooded her soul, the grief bled through the wound in her heart, buckling Orla's knees.

A farmer presiding over Orla as her jailer, held her arms tighter as she stumbled, almost collapsing. He proceeded to drag her through the mob, the mayhem building as each familiar person she passed sneered with damning condemnation.

With dread, Orla glimpsed Mary held tightly by the Witch confessor, a lewd grin plastered to his face. With a heart's flutter, Orla realised she had not seen Philippa and prayed that wherever Mary's daughter was, that she was sensible enough to remain hidden.

Within moments, the crowd had pushed the Warners and Abraham into the guildhall, William was dragged by two large farmers and dumped on the floor. Orla saw a dishevelled Abraham struggling against the strength of the Smith and Baker. His relative calm was betrayed by the quaking of his body. Orla found Abraham's gaze, and her stomach dropped with the fear she registered, glistening in his eyes.

Abraham rallied and shrugged off the Baker. With renewed strength, he pushed towards Crashaw and challenged him. "Without a warrant, you hath not the right to threaten us nor to make the damning accusations which would end our lives. You cannot jail us, or hold us against our will," he protested.

The light in the guildhall was dim, and the air was thick and dusty. A chair and pewter mug were placed in the middle of the room and Crashaw was pushing through the crowd to reach the drink. He rested a polished boot on the chair and drank deeply of the ale.

Orla was jostled through the door and her ears filled with the muffle of the sounds around her. The horde of people roughly pushed Orla and her sisters together, where they stumbled into an embrace. Assessing Abraham while he drank from his cup, the Witch finder's hand fumbled inside his coat and brought forth a rolled parchment.

Orla watched Abraham's face twitch and saw that he was failing to hide his fear. It appeared Abraham knew already what damning words the parchment held.

"Right here, Master Bones," and Crashaw shook the parchment out, "is the warrant you seek." Glancing over the paper, he raised his voice to address the room. "And it appears that your entire family has featured in its context." He winked, and positioned his body to face the townspeople.

"To all those gathered, let it be known that I am empathetic to the plight of the accused." His face exhibited a mock sympathy as he glanced at Orla and her sisters. "Hereof is the truth; these accusations are not made by myself, but that I have been requested to investigate and impart my expertise."

"And collect a bag of gold!" shouted Alice. A few people muttered in the background.

Crashaw frowned at her, and continued, "To this situation. I am a Witch finder yes, but I stand not alone.

"This shire hath cunning folk—Watchers and witness, all of you judges, all of you housing Witch finders within your souls. You brought me here." He gravely stated, "And thus, grounds of prosecution are made not by my rules, but in the law-abiding hands of your own parish." He gestured to Cardell, "The Reverend in his power of Godly magistrate hath appointed selected Searchers and Watchers which he holds in high esteem to determine guilt or innocence of the accused." Cardell beamed.

The Witch hunter held the parchment out and read out loud: "And so, I beseech you, thou shall sight this parchment as the warrant bearing the insignia of your presiding Lord and law maker, King Charles the First. I stand awaiting written amendments to this parchment by further witness and your own confessions." The crowd quieted and pushed forward, and Orla strained to hear.

"These names and crimes I shalt read out, are here forth charged: Abraham Bones: These goodly citizens did hear your proclamations of heresies at the earlier hour. First: Thine own words spewed forth, incriminating yourself as not a trusted Physician, but as a schemer to aid in the possession of innocent souls.

However, it is written here upon this parchment that you worked with the accused women standing here to solidify their vile doings with your guise as Physician. Second: It is written that the land on which your home resides, is located on the property of Thomas Hodge, which he has demanded thou to vacate numerous times prior. It is the belief of Master Hodge and witness that 'foul and evil acts' occur upon his land, which are intolerable and immoral." Gesturing towards Hodge, who nodded.

"That land is mine fair," Abraham angrily responded, "and my brother, William. Our border has always been disputed by Hodge, but this accusation is an outright lie! I can produce the title deed. The other charges are simply ridiculous." Abraham was seething.

"And so you say, Master Bones," and Crashaw continued,

"Thirdly, Abraham Bones, your accusations of Baker Reid deliberately baking fouled bread are here forth found to be diabolical and slanderous. Only a tainted soul of deviant character would cast such darkness on an esteemed member of the community." The Witch hunter took another drink of his ale, and faced off Abraham. "New accusations of heresy have just been added, as the good townspeople are witness today to these grave offences, namely that you have not been seen to attend church on the Sabbath, but instead, found rifling through church records on the Sabbath!" Crashaw wagged his finger at Abraham. "That you openly reject the doctrines of our God's word by questioning the very world he controls, namely blighted grain. Why would God create blighted grain to knowingly poison his beloved creatures?" the Witch hunter asked the room theatrically.

"And lastly, Master Bones, as witnessed by the good Reverend Cardell, mocking the Puritan's tradition of signing their allegiance to God, you have been signing a demon's book of your own making."

"Demon book?" Abraham choked, as he was suffocating in confusion and heartbreak. "If you are referring to our sickness journal, then it is an ongoing log of our remedies and cures. There is nothing devious nor sinister about this book. More foolish tale-telling by bored and noisy Good wives." Abraham frowned and eyed the town's gossips.

"Spells and hexes more likely," a known rumourmonger called out.

The Witch finder shook his head.

Abraham was trying to shout explanations above the din, but his voice was lost. Orla caught sight of him being wrestled to the ground.

Donne's voice cut through the shouting to quiet down.

The Witch hunter motioned to the still-prone body of William Bones. It seemed that the remedies administered were not working, and William was worsening.

"And there lies William Bones, accused brother of Abraham. Today we have witnessed his deranged ramblings, and by his own admissions, he has confessed to murdering his wife and babe, and knowingly poisoning the innocent daughter of Reverend Cardell." He gestured to William and slowly shook his head.

"His own community has watched William fall prey to possession by the Archfiend, as confirmed by his delusional ramblings and night rides through the countryside, howling like a mad thing." Crashaw nudged William with his boot. "Alas his soul is being consumed by Satan as we speak. But if we are to leave him unattended, the Devil will completely possess his body, and no longer will the goodly, pious citizens be safe in their homes."

The people next to William stepped back for fear of the Devil rising up right then and there, years of his healing servitude were all forgotten by the new charges.

Abraham was standing again, and advanced on Crashaw. "These accusations are fanciful and are only for making your purse heavy with coin! How now you come to our village and presume to reside over us like a Watchman or Magistrate!" Abraham's allegation was stirring, but he was roughly pushed back by a jailer.

Without answering him, Crashaw continued.

"Alice Warner, spinster, crone and accused Witch," he read out. Some people laughed at the title.

"What do ye care about my unwed bed, and since when didst being an old woman warrant a Witch trial?" Alice shouted.

"Alice Warner your charges," Crashaw continued. "For suspicion of witchcraft in frequent accounts: For the giving of fertility eggs to barren goodwives only to poison them with ill humours; for walking past Farmer Sullivan and cursing him with a severe look."

"Foolishness and balderdash," responded Alice with hands now on hips.

"He then reported his cock went cold and hath not been able to carry out his husbandly duties since that day," continued Crashaw.

A few people chuckled in the crowd, as Farmer Sullivan was known to blame the ugliness of his wife for his disinterest in the bed. For some, these accusations of witchcraft seemed farfetched.

The Witch hunter continued reading, a frown now creasing his face. "Alice Warner, thou art accused of the diabolical and loathsome acts of infanticide, and causing the deliberate deaths of mother and babe in birth, by laying of hands on their bodies, and the breath be taken."

He looked at her with raised eyebrows.

The air grew heavy with the gravity of these charges and gasps could be heard. "And the unholy, conjugal acts and convergence with Lucifer, Alice Warner, you stand accused and are no doubt guilty of these ghastly atrocities."

Orla squeezed the trembling hands of Alice. These were heinous accusations. The vehement anger was a betrayal to the sacrifices of a Midwife in such desperate times. Alice's face was contorted in hopelessness and grief.

The crowd started shouting insults at Alice but were quieted again by Donne.

The Witch hunter continued reading from the parchment.

"Mary Warner, known as Goodwife Lyttle, widow to the late Benjamin Lyttle." Crashaw smiled at her. All eyes found the quiet and pretty woman, quivering and quietly weeping.

"A year to this day, witnesses saw you call forth the Devil's power to heal your drowned child, Philippa, all accounts proclaimed, the child lay dead, and you placed your mouth upon hers in an unclean fashion, of which the child then stood alive and well."

His voice rose, "Upon that very day, little Bess Fairfield, the same age of your spared child, dropped dead where she stood, with naught explainable affliction."

Mary spoke for the first time, in between sobs, "My daughter fell into the lake; the water filling her lungs," she defended. "'Twas under the watchful eye of God that I emptied the water from her lungs and returned breath given from my own to my child. 'Twas a miracle of life that she returned," Mary stated weakly.

Some of the crowd jeered, and the Reverend heckled that only God bestowed miracles and did not take the life of an innocent in exchange.

Orla spoke up in defence, addressing the crowd, "How dare you all! Everyone knew Bess was dying of weakened lungs for seasons past. 'Twas an oddity that the child would pass the same day which Philippa was saved. 'Tis a terrible charge, and you should all be shamed!" Orla glared at the crowd.

Crashaw continued, eyeing Mary. "How now you've been in the service of the Devil, have you not?" interrogated the Witch hunter. "Did he command you to take the soul of an innocent in exchange for the breath of the Devil's spawn, your own daughter? Is it not true, Goody Lyttle, sister to Orla and Alice, you promised to partake in conjugal rights with Satan if he spared the life of your child?" Mary began to openly cry, but still Crashaw continued.

"On many accounts, you hath been seen dancing with demons at Witches' Sabbaths—maniacal and possessed, as you appeared to have lost your soul in a frenzy." He paused for effect.

"The Godly Puritans hath state that dancing incites lust and encourages eyes to watch with wicked thoughts. Thou hath been seen at Witches' Sabbaths, partaking in diabolical orgies and conjuring your imps by offering up the hearts of the dead babes you've collected. Naked and salacious, you were seen riding your goat and fornicating with other Witches and Satan himself." Mary swooned and looked as if she would be sick.

"Ridiculous and superstitious nonsense!" Abraham cried out, appalled at the humiliating accusations made on Mary. "Have you lost all sensibilities?"

"Shut yer mouth, quack, before I force it shut," threatened Donne.

The Witch finder continued, not looking impressed to be interrupted again:

"And lastly, Mary Warner Lyttle, it's alleged you drink the blood of dead babes which you steal from their mothers to ensure your maiden-like beauty, disguising the true hag which resides beneath the illusion." Crashaw looked impressed, and ran his eyes slowly down Mary's body.

"Dear God!" cried a woman's voice from the mass.

"'Tis true! Mary didst take my afterbirth, and other women's it's been told, and we don't know what she does with it," added another.

With each allegation read out about Mary, Orla hugged her sister closer. Mary's blonde head hung low, her hands over her face. Mary's body rocked, and her loud sobbing shattered Orla's heart. The humiliation alone would break her fragile sister.

Orla was disgusted by the fervour of envy and jealousy searing forth from the dowdy village women. Rumours of such abhorrent behaviour by begrudging women were common place, but that did not soften the betrayal.

They would see the pretty and youthful Mary condemned rather than be confronted by their own ageing and mortality. What insane world were they living in?

"The list of charges remains open until further interrogations are completed. Sisters Mary and Alice Warner, and Orla Bones, you stand accused based on the testimony of numerous, reliable witnesses." A few people could be heard agreeing, and yet more townspeople could be heard murmuring their surprise.

Orla heard Reverend Cardell laugh and his congregation of Puritans chant "Praise the Lord" whilst cheering Crashaw to continue.

The Witch finder continued drinking his ale like he was at a Sunday gathering, and not a proceeding condemning lives to death, then started reading again,

"Goody Bones, also known as Orla Warner," the Witch finder's voice drew out the vowels of Orla's name.

Orla thought she would faint and turned her gaze to the dusty floorboards below. The room quieted again, and the Witch hunter cleared his throat:

"Cast your eyes on the ringleader of the evil within the Warner-Bones' home." He gestured theatrically towards Orla. "These many seasons hath seen you, Orla Warner-Bones at the birth bed of countless women and their babes, to the sickbed of children and the homes of ailed families, your spare time being spotted traversing the countryside collecting God only knows what healing herbs. So you say, your actions are solely in purpose of aiding the innocents, but you are in fact an agent of Satan, a reaper of death in disguise as a comely Wise woman." He smiled at the gathered people and gestured to Orla. "Behold! Goody Bones," Crashaw gestured to Orla, "who is known to hath set hands upon the pregnant womb of a mother, only to kill the babe within, and then yanking the babe out dead from their mother. Witness hath seen the babes, terrible to behold, their bodies purple and distorted. Furthermore, how many of your own babes died before taking their first breath? Killer of even your own babies aye?"

Crashaw's words were hateful, bringing fresh pain to Orla's heart at her own miscarriages.

"How many children like the Dowsett children did thou pass by and blight with your Witch's taint, possessing them with hell-begotten screams and writhing, leaving them to die, black limbed?" he cruelly accused. The death of children forever weighed heavy on any healer.

130

"'Twas the ergot I hath explained, which took the lives of the unborn, their limbs decayed! And the Dowsett children, hath eaten the bread from the ergot!" Abraham desperately argued.

This time the Witch confessor backhanded Abraham, who stumbled, and was ready to retaliate, but two jailers now held his arms.

Crashaw continued, "Countless questions remain, Goody Bones, all of which your name continues to be uttered at these queer and terrible events. These unspeakable acts thou knows ye are responsible for."

"No!" Orla denied. "Devastating these deaths are, but I am not to blame."

The crowd muttered loudly, and a few people cried out in agreement. Crashaw continued,

"Of present day, you stand accused of blighting the grain of Farmer Wenden, if indeed it is a scourge, the blame falls on you. For it is known that you harbour ill feelings towards the farmer and it be known that thou hath been seen walking through his fields more than most. Your own husband collaborates this tale, blaming the sickness of this community on the blighted grain Farmer Wenden grows. This same grain, I say, is fouled by you, Orla Bones." Orla was gulping deep breaths. If it weren't for the strength of her sisters, she would have no doubt fallen to the floor.

"And the last charge," the Witch hunter paused for effect, "of bewitching the good Reverend's daughter, Faith Cardell, and even more disturbing, of poisoning her to cast her newly begotten babe from her womb. These acts of wickedness are immeasurably evil and beyond belief of anyone, especially a healer and Midwife." Shaking his head, "Thou hast been accused."

The Witch finder Crashaw stood pointing at Orla, and after the crowd erupted, downed the remainder of his ale. This would be a fast trial, and he began to consider where he would travel to next.

Orla knew the truth of these matters, as did the sensible citizens of their village, but most appeared to be blinded by the Witch craze, the blood lust. Confused and fearful, they needed someone to blame. Was it truly the ergot escalating their fears into demons and delusions? This is what Abraham had been hypothesising these last weeks.

Orla searched the faces of her community for compassion. Many were shouting and pointing fingers at her, some were backing away silent but with fear etched on their face, and yet a few others stood confused, shaking their heads with disbelief and with sympathy shining from their eyes. Orla pleaded silently for these people to help her and her family.

She noticed a couple standing in the corner, their heads together. After a moment, they looked up at Orla and nodded once. Orla watched them quietly leave the room. There were others who also left, either from fear of being in the same room of so many damned, or the sheer disgust of the inhumane treatment of their healers.

After a moment, Orla noticed Crashaw beckon to the Witch confessor. She overheard him say, "Dear Master Donne, let us not waste time," and winked. Donne swaggered towards the women and licked his lips as his eyes settled on Mary.

"Goody Bones and her wench sisters, Alice and Mary Warner," Donne called out with sarcastic tones, "You shall now be separated and held in rooms with a Watcher," and he elbowed Mary hard, "in case you think to call upon your goat and fly away." He laughed out loud, his mirth displaced for such a serious environment.

"And a chosen Searcher will seek yer bodies for any tale-telling Witch's mark. When this mark is found, and I hath no doubt it shall," Donne smiled knowingly, "I will prick the mark with this," he produced a long, blunted sewing needle from his coat, "and see if thou shalt bleed." The cruel needle looked dirty and for certain, a torture instrument.

Donne positioned himself in front of the sisters, and with a wider smile added,

"Alas, but first I believe shaving is in order." A few 'hazzahs' were heard in the crowd. The shaving of suspected witches was not only a humiliating method of breaking down a person's identity and self-worth, but also enabled the Searchers to view the scalp and genital areas clearly for Devil marks and Witch's teats. Donne's obvious exuberance made Orla's stomach churn, and she felt Mary clawing at her arm in panic. Alice stood clenching her fist, defiant with glowering hatred.

Many in the guildhall were infected by the glee that the Witch confessor held for these barbarous acts.

They laughed and thumped each other on the back in apparent congratulations of catching real life Witches, but secretly, most were happy to have the monotony of their mundane lives broken.

Orla again noted the uneasiness in the room and that the townspeople appeared split in the sudden and atrocious behaviour being subjected to their healers and Midwives. Wrenched from her thoughts, Orla was seized and dragged from her sisters out of the guildhall. She looked back to see Mary also being removed from the hall, her face a mask of terror and tears. Orla could not see where they were taking Mary for interrogation. Alice, it appeared, was to remain within the guildhall, the crowd taunting her as she fought to break free of the restraining hands. She did not see William. Orla could hear Abraham's voice, hoarse from screaming her name, fade as she was pulled away from the hall and into the twilight.

It came as no surprise that Orla's torture chamber was the home of Reverend Cardell. A makeshift table had been dragged to the centre of the barren room, and when Orla was pushed through the door, she quickly discovered that Faith had been removed from the scene. She wondered if the girl was also being tortured—'confessed' as they so put it—somewhere, or if the poor girl, God forbid, had succumbed to the ergot poisoning. Orla noted that in addition, the room also housed a rough table, where evil-looking instruments, including thumb screws, hammers, thick ropes, leather binds and tools from what looked like the black Smith's, were laid out. Was this her first ordeal? To allow her imagination to cause further panic? It was certainly working, as she choked back bile and dragged her eyes away from the contents of the table.

A dowdy matron arose from a seat in the corner, draped in the dark fabrics of the Puritan. Orla did not recognise this woman, but presumed this was her Searcher. This cold stranger was the person to shave her and scrutinise every inch of her body for a 'Witch's teat'—the teat which was solely used to suckle imps and her familiars. The thought was laughable that people of this age could believe such absurdity.

But there was no humour in the dark scrutiny of the Searcher. Her eyes shone with the zealous fervour of her convictions. These barbaric practices only still existed due to money grabbing, sadistic men like Crashaw, and his predecessor Matthew Hopkins, Witch finder general, and not because of popularity with the masses.

The Searcher's dour features beguiled a cold shadow in her eyes as she approached Orla. A scuffle at the door and Orla turned to see Reverend Cardell appear in the room. In the weak candle light, his smile was grotesque, and Orla could still see a vein bulging from his forehead, his eyes ablaze with a seeming fever. Perhaps he had ingested the ergot as well, she mused.

The Searcher's face darkened further and her eyes moved to Cardell. "This confession is not a side show, but the most sobering of all God's tasks. Thou shalt remain outside, Reverend," came the steel voice of the Searcher. "I shall call upon thee when the first examination is complete," her emotionless voice sent a shiver through Orla. The Reverend slinked back into the shadows, frustration and disappointment apparent in his disjointed movement. Orla contemplated the distance to the door and judged she could easily push past the woman and run for freedom. Following Orla's gaze, the Searcher placed herself between Orla and the exit. "If thou hath any thoughts of escape, there art brutes outside this door, awaiting thine departure and ready to partake their own searching." This thought seemed to amuse her, and a half smile found the Searcher's face. Still grinning, her dark eyes lighted:

"Goody Bones, I declare thou art not to blame for your consorting with the Devil. It is known that ungodly women as thee—those who do not abide by the Sabbaths' laws—are vulnerable to Satan's affections. Thou art a daughter of Eve after all, born into sin and evil. 'Tis only through the pilgrimage of confessions that there is hope of repentance and forgiveness. If found guilty of your accusations and thou hast confessed, then a merciful death and a Christian burial awaits. But if thou allows the devil to overwhelm your soul and sensibilities, the ordeals shall continue until your last breath, and a burial at the base of the gallows, unmarked and forever unnamed, as befits all crimes against state and church, will be your fate," the Searcher explained dispassionately.

Orla felt her mouth turn downwards in distaste and decided the woman was as mad and deranged as Cardell. As well, the Searcher appeared calculating and shrewd, making her all the more dangerous.

Orla struggled to stay calm, and ran through her options in her mind: Play along with this madness and flee at an opportune moment? Try and fight? Trying to manage her wits had nearly exhausted Orla's reserves, and she decided this was not the best time to strategize an escape. She would take her chances and endure the challenges, whilst being vigilant for an opportunity to free herself. Orla faced the Puritan woman and with bravado, looked her in the eyes.

"Turn thine wicked eyes from me!" she hissed and slapped Orla hard. "Look to the floor, and now, make haste and remove your clothing, including your smalls," commanded the Searcher.

The slap stung, and as Orla noticed there was nowhere to change, the humiliating sting of self-consciousness swiftly replaced the pain in her face. She removed her clothes and tried to cover her private areas. The Searcher made a sound in her throat.

"Do not pretend to show modesty, Eve's daughter, I know Satan hath maketh thee lustful and proud. Do not struggle against the lechery which lies within your tainted soul." She pushed Orla hard. "Now, lie down on the table," the Searcher commanded. Orla shivered with the night air, and the coarseness of the wooden table beneath her bit into soft flesh.

"Prudence, bring more light," the Searcher called out, and a young homely Puritan woman appeared from the shadows with more candles, a handmaiden to the Searcher. "Bring the light near as I examine the body for teats and a devil's mark." Orla thought Prudence looked petrified and stared at her wide-eyed as if being in Orla's presence could condemn her soul to damnation. Prudence moved towards the Searcher without taking her eyes from Orla.

The Searcher brought forth from a hidden pocket in her skirts a small knife. Orla froze and braced herself to fight or run. The woman pulled Orla's braided hair from her coverings and without regard, began hacking away close to her scalp. Her braids hit the floor with a soft thud. Orla felt tears of grief and violation well up. Abraham had always loved her braids. More hair was hacked away, and lastly, the Searcher began to scrape her scalp with the knife—blunted, removing more scalp than hair. Orla could feel trickles of warm blood run down her face. "This shaving, Witch, is to ensure you hath not hidden a magical amulet to beckon your imps or hide the devil's mark."

In a short while, Orla could feel the cold air assaulting her naked head, marking her as an accused Witch. The Searcher leaned so close to Orla's head that she felt the weak heat from the single flame on her scalp.

"Oohhhhhh!" the Searcher exclaimed and jumped back, startling Orla and Prudence. She regained her courage and ran her hands over Orla's head again.

"Never have I seen with mine own eyes! The lick of the Devil! The true sign of the 'Nocturnal initiation rites'!" The Searcher was ecstatic. "Your pact with the Devil, sealed upon you! Master Donne shall be pleased." Prudence backed away, looking ready to run. Orla could only think she had found a burn scar on her head.

"Thou art a foolish and cruel woman!" Orla cried, pushing the Searcher away. "That be scars from when I was a babe and the hearth fire didst burn me! Are you witless?"

The Searcher ignored Orla and was ablaze in her vindication. "Hand me the Witch pricker and assure Goody Bones does not move," the Searcher demanded of Prudence.

A large needle was taken from the table of assembled instruments.

Orla felt a sudden jabbing into her head. She cried out and struggled to sit up. "Prudence!" shrieked the Searcher, "Hold her down whilst I bind." Within moments, the leather ties painfully bound Orla to the table, her legs spread open. The cruel pricking of the needle continued all over her body. "Girl, bring that candle closer!" the Searcher's voice was a mix of irritation and excitement. The light flickered from Prudence's shaking hand, but the Searcher managed to examine and prick Orla's lower torso.

When the Searcher finally stopped, she had made her way between Orla's legs. Revealing her hidden knife, the Searcher quickly snatched a handful of Orla's pubic hair. Mortified beyond words, even the nicks made to the tender skin beneath were nowhere near the humiliation Orla was suffering. Within a few moments, Orla screamed as the pricking needle was now being used on her genitals. When Orla thought the examination could not get worse, the Searcher began pulling open her labia. Horrified, Orla fought the restraints and tried kicking at the Searcher's head. "Leave me be!" she cried out. "By God's witness, woman, you are a demon, not I!"

But to Orla's shock, her cries were silenced when the Searcher yelled, "There it is! The Witch's teat!" And she pricked Orla's skin again. "That which the imps suckle from! I hath found another mark! Confess now, Witch, confess to your wicked consorting with Satan and you might still die with a pure soul!" Her frenzy sent Prudence running out the door and a number of men, including Cardell, fought their way into the room. The excitement of discovering a genuine sign of a Witch overrode the Searcher's orders of staying out of the room. Orla was mortified and twisted her body to conceal her exposed privates from the inquisitive, yet leering, stares of the men.

"Gaze not onto the beguiling body of the Witch," spat Cardell, as he looked away. "One glance and thee shall fall prey to her wicked temptations." The men pried their eyes from the Witch, but with reluctance.

A distant scream belonging to Mary snapped Orla out of herself. Her body burned with rage and an overwhelming need to run and protect her sister, and Orla's own nakedness and vulnerability were momentarily forgotten.

"Ahhhh," said the Searcher, looking out the door, "that would be a confession in the making."

Orla was angry and shouted out to them, "I do not wield a devil's lick, nor a third teat for sucking demon familiars, but I do sport the marks of an ageing woman! Superstitious and bloodthirsty beasts ye all are. And you," Orla glared at the Searcher, "should be filled with shame for the lewd and violating work you do in the name of God!" A jailer advanced on her and stuffed a dirty rag into her mouth.

"When will the Confessor arrive?" the Searcher asked.

"I know not when he will finish with the sisters," answered a jailer.

Orla's eyes filled with tears at the thought of Mary enduring the same abuse. Her thoughts slid to Alice and Abraham, knowing their wit and inner strength would protect their sanity, but she was frightened for their fate. She also wondered if William and Faith were still living. She felt pity for them all.

She sought out the Searcher and pleaded with her eyes to let her go. The Searcher only stared at Orla and began reciting prayers. The first of her ordeals were complete.

The hour was late when the Witch confessor arrived.

Orla was near frozen, shivering uncontrollably without a blanket or clothes, and exhausted, as she had not been allowed to close her eyes. Another form of torture to weaken her resolve. She blinked at the shape advancing through the dim candle light.

The Searcher, forgotten in her incessant prayers, jumped up and met the Confessor halfway. Her excitement was like a child's on yule, and Orla again found herself feeling ill.

From across the room came Donne's booming voice;

"Woman," he addressed the Puritan Searcher. "Ungag her pretty mouth." He locked eyes with Orla and his mouth twitched.

The Searcher nearly dragged Donne to Orla's side, and pointing madly, she exclaimed, "When I doth shaved and examined the head, Master Donne, I found the Devil's mark. Bleeding it does not, but purple and discoloured it is exceptionally evil in the looking." Donne peered closely, and poked at Orla's head.

"And, sir," the Searcher brimmed with pride, "I hath found a teat! In the most lewd, unholy places," and without hesitation the Searcher went to Orla and pulled her labia apart for further examination.

Orla thought she would die from humiliation, but was distracted and sickened by the spittle which ran from Donne's mouth, an ugly grin appearing. It was then she noticed the wooden mace which he shifted into his other hand. Before Orla could consider what that was used for, Donne roughly thrust fat fingers into Orla, tracing and pinching the place of her alleged Witch's teat. Orla could see he was enjoying the examination and noticed the disapproval on the face of the Searcher. Orla squirmed to rid herself of his assault and tried to kick out, but she was too strongly tied. Donne appeared to enjoy her fight and clutched Orla by the hips.

"Witch whore, ye try to possess my cock now," and laughingly rubbed himself into Orla's leg. "Still wet me cock is from spreading yer sister during her confession, but aye, just a sight of ye and it springs to life." The jailers at the door made lewd comments and many were laughing. His words were a hot blow, and Orla wondered with grief which sister he referred.

"A pox on you!" Orla spat.

How had life taken such turns? Orla and her sisters had spent their lives dedicated to helping others, yet, within a few hours, they would be condemned and doomed to the gallows, but not before they were tortured and raped first.

Tears flooding her eyes, Orla began to whimper.

Donne then took the needle and proceeded to further prick the teat. The Searcher, now eyeing the scene with her Puritan values, was plainly disapproving. She opened her mouth to protest the man's unscrupulous methods, but she caught a murderous look from him.

Removing his fingers, Orla was whimpering and sobbing. "Do we have ourselves a confession now, lovely one?" Donne whispered in her ear and then bit down on it.

Orla cried out again, and with renewed strength fought to grab Donne's hair with her hand. "No, ye don't, bitch," and slapped Orla so hard her teeth jarred.

The Searcher moved closer to the Confessor and asked, "And now, sir?"

"Did thou not get a confession from the wench?" he sneered.

The Searcher held his glare but cast her eyes down as she replied, "Nay."

"Well, then, ye know the next step of the trial—string the Witch up!" barked the Confessor.

The gathered men came rushing in, eager to be a part of the process. Within moments, heavy ropes were fed through the rafters in the ceiling and a pulley fixed in place, erecting a 'strappado', a device Orla was sure had been made illegal many years prior.

Orla was shivering uncontrollably and her mind was starting to distance itself from the room. She barely registered the roughness of the floor, as she was dragged from the table to the ground, her elbows and wrists bound tightly behind her back. Her shoulders ached immediately with the unnatural pulling, but the pain was intensified as the men fed the rope hanging from the rafter through her own tight knots.

"Now hoist!" commanded Donne. Suddenly her binds tightened, and Orla's shoulders burned a horrific pain as rope bit into flesh and her joints were forced into unnatural angles.

The pain was unbearable. "Halt now, you'll break my arms!" shrieked Orla. She could feel that her own weight was tearing muscles from the bones, as they were never meant to be stretched and hung like this. Orla felt a popping sound and screamed out in pain as a shoulder dislocated.

Why haven't I fainted yet? she thought, pain blinding her. There was a roar in her ears, and she realised it was the cheering of a growing crowd. They were themselves clearly possessed. Entangled in the Witch craze, they had lost all sensibilities, worsened from the hallucinating effects of the ergot slowly poisoning mind and body.

Orla was suspended from the ceiling and below she could see the sadistic grin of Donne. "Art thou ready to undergo the interrogation and confession?" His eyes hopeful, he slapped the mace loudly against his leg.

When Orla remained quiet, he continued,

"This trial is simple: confess to your diabolical dealing with Satan—those which led thee to the murder of babes and the poisoning of children. And tell me what the Devil promised in return." Taking Orla's dangling feet, he pulled. Orla screamed as she felt a searing, tearing pain though her muscles.

"You were seen by witnesses carrying dead babes to the forest, is this not true? Confess—how did the Devil seduce thee into feeding them into the hellfire?" His interrogation made no sense to Orla, and she reeled at his words.

"Clearly, Satan does keepeth you from confessing, but more pain I shalt inflict." Donne smiled and struck the soles of Orla's feet with the mace, the pain so excruciating, she blissfully blacked out.

Orla could distantly hear the protest of the Searcher, but her voice was lost in the cheers of the mob.

"It is known, Witch, that Goody Walton, a Godly, Puritan woman, did step in front of you at the market. It is known that thou did smite her with your Witch's glare. That day, the poor goodwife was found to fall down into a fit, frothing from the mouth and a writhing of limbs, hours after she was crossed by you. Truth it is, Witch, you did curse Goody Walton as thou art known as a hater of the good faith of the Puritans?" He smacked Orla with the mace to assure she was listening.

"'Twas your work, was it not, Witch?" He searched her face for defeat. "Confess and ye shall be cut down, warmed and fed," Donne said, his voice sickly sweet.

When Orla continued to be silent, he continued with the charges.

"Is it not true that you hath cursed the goodly Reverend Cardell in his own home, and is it not true that thou hath poisoned his only daughter, a Godly child, with intent to murder her?" The Confessor brought his face close to Orla, "Bring peace to thyself, Witch, and confess that you work the Devil's bidding to bring chaos and evil to this peaceful town. Yay, but this is true?" he pressed.

If Donne expected Orla to confess after his tedious litany, he was wrong. Orla was delirious with the torturous pain her body was captured in. But still she clung to the righteousness of her actions as a Wise woman and Midwife.

Orla had never intentionally meant to cause harm. The notion of the Devil's dealings and possession was ludicrous. She closed her eyes against the vision of Donne and attempted to shift her weight against the torn and dislocated muscles.

"As my witness," the Reverend's voice rang out, "Behold the Witch's silence is proof that her devotion to the Devil is steadfast." Orla had forgotten the Reverend still remained to hear her confessions.

"Leave her now, goodly people, and return to your homes." They retreated with reluctance.

"Bring forth the Watcher," Donne commanded and gestured the Reverend to stand back.

A stern-looking woman of middle age breached the threshold and glanced up at the accused, body hanging from the ceiling. She had seen this variety of torture before—though outdated, it often delivered many interesting confessions.

She noted the Reverend Cardell, a fervent member of the Separatist movement, approaching her. His face was animated and flushed as if he suffered a malady. She withdrew slightly as he leaned closer. "Watcher, it is your task during these long dark hours to 'Wake the Witch' and not allow her to sleep." He motioned to Orla, "You will watch with pert the movements of this Witch tonight, ensuring her familiars do not make their way inside and free her."

The Watcher looked calm and nodded. She was not a fearful person, and hence why she was often employed for this task. She actually enjoyed partaking in the sleep deprivation torture, as it made her feel powerful, and brought esteem to herself in the Puritan community. "Throw in some bread and water for the Watcher," called Donne, who without haste, left the room. In a moment, food was given and the door shut.

Throughout the night, Orla pleaded with the Watcher to release her from the agonising binds, but she was always met with silence. When her arms were not burning from pain, they were numb.

Her back and neck hung at awkward angles, and as much as Orla tried to send her mind somewhere else, the pain held her captive. The night was endless, time marked by distant intermittent screaming. Orla recognised the sound as Mary, and a few times Orla was certain the screaming belonged to Abraham.

Orla sobbed pitifully and had no concept of the passage of time. She was acutely aware of her frozen body, her feet swelling from the bruises and broken bones acquired from the beating.

"Thou and thine sisters, concocting poisons in thine cauldrons, and then giving diabolic salves to babes and children," Orla heard the accusation through a thick veil of semi consciousness. "Simply confess, Goody Bones, and we shall release you from your bindings," a voice floated on the air around Orla. The voice was a mixture of the Watcher and her mother's. Orla was beginning to hallucinate.

"But I am innocent, Mother," whispered Orla. "A healer I am, just as you were. So beautiful, and not a Witch," her words fell on deaf ears.

The Watcher believed all beautiful women were in partnership with the Devil. How else could some be given such beauty and others, like herself, be punished with homeliness?

She eyed Orla's naked body and fair looks with a begrudging envy.

The Watcher was attentively staring at Orla's suspended body when the Searcher, Donne and Witch finder Crashaw returned at sunrise.

Orla was pulled from her blackness by the fumbling of Donne's hands on her body.

"This is the way to wake a Witch, unholy that you are," he cooed. "I like this too," and he grabbed his crotch lewdly. Orla, snapped back into consciousness, by the hollow sound of Crashaw laughing, tried to kick out, but the jarring pain of the mace on the soles of her feet abruptly stopped her kicking.

Orla was clinging to threads of sanity and the Witch finder's words were blurred to her ears.

"Your sisters and husband have confessed themselves as servants of Satan, 'tis your time," his announcement cut through her fog of pain.

Delirious with agony, Orla's mind was playing tricks. A voice in her head told her to not believe him. Of course Abraham would not have confessed anything. Nor Alice for that matter. Mary, well under promise of keeping Philippa alive, what mother would not sacrifice herself for her child?

"Searcher—woman," Donne bellowed, still with his hand on Orla; the Searcher startled. "Earn yer coin and listen well," he proclaimed. "As the wench keeps her oath of silence with the Devil, we move to the next trial and work to extract a confession, by any means possible," and Donne winked at the Searcher. Affronted, she once again frowned, disapprovingly, at the confessor and his crude methods.

The Witch finder took a step and turned Orla's swaying body to face him, "As thou art been silent throughout the night Mistress Bones, faith will be your next trial." And shaking Orla to ensure she was listening, Crashaw instructed her, "The trial is this: With naught stumbling or error, you will recite the Lord's Prayer as all goodly women, like that one," he thrust his chin towards the frowning Searcher, "should be able to do in entirety. One mistake and the Puritan will enlighten me, further damning your soul." He nodded.

Orla had no awareness of what was being said between her jailers. She felt as if she had risen out of her body to a place where she would not feel the scolding burn of humiliation, nor the violation of her body. Orla blinked as the new day brought light to the shadows. She vaguely wondered how such a weak light could bring warmth, as she could not feel the cold any longer. Orla's mind fought to release her tortured body from the pain, and returned her to the summer's warmth of the fateful day she first met Abraham. His lanky body was cloaked in silhouette, but as they drew nearer, his face alighted from the morning sun. The soft, gentle face Orla had grown to love, floated in her vision. Orla could hear his laughter from the days shared tending to the soldiers, and she could still feel the warmth of his lips on her hand as they parted. Orla imagined for the thousandth time the look on his beautiful face when he unwrapped the oaken heart she had carved for him. To this day, he still wore it, tied around his neck, resting on his heart. "*Meus Dilectus,*" she could hear his whispers, an abbreviation from the Song of Songs in Latin, "My beloved is mine." Orla felt her face relax.

"Ahhhhhh, look at the Witch smile! Thou hath done well, Master Donne," the honeyed voice of Mathew Crashaw cut through Orla's delirium.

To her dread, Orla was again conscious and still suspended from the ceiling, naked and cold under the salacious stare of the Witch hunter. He looked fresh and immaculate, in contrast to his soiled and grubby companion, the Witch confessor.

Crashaw said to Orla, "Thou shalt confess as thy sisters have done, and this ordeal shall come to an end. Confess, Goodwife Bones, of thy consorting with the Devil, and with the killing of babes to appease the Devil's hunger. Confess thou art seduced to lie with Satan. Yes, Orla," and her name became forever tainted from his usage, "confess, and your soul shalt be cleansed and thine family spared."

Despite herself, she began to cry.

The Witch finder sighed. "Searcher, come hither so we may commence the Test of Faith." Orla was aware of someone shaking her. Chin slapping her chest and head jarring, Orla did not care. Snap her neck for all she minded. Suddenly a stinging slap brought her back to her appalling surroundings.

Her eyes focused and the stern face of the Searcher became distinguishable. Orla thought she saw something new in the eyes—pity? For certain she must be delusional.

"Goodwife Bones, 'tis the hour for thee to leadeth us to thine truth." The Witch hunter stepped back.

"Confessor, Searcher," he called, "Begin."

Orla's head was swimming, and she could feel a bruise surfacing from the slap. She looked up into the faces of her three jailers and frowned. Something was expected of her. Something important.

The Searcher repeated the demand, her voice slow and far away, "Begin by quoting the Apostle's name of which the Lord's Prayer is found."

What? Why would they ask this? Orla thought, and her fuzzy brain tried to clear.

She had never been much for the studies of the Bible, and certainly not to the rigour of which the Puritans demanded. A name popped into her mind— "Matthew," she muttered.

"That is correct," came the steely voice of the Searcher. "Now, recite the Lord's Prayer, without mistake."

Orla felt an odd sense of defence rise up. "In Latin or in King James' English?" she giggled in her mind. Through squinted eyes, Orla looked at her jailers; Donne looked confused, the Searcher looked curious and the Witch finder looked slightly impressed.

"English, Witch," came the rasping growl of Donne, and another head-jarring slap rendered Orla practically unconscious. There was a scuffle and a heavy weight slammed into the table.

She twisted her neck around to see that Donne was sprawled on the floor. Cleary, even the Witch hunter had tired of Donne's sadistic behaviour.

"The prayer," came the calm voice of Crashaw.

Orla's mind seethed. Visions of her mother, her sisters, all at Sunday church. In unison with the congregation saying the prayer. Her mother's naked body swinging in the tree, the wailing of countless women in childbirth, faces of dead babies staring accusingly at Orla; arriving to church each Sunday, and watching as the congregation increasingly wore more black and brown and the village people increasingly quoting from the Bible—the Bible. The Lord's Prayer. She must recite the Lord's Prayer.

"Matthew 6:9-13: Our Father which art in heaven, Hollowed be thy name." Orla's voiced choked from dryness. "Thy kingdom come, thy will be done—was it 'in' or 'as'… in earth, as it is in heaven." Orla glanced at the Searcher who nodded slightly. "Give us this day our daily bread. And forgive us our debts, as we forgive our debtors." Orla would not be forgiving these debtors. "And lead us not into temptation, but deliver us."

Orla stopped—deliver from evil? Deliver from the devil? Deliver from these evil people? Her vision went dark and swam; blindly she continued, "Deliver us from the Devil: For thine is the kingdom, and the power, and the glory, for ever. Amen."

Orla sighed and nearly fainted for the umpteenth time. She had proved that she was a goodly woman of faith. Regardless of assumed devil marks and a ridiculous Witch's teat, she had recited the prayer with perfection.

Orla opened her eyes to the three faces; Donne looked again perplexed; the Searcher's mouth was firm, but her eyes held pity; the Witch finder looked cold. "Goody Bones, thou art failed this test, and thus hath proven one more time to be a Mistress of the Devil." Orla was confused.

"Thou art mocking God as you replaced 'hollowed' be thy name, when well known the word is 'hallowed'! This is a depravation of the words, as it signifies a void rather than the Lord's love, thus making so a curse and not a prayer!"

"Stumbling over earth and heaven, was your second failing, and lastly, delivering us from the Devil—only one possessed would see that we are not delivered from the Devil, but delivered from evil!" He shook his head in apparent disappointment.

"The rest of the accused are still under confession, so thee shall wait here until called. In the meanwhile, cut the accused down and dress her," Crashaw commanded of the Watcher and Searcher.

Orla heard Crashaw's words through her befuddled brain, but she didn't understand, until she had fallen painfully onto the hard floor, her torn muscles and dislocated shoulder releasing a new scream of pain.

The Searcher found pity for the woman and forced a strong brandied drink down her throat, with a promise to ease the pain enough for her next trial. Always the herbalist, Orla's brain went through the catalogue of herbal simples she knew to disguise pain. The drink was soothing but did little to ease the burning pain Orla was suffering. She sat quietly and allowed the woman to wash and dress her. All the while she desperately worried for the fate of her family.

It was not until late in the day that Orla was called forth.

Hands bound, Orla was helped outside the Reverend's house by the Puritan women. Each step was anguish, and she cradled her dislocated shoulder with the other hand.

A crowd of townspeople made a path for them to walk through. Some looked at Orla with disdain in their eyes, while some refused to make eye contact. Orla noticed there were others on the outer edge of the crowd looking worried and talking in whispers.

Orla was roughly guided back into the hall where her breath caught.

Standing in line, was her family. Three of the four were shaved like herself, the hair remaining only on Mary.

The Witch hunter stood with Reverend Cardell and announced to the town's people the outcome of the trials.

Mary stood silent, eyes distant. She was the only accused to plead guilty from the beginning of the first ordeal. She was promised that in exchange for her confession, her daughter Philippa would be free of accusation and persecution.

Mary confessed and affirmed all allegations.

Alice's face was bleeding from countless scratches made by the torture of fingernails and knives. Orla was shocked, this inhumane treatment was abhorrent and illegal. Alice looked beaten and years older than her true age. Under horrendous stress and pain, Alice had not confessed.

Her plea was not guilty; however, she was found guilty on all counts.

William was too delirious and in and out of consciousness to offer a plea. He was found guilty of poisoning Faith Cardell and conspiring with the others to blacken the name of the goodly citizens.

Abraham was visibly shaking and holding what looked like broken thumbs from the thumbscrews. His eyes were red and swollen. He had pleaded not guilty to heresy and conspiracy with the Devil, yet he was also found guilty.

Orla stared into the eyes of her husband. She had never seen such despair. His eyes welled with tears as Abraham gazed at Orla.

Crashaw's voice brought Orla back, "Without doubt the accused, Alice and Mary Warner, with Abraham and William Bones, have been found guilty of Crown offences. These crimes are of malicious intent to undermine the good will of God." He paused and looked at the cursed souls before him, "and thus the punishment is death—you will all hang until dead."

Murmurs from the crowd followed this announcement. Some people cheered, a few berated the Witch hunter.

Orla's heart split and she heard her sisters cry out. Crashaw turned to Orla and with a smile pointed at her. "Since you, Goody Bones, have refused to enter a plea, then I have no choice but by decree of King Charles, I commit thee to Judicium Dei, to be judged by God by an Ordeal of Water."

He was visibly excited when there was a gasp in the crowd, and Orla could hear Reverend Cardell laughing. "If God grants a miracle on thine behalf, then you shall sink to the bottom and be found innocent."

"And dead!" Abraham shouted. "One does not survive these barbaric ordeals!"

A hand smothered Abraham's next outburst and Crashaw patiently continued, "However," and he raised his eyebrows for punctuation, "if you

Goody Bones float to the top, then clearly the Devil possesses thee." Someone gasped.

"As it is known," he continued, "Witches hath renounced baptism, and water being God's Divine force, shall forsake them by ejecting to the surface." Crashaw finished and looked satisfied, though his sentencing was received with mixed reactions. A few cheered, more stood in silent shock and a small gathering of people hurried outside and away.

Crashaw glanced at the man hungry for the land held by the Bones brothers, and nodded once, as he envisioned a heavy purse at the end of these proceedings. The farmer nodded back and smiled.

As the words sunk into the crowd, Abraham cried out and rushed towards Orla, only to be pulled back by the guards.

Orla slid to the ground as her legs gave out and cried uncontrollably. Her family would hang, and she would be drowned. How could their lives of selfless caring and healing their community come to this?

She was led to a small cell and curled up on the straw floor, exhaustion and heartbreak sending her to a restless sleep.

The next morning dawned, and Orla was yanked from the cell and dragged outside. She looked around for her family but could not see them. The condemned had all been separated for fear of joining forces and conjuring the Devil to assist in their escape.

A crowd was gathering and people either stared or spat at Orla.

Tears stung her face as she shivered in fear and humiliation.

As Orla was led to the river, her breath caught as she saw the ancient oak tree in the centre of the town now sported four nooses dangling from a huge branch. Beside the tree, her family stood shackled and trembling. Philippa was being led away, crying, by a woman, while Mary stood sobbing beside Alice.

Reverend Cardell was standing, reading from the Bible, and tossing water in their direction.

Orla called out, and breaking free of her captors, ran to her family. She caught Abraham in her arms, and then clung to her sisters with sheer desperation. Alice took Orla's hand despite her shackles and said chokingly but with her usual strength, "You be strong and the clever girl you are, you can beat them sister, you can beat this!" As Alice was pulled away, she nodded her head with conviction.

Orla took Mary's chin and held it close to her face. "I promise thee, Philippa will stay safe and will grow into a beautiful and gentle healer." The words choked Orla, as Mary's eyes filled with tears. Orla then turned to Abraham, who began covering her face with kisses. The jailers had rushed to them and were trying to separate them. "*Meus Dilectus,*" Abraham's voice was hoarse and defeated, "my love, my rising sun, our—" and Abraham was torn from Orla, his shackled arms reaching out to her, as Orla was dragged backwards. "Our love will be forever, we shall reunite in the afterlife!"

And he raised the oak charm of the rising sun Orla had carved for him all the years before and kissed it. "Abraham! I love you!" she sobbed. "I love you!" And her eyes blurred the last sight of her family, as she was dragged down the hill towards the Colne.

The river was full from a recent deluge and darkly churned.

Orla was pushed towards the muddy shore, where she stumbled on a large stone and fell to the edge. Her heart was pounding as she eyed the darkness of the water.

She was roughly bound with a rope and pushed into the bottom of a small boat. Two jailers rowed them all a short distance from shore.

The Witch hunter and Cardell were rowed out in a separate boat. The Colne river had a swift current, which made reaching the side of Orla's boat difficult. It took numerous tries before they were alongside the craft, and then Orla was made to stand up in the unstable boat. One man lost an oar in the current as he checked the water's depth, seeking the deepest point of the river. A wooden chair was passed down from the front to the rear, and Orla was pushed into it. The reality of her life, now measured in moments, set in.

Panicking, Orla began kicking and fighting against her captors. The crowded boat pitched and teetered as numerous hands attempted to tie her legs, arms and waist to the chair. Orla slammed her head into one man's nose, who stumbled back as blood ran down his face. She also managed to kick another overboard, as she was now fighting for her life.

Crowds of people began emerging from the thick reeds and willows which bordered the riverside. They stood and watched with interest and horror at the drama playing forth. Only two men remained from the other boat, who were struggling to get Orla overboard, and still she fought, biting one man's ear nearly off.

The Reverend was screaming at the men to finish their work and get the Witch overboard, while Crashaw's smile was replaced by a frown. This was not going to plan. Though an Ordeal of Water had not happened in many years, the Witch hunter had carried them out with success and little theatrics.

As he pondered the many failings of this trial, he watched dispassionately as Orla's boat pitched from the current, and the last man standing slammed into Orla's back. The chair lunged forward as Orla screamed and hit the water. Immediately, the chair and Orla were swallowed up by the churning current.

The freezing water tore her breath away as Orla swiftly began to sink. She frantically began fighting the ropes as she tumbled beneath the water. Her feet were pummelled by river rocks, and the pain from her torn shoulder was hot and searing.

Orla's lungs quickly began to hurt, and the panic of drowning fuelled new strength to battle the ropes. The chair collided into a submerged boulder, propelling the chair and Orla momentarily to the surface.

With just enough time to exhale, Orla noticed that there were people running alongside the riverbank, and then she inhaled as the chair sank for the second time. The fresh oxygen fortified Orla with enough strength to kick her legs free from the ties, and she attempted to swim.

The chair suddenly wedged itself on the river floor, inhibiting Orla from travelling any further down the river. She struggled to untie the knots binding her wrist to the chair, but her lungs were ready to explode. Exhaling the air from her lungs, heart pounding, Orla launched her body forward as a last attempt to dislodge the chair. Wide eyed, the water was rushing into her lungs, and images of sunshine, her sisters laughing, picking herbs, making love to Abraham, newborn babies, all filled her mind. *This can't be how I die!* her mind screamed. *Alice told you to fight, so fight.* With one last bit of strength, Orla lunged and freed the chair, which ascended quickly to the surface.

Her mouth touched the surface, expelling water and air, followed by fierce coughing. Orla saw hands and legs in the water, and within seconds, she was being dragged out, her head supported as she spluttered and coughed up the river water. Familiar faces dragged her further up onto the rocky shore and freed her hands from the bindings. Far up the river Orla could just make out the other boat which appeared near capsizing. The Witch hunter and Reverend had their backs to her, struggling.

A young couple Orla had recently helped deliver their baby to, and an older couple Mary and Alice had treated for years, were there trying to get her to stand. "Hurry now," the young man said urgently, "We have your husband's horse readied with your healing things, and you must make haste!" Stumbling with exhaustion and still coughing, Orla was supported by other people on the shoreline, up the embankment. There she saw not only Abraham's horse tied with saddlebags, but Philippa on Mary's pony. Looking distraught and shocked, she sat fidgeting with the horse's reins. "Aunty Orla!" Philippa exclaimed, "Thank God thee are well!" Orla didn't think she was well, but certainly alive and relieved to see her niece.

"Please Mistress Bones, get on the horse and ride hard from this evil place," the young woman pleaded.

Orla's heart dropped. "But what of my family, I cannot leave them," she cried, and strained to see the distant tree.

"Goody Bones," the older man said, "not all of us are the cruel villains who have betrayed you and your family. Many people will fight for them as best as they can." Orla read kindness in his eyes, but also sympathy and sadness. It was clear he did not believe anyone could help them.

Orla was helped onto the horse, and nodding to her niece, they urged their horses into a swift departure. For the second time in her years, Orla was running for her life.

Wiltshire, 1666

Sixteen Years Later...

Abigail awoke with a start, bolting upright.

Frantically trying to recall or place names with the strange things she saw, her eyes darted from wall to wall. She looked down and discovered that she wore a white shift, worn but clean and smelling of Lavender. Remembering the many holed and bloodstained garments she had previously worn, Abigail was not surprised to find them gone.

Looking around, the snugness and hominess of the room quickly replaced her anxiety with curiosity. The clean floors were thick with drying herbs, their aromas still lingering in the air. To the side of where she had been sleeping, hung a large cauldron over hot coals, with black liquid thickly bubbling up. She wrinkled her nose with the bitterness the exploding bubbles released, contrasting the freshness of the other scents. Casting her eyes to the ceiling, she observed that not a patch was clear from hanging plants. Most of them were well dried, though she observed, that in the darkest corner, newly hung flowers were loosely bundled in small groups. Some of the pretty flowers she recognised, but most were new to her eyes.

Every available space seemed committed to some unusual purpose. The longest wall, which was still short, contained shelves made from ancient trees, crammed with various sizes of clay pots, an assortment of dark glass bottles, various grains and cloth cut and sectioned to size. There was a large mortar and pestle upon the small but functional table, and two simple chairs were neatly tucked beneath.

On one shelf, there were clear bottles containing what looked like flowers in a kind of oil or fat. Most were yellow in colour, but a few held bottles which were a pale red.

The smallest wall housed a substantial collection of worn books. There were a surprising number of them, more than Abigail had ever seen in a home.

She determined that whoever was the keeper of this room was by observation an educated person, with knowledge of healing, more than likely, a man. This realisation of a male inhabitant rekindled her anxiety. Abigail had been given a lasting impression of men's greed, and so fuelled by these memories, struggled out of bed.

Concerned that she wore only a shift, she looked around for her bundle, but noted only empty wooden pegs. Abigail saw her father's knife laid out and snatched it. She then quickly spied her once muddy boots, which were now newly cleaned, waiting on the hearth. Grabbing her boots, she went for the door.

The worn door was swaying in a gentle breeze, which gave Abigail a quick escape. Throwing it open, she was momentarily blinded by the morning sun.

Squinting she was startled to see the back of someone, hunkered down with their hands in a prickly plant. The head was covered with a large straw hat, the sleeves rolled to the elbows. Still crouching down the figure quietly inquired, "Leaving so soon, and not even with a tummy full of breakfast?"

Abigail stopped. A woman's voice was behind that great hat. Releasing a sigh, the woman stood up, hands supporting her back, and one shoulder hung lower than the other. She turned to face her guest, and Abigail stared at the person before her.

Little over her own modest height, the woman was by no means tall.

Her age exceeded her mother's, and Abigail was taken back by the sea of thick grey hair hanging immodestly loose. The woman's forehead was creased with many deep lines, dark brows accented keen, green eyes. "I am called Orla," her tongue lingering over the 'r' as if not in a hurry to finish the word. "My second name is Flower...once my mother's name," she explained with circumspection. Abigail had heard an accent like that before from somewhere in the North. Orla Flower sounded like a character in a song.

"You have slept for a day, and through the night. I thought that the sleeping draught I gave you was too strong," she mused. "One would believe, young lass, that sleep was needed. By the awful looks of your head and skin, it would seem a wild creature had tumbled with ye." A half smile appeared around Orla's mouth.

Abigail struggled to recall, but held no memory except her stumble into the darkness, she was touched that this old woman 'Orrrla' had managed to drag her back, and care for her. She allowed herself to relax a bit but was still wary. "I am Abigail Midwinter of London," she introduced herself holding Orla's gaze.

"Abigail, hmmm, that meaning is 'father rejoiced'," she said, looking to the distant. "Yes, I believe he would rejoice with such a girl as thee, but, alas, Abigail is not the name of a country girl. You will have to simply be Abby; that is of course, if I decide to keep ye," Orla added with a wink.

It wasn't the shortening of her name which distressed her, as her brothers had called her Abby since she could remember; it was the fast realisation of a new life and the prospect of living as 'a country girl'.

The sound of the statement so final. The reality fell like a rock, that no one was awaiting her return to Pudding Lane. She crumpled where she was in a flood of tears, the last weeks robbing her of all strength, courage and now her identity.

So consumed by her despair, she was not aware of the warm arms encircling her. It was the quiet murmurs and the stoking of her loosened hair that brought Abigail to her senses. "Sshh lass, Abigail is a fine name, I am a wicked old woman to send you into such a fit of tears!"

At the words, Orla freed the curls from Abigail's sodden face and smoothed the coppery hair behind her ears.

"I...I like Abby," and a thin smile materialised. "It is not that, it is—"

Orla put her finger to Abigail's lips. "Sssssh, so much pain to put words to, wounds still open and bleeding.

"'Tis not the moment to speak of dark memories, there is plenty of time once you are more of sound body. Now, let's break our fast, as I am hungry after my stint in the garden." Orla stood up and encouraged Abigail back through the thick door into the coolness of the house.

After a delicious breakfast of oats, seeds, honey and rich milk, Abigail's head of thick fog was clearing. Orla was silent through the meal, getting up once to stir the unknown concoction in the pot.

At the end of the meal, Orla removed the cauldron from the heat and set it down heavily upon the hearthstones. Musing over its contents, Abigail watched the black bubbles slow and finally recede. Though the terrible bitterness was suspended in the air, it somehow held a note of recognition.

Abigail was reminded of her death oath to her mother and stood up to fetch the bottle from her bundle. "Yer bottle is there," came the voice of Orla, startling Abigail. She pointed in the direction of the shelves. "Not to be nosy, but I couldn't allow you into my home without knowing if danger lingered." While

Abigail had slept, Orla had carefully smelled and tasted the last drop of the remedy earlier. The herbal syrup had somehow been familiar to Orla, but she could not recall why. She had fast concluded that the syrup was a potent and well formulated plague remedy.

"Tell me lass, how did this remedy come to be in your possession?" Orla queried. What was clearly a painful memory for Abigail washed over her; "My mother bought it from a London Plague Doctor, after…my brothers died." Swallowing she continued. "I thought her mind was unhinged at the time, but it would seem it held healing properties after all." Abigail gestured to indicate that she was still alive.

Orla gave Abigail a once-over. "Blessed you are, as indeed you breath, where so many on this morrow do not. 'Tis why your clothes, and the cloth you carried has been burned." And she returned to the great pot, noting the consistency was perfect.

Taken aback from the confession, Abigail stopped from recovering her medicine bottle.

"Disrespect not intended, Mistress, but what came over thee to burn my things?" Abigail asked incredulously.

Orla turned from her stirring of the black liquid and looked at Abigail with sharp eyes.

"I know your plight, lass, a journey of folly from the blight of London. I know that ill-fortune has marked you." Orla stood and pointed. "What is held in this great pot is a stronger brew to what you carried in that bottle. If you could survive from the flames of hell itself alive, survive a blighted road, then to know the contents of that bottle was made my business." Orla stared. "As for the burning, the seeds of plague live on within fabric; I had to rid the scourge from my home." Abigail frowned and countless dead faces swam past her eyes, but she focused to hear Orla. "'Tis why your head," she pointed, "and body hold bruises and wounds inflicted by those that saw you as the walking dead— Abigail, you were seen as a carrier of the black death." Orla softened her look as she noticed the poor girl trembling and motioned her to sit down. Orla continued, "Everyone knows that the plague was bred in London and carried forth by those escaping its grim jaws."

"The royal family is no exception. A merchant from Salisbury travels these parts every other passing moon and brings with him the news. When the royals figured out that their expensive Surgeon and flashy trinkets were no match for the plague, they upped and left their castle and escaped to Salisbury." Abigail nodded as she had indeed witnessed their exodus. The wealthy woman in the black carriage leapt into her mind.

"Countless lords and ladies arrived, each bringing large chests of clothing and wagons full of food. All crawling with the plague, each one an executioner." Orla's voice was distant. "They may be witless fools, but I am not." Abigail stared at the bottle across the room, intrigued by Orla's opinions on how the plague was transmitted. Abigail wondered how this woman could know about her plight and knew enough by the looks of the black liquid to reproduce it so quickly? So many more questions pushed their way into her head, and in a rush, she fired questions at Orla.

Waving her hand in response, Orla said, "Rest now, lass, there will be time enough for questions and answers."

Orla returned the empty bottle to Abigail and also produced a wooden spoon from the shelf. She motioned to the cauldron holding the mixture, inviting Abigail to take a spoonful. Orla deftly braided her hair and within a moment, went outside, leaving the light streaming through the doorway and Abigail to her thoughts.

After consideration, Abigail choked down a spoonful of the mixture. It certainly did taste like the substance from her bottle, and she grimaced with the bitterness. Clutching the empty bottle, Abigail recalled this was the last thing her mother had given her. The pain in her heart silenced her other bodily complaints.

Carefully placing the bottle back on the shelf, Abigail dressed in the skirts and bodice Orla had left out for her. The fabric was worn but soft, and delicate embroidered flowers adorned the edges. Judging by the size and cut of the bodice, the clothes did not belong to Orla but had once draped the curves of a buxom young woman. The bodice hung awkwardly on Abigail's shapeless body, but she thought with time she would grow into the clothes nicely. These were clothes for a woman and not a child, and Abigail overcame her feeling of immodesty to make her way outside to face her seemingly new life.

"Ahh, those clothes suit you well...they once belonged to my niece, bonny that she was," and Orla's eyes clouded for a moment. "Don't worry, you'll grow into them in no time. Now come hither, and aide me with clearing of these weeds."

The day was busy with what seemed endless tasks. The sun was warm on their backs as they collected leaves from various plants in the garden, then they made their way through the trees collecting mushrooms at the tree trunks.

At yet another location, Orla exclaimed when she spotted what looked to Abigail to be small mealy berries resembling a tiny apple. Abigail was fascinated by Orla's enthusiasm in a plant she would have easily passed by.

They picked what they found, Orla calling them "May-blossoms". She explained that usually this plant flowered in May and soon after the fruit would appear. These were late bloomers, Orla blaming the unseasonably hot weather. Abigail was focused on mirroring Orla's methods, and though she was eager to ask questions, she held her tongue. Her father used to tell Abigail that observation often answered questions.

When the sun was high and warm, they shared a quiet lunch of soft cheese and crusty pumpkin bread under a huge tree.

Orla seemed at a distant place and spoke little during the meal. Abigail pondered her future and imagined a dozen options of what Orla might do with her.

Abigail's parents had always taught their children to not be impulsive but to wait, and answers would come. For Abigail, this was a challenging exercise.

After lunch, they wound their way back to Orla's cottage, stopping occasionally for Orla to examine a plant or add roots to their collection. Abigail noted that Orla's shoulder hung at a strange angle and when inquiring, Orla stated it was an old, poor-healing injury.

By the time the two goats, Sally and Sadie, were milked, and a few eggs were collected from the relaxed chickens, the light of the sun had softened to an orange hue.

Carrying the last pails of water into the house, Orla smiled and said, "Fine work today, Abby, now wash the dirt from your hands and refresh your face; oh, and don't forget to leave your boots outside."

Once again. Abigail was surprised. She couldn't recall ever taking the time to wash, outside of their once-a-month regular session. Noticing the look on her face, Orla explained, "It is in my teaching that the earth carries things that should not be rightly eaten. Just as you would rinse the soil from food growing, so you should from your hands." With that, Orla gave her own hands and face a quick wash and turned to cracking the fresh eggs into one of her earthen bowls. The cool water did indeed fill wonderful on her sticky face, and to see the whites of her hands reappear after washing was satisfying.

Abigail re-braided her escaping curls and gingerly touching the sides of her head; she was relieved to feel that her wounds seemed to be healing. Her body was still tender in many places, and after the day's exertions, she was without doubt, weary.

Abigail returned to the main room and was invited to occupy one of the two chairs. Supper arrived soon, once again a delicious meal of eggs, fresh goat's milk, soft cheese and garden herbs, all blended and folded into a crust, baked quickly in the heat of the coals. Abigail was abashed by her unyielding hunger, and Orla was pleased to oblige with seconds and thirds.

"A young lass should eat hearty to help make her a strong woman," Orla said with a smile. When the last crumb was licked from fingers, Orla explained, "Your supper finished, I must tell ye, and sorry I am, but I mean to cut those fiery curls of yours." Abigail leaped up, casting aside all social graces her mother had attempted to convey.

"Have you lost all sense," she cried. "I have not questioned any of your actions, standing silent while you have performed oddities without a word to me otherwise. But I will not have you hacking my hair to a length which makes me indecent, no matter the secluded life you have in mind for me! Keep clear with your happy knife!"

Orla observed the young girl with a slight furrow to her brow. She began slowly unwinding her own abundance of milky hair, green eyes never straying from the youth's. "It is in my teaching that vermin which thrive in the comforts of hair, they can carry vexing and grave humours, which can be passed through to the heart of people. Remind you I will, that not so long ago, thou were spurted forth from a cesspool of sickness. By taking the food which the vermin devour and cleansing the head of vermin, only then do I fear not the contagion," explained Orla.

Abigail gaped openly at Orla. Abigail thought to herself, *Her mind is indeed unhinged! How could anyone be so preoccupied with such queer thoughts of cleanliness?*

Out loud she said, "I cannot understand your needs of me, Mistress Flower, I hear your words, but never have such things been requested." Breathing deeper she questioned, "Must I really part with my hair—it is my mother's hair you know, she was the one with this colour. And, and, what next shall you have me part with? And what will become of me? My own blood kin has cast me aside, how long will I be welcomed with you?" Tears threatening, Abigail knew she was babbling, her father always insisting that she speak clearly, but she was overwhelmed. Gesturing, Orla pointed to the empty chair.

"Your hair shall grow back, Abigail. Now, sit ye down, so much leaping about does no good after such a bountiful feed. Some tea from the garden to ease your disquiet, and then we shall trim those locks," Orla said with finality. Abigail feeling defeated, nodded and sat down heavily.

The tea arrived in chipped earth ware, but the tea, a slight yellowy colour, had a soft and pleasing taste. Abigail cautiously sipped her hot drink.

Orla brought out a plate chipped as well, with pale biscuits on them, and sat them before Abigail. "From what I can gather, thou art left in the wilds of the world, without family. In your own time, your tale shall come forth. I, too, am without ones to love." At this confession, her eyes fleetingly clouded, but was quick to recover.

"I see that it would suit us to be housed together. Each winter I feel the cold more and more, and each summer my eyesight further withers. It gladdens my heart to have such a spritely lass as yourself to companion me on my lengthy days." Orla smiled and continued, "Your head is not befuddled with nonsense, and I do believe you could learn the ways of my teachings, the ways of generations of Flower women, Wise women of my family," gesturing to the drying herbs and earthen pots.

"To have this knowledge, you could wander the lands, with always a penny in your purse, and a purpose to your life." She smiled encouragingly.

"Many a morning, Abigail, I have awoken still smiling from dreams of a girl like yerself to share my mastery with." Orla sighed and smiled. "You have my promise that I shan't be wicked to thee, nor take a switch to your backside. Feed you I will, with foods while the earth provides it. Evermore, shall there be shelter for you during the bitter winters. I ask that ye always be truthful, and that your tasks are completed to your best attempt. What sayith you, Abby?" Orla asked, and she sipped her now cooling tea.

Abigail nibbled one of the buttery biscuits and contemplated her circumstances. She would be 14 next month, and was by all means, a living miracle. Whatever God's reasons for punishing the people of England, the scores which had succumbed to death, somehow, she a simple Smith's daughter, had dodged the falling of the Reaper's sickle. Through a curious serious of incidences, she now had the golden opportunity to start a new life with someone whom seemed interested in her and whom was willing to accept her as family. The intrigue to the teachings of whatever Orla spoke of was also tantalising.

Worry still shadowed her that Orla might not be of sound mind, but Abigail decided that she would take her chances, as there was not another choice available.

"If you would take me into your home, you have my word that I would be a hard and eager helper, as well as an attentive pupil. I know some letters from my brothers, and my writing hand is fair. If you believe my hair must be shortened, then I believe it to be of truth. Thank you," she quietly finished. Orla smiled, and reaching out with a sun-browned hand, she ran two fingers down Abigail's freckly face, where it lingered for a moment.

"Come outside, so I can cut and lather your hair." Taking a large cake of soap from near the door, and picking up the kettle from which the tea had come forth, Orla stiffly made her way outside into the setting sun. Without wasting time, she set Abigail down on the milking stool, and with care, lobbed the ends of her long hair off. The lightness from her head was registered immediately. From where it had hung long past her chest, she could now see that the ends only touched her shoulders. Trying not to cry, Abigail tugged to straighten her curls to add length. Instructed to remove her clothing and shift, Abigail sat while the old woman poured cold water from the bucket over her head. Gasping and shivering, Orla was already making haste with the slightly abrasive soap. Through her shuddering, she noticed the sweet smell of the soap like a spring's morning. She did not realise how much filth had accumulated on her skin, until muddy streams flowed off her body to form pools at her feet. Another shock of cold water brought yet another scrubbing of her head. The final rinsing was with the warm tea water, which was delicious on her freezing skin. Orla threw a small woollen blanket over her, and instructed she come in and warm up by the fireside. With another cup of warming tea in her hand, she sat placidly while Orla rubbed into her scalp a kind of liquid which was strong with the smell of Lavender and other assumed plants she did not recognise. By the end of the treatment, Abigail felt sleepy, and more clean than she could ever remember. Orla gave her an oversized chemise to sleep in, and curling up on the straw pallet Orla had made for her, Abigail slept peacefully for the first time in weeks, without dreams and without nightmares.

Wiltshire, 1669

The winter had been long, but the earth rejoiced spring with an abundance of buds and flowers.

Many lives had been lost during the Great Plague, but those spared had bravely rebuilt their lives. Orla reflected that there was a greater number of gravestones than living citizens. What lives the plague had not stolen in London, were left to be devoured by the great fire, which swept through the Great City the same summer.

Orla had also mused many times if the affliction that had tormented the people of London—who were seemingly the worst affected—was due to the consumption of blighted bread, as Abraham had speculated all those years before. If by consuming the ergot, the humours of the body had weakened, would it make the body susceptible to malignant miasma like what the plague brought.

She had shared these thoughts and teachings with Abigail, and had spent a great length of time asking for her account of London before she had escaped. Blessed indeed this child was, Orla thought for the countless time.

Orla stood stiffly from her collecting, quietly cursing the winter and her age, and shielded her eyes from the sun. She smiled at the lanky lass, reaching for newly flowering Elder, her hat as usual forgotten down her back. Such pride and happiness Abigail had brought to Orla's life these last few years.

It was during the long cold winter nights that Orla's harrowing life had been revealed to Abigail, ending with the bitter loss of her niece Philippa, seasons prior to Abigail's arrival. The tale had never been repeated, and Abigail had openly cried with Orla over her horrific ordeal and the loss of her family. The two women shared not only loss, but the uncanny will to survive.

Abigail's respect and love for Orla grew each passing month.

A busy year of birthing babes had made the young woman into the makings of a competent Midwife. Abigail was a swift learner, and importantly had an intuition for pregnant mothers and their babes, a skill which was born and not taught.

Though still young, local villagers were beginning to trust the hands of the Wise woman's apprentice, appreciating her patience and gentleness. The Flower women were an essential part of their community.

Abigail had also shown great promise in her skills with herbal simples. Orla had not met one so young to comprehend the complex formulations and methods of manufacturing the herbal syrups, salves and other compounds within their dispensary. The young apprentice even successfully experimented with methods of preservation of herbal syrups and salves, which Orla found surprisingly useful and was shamed that she herself had never considered them.

Reminiscing on Abigail's talents, Orla's smile suddenly dropped.

Around the Elder tree appeared the local Preacher's son, Nathaniel. Startling Abigail, she cried out but then fell into a fit of giggles, something Orla noted was done often in Nathaniel's presence.

Producing a posset of flowers from behind his back, all work was forgotten by Abigail as they sat down in the grass, heads together in a shared secret.

Orla tried to see him through the eyes of a young woman: tall, strapping and exuding plenty of charm.

She could see the attraction, but the fact that he was the only son of the Puritan preacher, no matter his apparent lack of typified piety, did not win her approval. Nathaniel was often in their kitchen, quietly observing the making of their many healing droughts. Though, he would sometimes blurt out that "when he was a Physician, he would do something this way", which was opposite to the methods Orla used. She was open to change, but Nathaniel offered not this alternative. He spoke often of travelling to London and studying to be a Physician. But these thoughts were fanciful as far as Orla was concerned, as his father was a Man of God, and without means. Nathaniel would naturally be expected to walk in his boots by preaching, or find a trade's guild to join. Neither of these options appealed to the fancies of an aspiring healer, and Orla had originally smiled as she reminisced on her own husband's love of being a Physician.

But as time went by, Orla observed surfacing cruel traits in Nathaniel, such as his ill treatment of the village dogs and the feeble-minded. Orla grew doubtful that this dark young man could nurture a healer within.

Of recent, Orla had stumbled upon small, dead animals in the neighbouring forest. At first glance they looked to be ravaged by another animal, but a Wise woman's eyes are sharp, and on closer examination, the poor creatures had been dissected and left to die. Only human animals could be this sadistic, and this worried Orla. Did this person live amongst them, or was it he, Nathaniel, a neighbouring villain? Orla had not told Abigail, as the girl on occasion was still haunted by nightmares, which she did not wish to provoke.

Orla looked over and noticed Nathaniel staring at her. She looked away uneasily, as Orla had more than once observed a lengthening shadow in his eyes. Increasingly, Orla kept Abigail busy in order to avoid being in the company of this dark young man.

Weeks passed, spring turned into summer, and the sunny days grew long.

Orla and Abigail took advantage of the lengthy daylight to be up early to harvest dewy-fresh flowers and tender leaves to add to their dispensary. Days were busy making large batches of salves and honeyed cough syrups, preparing for the anticipated cold winter ahead.

One afternoon, whilst decanting hot syrup into pots, Orla heard a fast-approaching horse. Turning to Abigail, "This rider seems to be in a hurry—be a good lass and greet them." Abigail nodded and wiping her hands on her apron, stepped into the bright light.

An excited youth from the village struggled to control his horse, as it danced around Abigail. "Fetch the Mistress Flower, as she is needed off the second path from the Brook's farm. A lass has been…" and his eyes grew wide, "torn apart."

Abigail frowned, "What folly is this? How—"

She was interrupted, "Make haste, girl, and summon the healer!" And he forced his horse around and galloped off. Abigail stood frowning at the dust behind the departing rider.

"What be the commotion?" irritation showing in Orla's tone as she was interrupted from her task.

Turning to her mentor, Abigail explained, "The shopkeeper's boy has said you are needed in an urgent matter—a girl has been—torn apart?" Abigail's voice questioned the message and pointed towards the Brook's farm.

Orla looked surprised, but turned quickly to gather her healing bags. "Gather the horses, we shall both attend, and get to the bottom of this queer beckoning."

Moments later, the Wise women came upon a large crowd of villagers gathered near the Brook's farm. A few women were tightly crowded, and holding their mouths as if a sickness had overcome them; others were saying the Lord's Prayer. "It's little Agnes Miller!" one woman explained, stumbling backwards and nearly fainting.

"Has anyone called to the lass's parents?" A voice asked.

"Yay, they ride now from the mill," answered another.

Orla dismounted and pushed through the crowd. A stench of rotting animal and a swarm of flies assaulted her senses. What she saw made her stumble backwards, and she pushed Abigail back. "Wait here, lass, 'tis a shock to behold—attend the Taylor's wife who is in a swoon." Abigail was stunned. Orla had always involved her in healing. She knew it was terrible by the paleness of Orla's face, and so rushed over to tend to the shocked villagers.

Abigail had heard the woman, but questioned her again, "Agnes Miller? Goody Miller's daughter—around my age?" The woman nodded and looked like she would vomit. Abigail helped her to sit on the ground, and tried to hide the shock she felt on learning this news.

Orla advanced towards the corpse, and could see concealed in the undergrowth was the naked body of a young woman around Abigail's age. Her head was at a grotesque angle and her limbs looked as if they had been broken. Orla looked at the face and indeed recognised her as the Miller girl.

Orla had seen injuries like this from falls of great heights, large animal tramplings and, on occasion, goring from boar or bull. But she had never seen before what had clearly killed the girl. From throat to pubic region, she had been cut and opened up, many of her internal organs removed. Orla recoiled, shocked, and tried to control the bile rising in her mouth.

She fought the urge to run away from the shocking scene, as she knew she was at this time the only person who could offer explanations.

Taking a breath, she regained her focus as a healer. "Clear these flies as I look closer," and Orla squatted down to examine the cut marks. A few onlookers ventured forward to swat the swarm, but the rest stayed back.

Orla looked closely at the cut at the girl's throat.

It had been skilfully sliced by a thin blade, with precision—much like the lines from a Surgeon's knife and not the thick blade of a hunter.

Her neck was clearly broken, as were her limbs, as they lay in unnatural positions.

Orla's eyes moved to the rest of the body. It was rare to get an entire glimpse of the internal makings of a body, as it was prohibited to perform dissections on a deceased person. A healer could spend a lifetime caring for people and never see so much revealed. Orla carefully concealed her curiosity and addressed the terrible issues at hand.

One of the Petty Constables, a peer appointed member of the community, was called for, as was the town Watchman. The district Justice of the Peace had been summoned but he had to travel from Chippenham, which could take a day.

The girl's body would need to be taken to the public house and laid in a large room, as was protocol during an investigation. This was the largest public gathering place, and the local townspeople would need to be interviewed.

"Abby," Orla called out, startling her, "bring me that small horse blanket there in the saddle bag." As Abigail handed the blanket to Orla, she tried not to look, but her eyes were drawn to the grisly scene.

Abigail had not known Agnes well, but they had always exchanged pleasantries. It was beyond horrific that this innocent young woman would lay so exposed to the world. But, unlike her mentor, Abigail's curiosity as a healer outweighed her revulsion.

Like Orla, Abigail took note that Agnes was not actually 'torn apart' as reported by the grocery boy, but more 'dissected'. There were voids in her body, where organs had recently been.

Orla threw the blanket over the girl's naked body. Abigail was pushed aside as four men roughly lifted the wrapped corpse and placed it on the back of a wagon. An arm fell out of the blanket, and one of the men awkwardly tucked it back in.

Orla noticed straight away that where the body had been lying, there was little blood. This surprised her, and forgetting that Abigail was probably in shock, turned to her as mentor and student.

"Is there something missing here, Abby?" Orla gestured to the flattened grass and imprint of where the girl had been laid.

Abigail, already puzzling at inconsistencies, paused for a moment and asked, "Where is the blood? Bless me, but wounds such as this…this," and she waved her arms, "butchering, should have left pools and splatter," she gestured to the nearby saplings which were clean.

Orla nodded her head once and a small smile confirmed Abigail's thoughts.

"Was poor wretched Agnes butchered somewhere else and her body disposed?" The thought was startling and unnerving. Abigail, feeling anxious, looked around, "Forsooth! Could the wicked villain still be amongst us?" she queried, eyes wide.

A good question, Orla thought to herself, but one she did not wish to verbalise.

As Orla well knew from previous experience, country people were skittish and swift to grasp superstitions for explanations, and were quick to point fingers of blame.

"Let us ride to the tavern. Perchance we can gain more insight; as well, the Millers may well have need of a calming tonic," and Orla climbed up on her horse.

Upon arrival at the tavern, Orla and Abigail found the place bustling with people, and Orla noted that the Watchman and Constable were trying to maintain peace, but to little avail.

The Millers had evidently arrived, as the sound of wailing was clearly heard from inside.

Orla turned in her saddle to Abigail, "Hold thee tongue inside, and let me talk. Expected we are to assist in this inquiry, as without a Physician for miles, the law makers and clergy will with haste, be wanting some answers." Abigail nodded her understanding.

As they were tying up the horses, the local Reverend was hastily seen entering the tavern, Nathaniel fast on his heels.

Orla gripped Abigail's arm and harshly said under her breath, "Stay by my side, lass, and do not approach the Reverend's son—this is naught the time for you to lose your head in giggles and nonsense." Abigail was surprised and abashed by Orla's perception of her behaviour around Nathaniel. Did she really act the fool? And Orla added, "Trouble we don't need from the Reverend or his Puritan flock."

Not able to ponder this odd outburst further, Abigail accompanied Orla to the back room where the Miller's daughter was laid out. The Watchman and Constable stood by with the Miller, while his wife was being consoled by the Reverend with soothing words. Nathaniel stood back a few feet, staring at where the body lay atop a table.

Abigail avoided Nathaniel's glance as instructed, and made her way one step behind her Mistress to the law men and the Miller.

"Mistress Flower, we'll be with you," greeted the Watchman, and the Constable touched his hat.

Orla responded with a polite, "How now, gentlemen of law?"

Now that the pleasantries were complete, Orla explained that she would "examine young Agnes's body in hopes of finding clues to her terrible demise".

The lawmen seemed relieved that they were not expected to partake in this unsavoury examination, and they stepped out of the Wise woman's way.

Though reluctant to have to view the grisly scene again, Orla knew the villagers expected some answers, and that she, their healer, would have some ideas. She gestured to Abigail to move to the other side of the body.

Pulling the blanket back, Orla tried to dispassionately evaluate the corpse.

The scratches at her throat were curious, and on closer examination, Orla could see finger-sized bruises. Lowering her voice, Orla said to Abigail, "This girl was strangled first; these scratches would be from the poor girl trying to claw the hands off from around her throat." Abigail swallowed and nodded her understanding. Orla then ran her fingers slowly down the small bones of the girl's throat, then stopped and squeezed a lump.

"This broken bone in her throat is more proof that Agnes was strangled," Orla stated without looking up. "Notice that her lips and fingernails are blue, but why break her neck as well?" she asked out loud. Orla looked at Abigail, "God was merciful, as the lass was dead before the beast could mutilate her."

Orla could hear the girl's mother begin to sob again, and she motioned to the Reverend to take the mother outside before she lowered the blanket further.

At a second glance, Orla caught the look of Nathaniel gawping at the corpse. A cold shiver ran through her, as unlike the rest of the people in the room, who were avoiding looking in the direction of the body, Nathaniel stared with a glint of something in his eye. Orla could not place it; not curiosity, not pity, but satisfaction or even pride? Her heart skipped, and her stomach dropped.

Nathaniel caught Orla's look and smothering a smile, quickly turned his head and hurried out of the tavern.

"Mistress Orla," Abigail's voice called to her from a faraway place. "Mistress, what vexes thee?" Orla returned to the scene, with her apprentice looking worriedly at her.

"Tell me, child, where does the Reverend's son spend his days when not fawning after thee?"

The question surprised Abigail, and she frowned in confusion. "I do not know," she stammered. "He is often about studying his healing books—the ones you have given leave to borrow."

Orla held her hand up. "Yes, I know…let us finish this dreadful task, and then we shall speak further over our supper."

Abigail struggled to push the odd question from her mind, as she and Orla methodically completed the examination.

At the end, both healers had a better understanding of what the body looked like from inside, but also they had seen first-hand what atrocities had been carried out on the innocent Agnes Miller. Orla could see that the heart, lungs and stomach were gone, but other organs remained. Most disturbing was the void where once was the young woman's womb. "Why take her womanly organs?" Abigail asked, visibly shaken by the sight. Orla looked up and could see Abigail looking pale and trembling.

"We are done here," and Orla pulled the blanket up over the body. She then draped her arm around Abigail's shoulder and guided her away from the Agnes' remains.

The Watchman met the Wise women leaving the tavern. Orla wasted no time in reporting her findings, "The Miller lass was strangled, then her limbs and neck broken." She looked from one to the next, while the men shifted uneasily. "She was cut with a small, fine blade from throat to groin, and many of her internal organs removed, particularly," and Orla's voice caught, "the ones which make her a woman." She looked down, as the men gasped. Nothing like this had ever happened in their living history. Orla took Abigail by the arm, but before she left, she added, "Inform the Justice of the Peace when he arrives, that when the missing organs are found, likely the knife and her blood will be with them." The men mutely nodded.

The grisly examination complete, Orla wanted to hurry home before the shadows lengthened further. She had a chill, and despite pulling her shawl tighter, it did not abate. Orla could not shake the feeling and thoughts that somehow Nathaniel was involved in the terrible butchering of the girl.

(New Chapter)

Abigail had awoken late, and was surprised that not only was there a plate of her favourite oat hotcakes on the bench top, but that Orla had not roused her for morning chores.

Orla had not spoken of the brutal death of Agnes and in fact, had said very little once they were home last night. Abigail had wanted to further discuss the enigmatic remarks and questions Orla had asked about Nathaniel, but knew better. She would have to wait for her Mistress to initiate this topic. Despite Abigail's fatigue from the stress of the previous day, she had slept poorly.

Soft voices could be heard from the front of the house, and Abigail moved closer to the door to hear better.

"'Twas identical in Chippenham…the girl we found like the Miller's daughter," came a male voice. Abigail stole a look outside, and standing in front of Orla was a well-dressed, portly man, who seemed out of place on the dusty path. He must be the Justice of the Peace.

"Bless me, but another girl has been murdered?" Orla was taken aback. "In the same fashion?" and she lowered her voice. The man nodded once, soberly.

"The poor girl had her throat cut, and she was opened up like a hunted animal," the man crossed himself.

Orla shook her head slowly, "Godso, how can such evil walk amongst us?"

Abigail suppressed her shock, but strained to hear more.

"I know not, Mistress," and his brows went up as he spoke to Orla, "but I would ask you to make haste to Chippenham to examine the wretched lass with our Wise woman, and determine, if there are," and he lowered his voice, "ummm, similarities to the Miller girl," and he added, "The Devil is indeed amongst us, Mistress."

Abigail knew by the set of Orla's mouth that she was not happy with the request, but also knew the healer would concede. Presuming that she would accompany her Mistress, Abigail hurried to dress and ready themselves for the half-day ride.

With the sound of hooves fast departing, Abigail knew the man had left. In a few moments, Orla stepped into the cottage. "Ahhh, thou art up at last," and stopped.

"What are you packing?" Orla quizzed Abigail and frowned.

Abigail, suddenly aware that she had been eavesdropping, blushed and hurriedly explained herself, "Mistress, I overheard you speaking with the Justice of the Peace…and I, ummm, presumed that I would accompany you." Abigail looked at her hands, as she knew Orla was unhappy with her.

"Abby, you should not be listening to these terrible tales, and this is naught an adventure that I shall be requiring your presence," and she added hurriedly, "You do not need to see this horror again." As Abigail's face fell, Orla continued, "Those winter syrups won't finish themselves, and the honey from our bees must be collected to make this," and noting Abigail's deflation, added, "as well, Goody Barter is well to have that babe delivered in a day or so, and there cannot be both Midwives away." Orla knew that Abigail could not resist the opportunity of birthing a babe, especially on her own, and smiled at her.

Abigail immediately brightened, both with the prospect of a new babe and the trust endowed by her mentor. "Oh yes, I promise to bring all the simples and oxymel for Goody Barter and her babe," and Abigail was swift to forget about riding to Chippenham, as she was already thinking about what to pack in the birthing bag.

"That's a good lass; now I must make haste, as the Justice of the Peace wishes me to view the poor girl and return on the morrow." Abigail looked up, realising that Orla would be gone throughout the night. Orla had often left Abigail in her bed when healing was called upon in the night, but she usually returned within a few hours. Abigail felt apprehensive about the prospects of the night alone.

Reading her mind, Orla came and hugged her. "Ye shall be fine, my Abby-lass, after chasing the goats for the evening milking, finding the eggs from the hens, preparing the bread for rising, your knitting and darning, ye shall sleep like a babe!" And Orla kissed her on the forehead.

Though Orla felt uneasy about leaving Abigail, she was duty bound to attend this death with the other healer, and besides, Abigail was a very capable and mature young woman. Nonetheless, Orla brought the pitchfork inside, and made Abigail promise to latch the lock when she came in for the night. After gathering a few items and some bread and cheese, she waved goodbye to Abigail standing in the front yard.

Orla had been right, it was a busy day, and before long, the sun had set low in the trees, alerting Abigail it was time to come inside for the night. After a simple meal of pickled eggs and a slice of the fresh corn bread she had baked earlier, Abigail soon fell into a slumber.

The scuff of boot on the pebbly walkway awakened Abigail. Immediately, her heart was pounding, and she could see by the yellowing light of the moon that the hour was late.

She slipped out of bed and quietly made her way to the door and pitchfork.

All who knew the Wise women were aware of the little bell attached to their gate. If service was required after hours, they were to ring it twice and await to be attended. All was quiet, and the bell had certainly not been rung. Just as Abigail was thinking her mind was playing tricks, the latch on the door rattled as if someone was trying to open the door from outside. Scared now, she grabbed the pitchfork and called out with as much bravado as she could muster.

"Who goes here, and what do thee want?" Abigail's voice was hoarse from sleeping. "Wherefore your visit to see the healers? If so, state thy name."

There was a heartbeat of silence, then, "Will you not open the door? 'Tis I, Nathaniel."

Relief washed away fear, but was replaced by a level of apprehension. Abigail's thoughts returned to Orla's odd remarks and questions about Nathaniel; as well, she recalled his own odd behaviour at the tavern.

Not to mention, it was completely inappropriate for a young gentleman to be at the door of a young woman unaccompanied and at this hour. No one, especially Orla, would approve. But yet, her heart skipped a beat with the excitement of seeing Nathaniel, despite the hour. Trepidation was replaced by intrigue.

Abigail unlocked the latch and opened the door a crack and peeked outside.

Nathaniel stood bathed in moonlight, his dark hair outlined the paleness of his face. His usual neat clothes were dishevelled and he stood trembling.

Concern vanquished caution, and Abigail pulled the door open. "Nathaniel, what vexes thee? You are trembling and a mess…are you hurt?" The eye of a healer assessed him for any tell-tale sign of illness or injury.

He smiled, eyes alight. "I am all the better with the sight of you, my beauty." And reaching for Abigail's hand, he kissed it.

Confusion washed over her. Orla, and her parents before, would certainly be disapproving of such bold behaviour, and yet the warmth of the kiss lingered on her hand. Trying to gather some composure, Abigail wrapped her night shawl around her shoulders tighter. "If you are not unwell, then you cannot be at my door," she stammered. "My Mistress is attending a matter over night, and 'tis not appropriate for your presence here, alone with me." She was impressed with herself for sounding so convincing.

Nathaniel continued to smile and tilted his head to the side in the way Abigail found irresistible. "Alas, young Mistress Flower, your body and eyes beguile your words. I know that thee is happy of heart to see me on thine doorstep." His smile deepened, "Join me for just a small walk beneath the moon's ray—'tis a glorious warm night, and I know your soul will alight with the mysteries of the world illuminated in moonlight." He could not see, but knew that Abigail blushed and by her stance, Nathaniel knew she would accompany him.

Closing the door for privacy, Abigail pulled her skirt over her sleeping chamise and tied her shawl well. A far away memory flooded her thoughts as she had once before stowed away into the night with her brothers. That action had been folly and had haunted her dreams for years. The nagging voice of her father in her head made Abigail turn to retrieve the little knife she had taken from his forge all those years before. Blinking in the darkness, she could not see it. Feeling along the tiny shelf, it was certainly not there.

"Make haste Abigail," came Nathaniel's voice, and Abigail pulled her boots on, and telling herself she would locate the knife in the daylight, she set out on her romantic walk.

Stepping outside, he offered his arm. Entwining her arm into his, Abigail noticed that not only were Nathaniel's clothes dishevelled, but they appeared deeply stained, which was unusual for the meticulous young man. She also noted an odd smell about him, which was vaguely familiar, but she couldn't identify it at the moment.

Nathaniel led Abigail off the road, and they walked through the trees. He was quiet, but would point out the different owls by their calls, and very soon, they were walking through the outskirts of Farmer Brook's land.

Abigail stopped and looked around, as it had only been days since the body of Agnes had been found here, and she again felt uneasy about leaving the house at night.

"I should get back," Abigail said nervously. "Many chores I must attend before my Mistress returns on the morrow, and awake at dawn I shall be." And she pulled herself out of his arm.

Nathaniel caught her hand. "Not yet, my lovely, only a short while—there is something I am pert to show you," and he then placed his arm around Abigail's waist and began walking faster down a narrowing path and thickening trees.

"Nathaniel, no, I must return home," and Abigail stopped and tried to pull away, but he held her tight. Now struggling, Nathaniel locked his other arm around her, and hurried her away. Abigail began dragging her feet to slow him down and cried out, "Stop, release me now, Nathaniel, stop!" But he only held her tighter and began running.

Branches were now slapping Abigail in the face, and her skirt tore on a low stump. The path had turned into thick brush and though she cried out, he did not slow. As Abigail was being dragged along, she searched Nathaniel's face for an answer to this now erratic and disturbing behaviour.

In the years of knowing him, never had he given her reason to ever feel fearful. Now she was afraid of his actions and what she saw. No longer the face of an inquisitive and impish young man, but now the face of a stranger, angry, unyielding and a mouth curled in a cruel smile.

In the distance, hidden by trees, Abigail spied a little hut. She was not familiar with this corner of the forest and could not gain any bearing of where she was.

"Nathaniel, please be merciful," she begged, "tell me why we are here and why you are treating me so disrespectfully?" Abigail was trying hard to keep her fear in check and not panic. She knew that one could stay more focused that way.

Not replying, Nathaniel yanked Abigail over the narrow, broken porch and pulled her through the door. Dropping her, Nathaniel turned and locked the entrance.

Abigail slumped on the floor as she regained her breath, and that was when the mouldering smell assaulted her nose. It was the same odour on Nathaniel, and gagging, Abigail recognised it as the stink she had smelled all those years back in London: rotting corpse.

The sound of the fire steel made her recoil, and then a weak light from an oil lamp cast shadows in the room. Darkened shadows, alight by the lamp, revealed familiar shapes. Abigail's breath caught, and her attempt to fight panic dissolved as she pushed herself off the floor.

From every available space, hanging from the rafters were an array of dead animals. From wild animals to lambs, cats and dogs—people's beloved pets. Some were missing limbs, most had been gutted, and all were mutilated in one form or other. Trying to keep the bile down, a cool sweat forming on her forehead, Abigail backed towards the door.

Blinking in the gloom, she could see in the corner of the room a table and identified a human body laid upon it. Her breath caught and Abigail screamed. Turning, she hit the door and began clawing at the latch to open it.

She was roughly captured from behind, and Nathaniel's hand, now clammy, stifled the next scream. His scratchy beard cut into her neck.

"Ssshhh, I would show you my work," his voice was thick. "Like you, I am a healer. Only I can see peculiars and diseases through the skin—perhaps through to their soul. But treat them with potions and spells, I do not." Abigail could feel Nathaniel shake his head. "For I sever the diseased parts from bodies—they will call me Surgeon." The statement hung heavy on the air. Abigail's mind flashed to his father, the kindly Reverend, and as if reading her thoughts, Nathaniel replied, "Nay, I shall not be like mine father, the righteous Reverend. Fool he is with misguided beliefs that souls will be saved by the wishes of an unjust God. Damn you, Father, and thy God." He spat the words with disdain.

Nathaniel's blasphemous words surprised Abigail. She knew he was not close to the Reverend, but the maleficence Nathaniel expressed for his father was blatant. He pulled Abigail away from the door and dragged her towards the table. Abigail had lived with two brothers—she fought hard and bit the hand over her mouth. "Thou art a fiery polecat," Nathaniel laughed, and squeezed her mouth tighter.

With a few steps, they were beside the old table, and a suffocating pall of horror fell over Abigail as she stared wide-eyed at the body. She looked familiar to Abigail, but decay, hastened by the warm weather, had obscured the finer features.

Her gaze was torn from the face, and down to the girl's throat which had been similarly cut as Agnes'. Clearly, this was the depraved undertakings of Nathaniel.

Abigail shut her eyes from the abhorrence before her and struggled to free herself again. But Nathaniel held true, and he swivelled her head towards the bottom half of the torso.

"Behold," he pointed at a small exposed organ above the pubic region, "wherefore females grow babes, and I know not yet what the purpose of the rest are," and he gestured to the exposed cavity, "but together we shall partake in glory as we discover." His smile made Abigail's blood run cold, but she tried to not show her fear.

"Pray what doust speak of?" Abigail's voice was thin and small.

"Autopsy of course," Nathaniel replied, as if this was a common act, though long an illegal practice. Out of his pocket, he withdrew a small knife. Surprisingly, Nathaniel offered it to Abigail. She strained to see the knife clearer in the weak light, and immediately recognised her father's forge knife, the one she had missed.

Realisation and dread surged over her. It had been Nathaniel who had taken her knife with the fine blade.

"You stole my father's knife from my home and mutilated these women?" she accused incredulously.

Nathaniel laughed, "'Twas the finest knife I could wield for such delicate work—my thanks to thine father."

Abigail reached out for the table to steady herself from fainting. She quickly redrew her hand as Abigail realised it touched a pool of gore. Her body rebelled, and she vomited.

Nathaniel recoiled.

"Thou art afflicted by a swoon and vomit. Perchance Abigail, you have not the wits after all for this task," his voice was so dry, it could have snapped.

Abigail's mind reeled. There was a very real chance that Nathaniel would slaughter and dissect her just as he had the other young women. Yet, at the moment, he wanted her to share in the learning? In the excitement? This could buy her time.

Abigail gingerly accepted the knife into her shaking hand.

"I can do this." She steadied herself. "Forsooth, such a clever Surgeon thou art," Abigail played to his ego, "I shalt be humbled to stand together with you, my...love," Abigail choked on the word, "and walk, entwined, the road of revelation." She leaned into the body to look closer at what she could dissect.

Abigail could then feel Nathaniel relax and he released her. In a heartbeat, Abigail whirled around and thrust out with the knife. She could feel it slice into soft flesh; she withdrew and swiftly stabbed again, not knowing the target, only knowing that the knife was true.

"Bitch!" Nathaniel howled, holding his right shoulder which spouted blood, and he slapped Abigail hard in the head.

The blow sprawled Abigail to the floor, and her father's knife flew out of her hand. Her head was spinning and her eyesight went blurry. She saw Nathaniel stumble towards the door, fumble with the lock and lumber over the threshold.

Abigail heard an outside lock on the door slide into place.

She was momentarily safe, but not free.

Clearing her sight, Abigail looked around at how she could escape. She tried to not think of the monstrous things done to the poor girl on the table. A swift assessment found that the hut was windowless, but she noticed that a pale light was beginning to shine through various cracks in the walls. It must be the dawn light. She was surprised that so much time had elapsed since leaving her house.

Abigail quickly realised that the hut was old and not maintained, and started to find areas between the boards of the hut where light shone through the most. Near the doorframe were two cracked boards, and one looked as if it had fallen away. Abigail pried and shook at the loose boards. At first, they only creaked, but adrenaline fuelled her strength, and pulling hard, a board broke loose. With her feet she stamped out the other board, and the full light of the morning streamed into the hut.

Remember her knife, Abigail searched the floor on her hands and knees, eventually finding it.

Before she left, Abigail took her shawl and covered the dead girl's face.

"I promise to bring help, and return thee to your family," she said to the corpse.

Abigail squeezed through the broken boards and started to run down the path. Panic and fear charged her strength as she fled. A thorny branch tangled in her hair as Abigail blindly crashed through the trees.

Around a bend, she suddenly collided with a man. Abigail began screaming and slapping at him as the man tried to calm her. Very soon, she recognised him as the Petty Officer from town.

"Whoa, lass, slow up." He held her arms.

Relief washed over Abigail, but she was still wild from fear and shock.

Her teeth chattering, Abigail began babbling to the lawgiver of her terrible plight, "'Twas the Reverend's son Nathaniel, who, who, butchered the girls, and he tried to kill me as well!" Her eyes darted about, fearful of the shadows. "He stole my knife, and he dragged me to the hut, and—"

"Me thinks you best stop yer blithering and save the tell-tale for the Justice of the Peace." Abigail now looked the officer in the eyes, and where pity and compassion should have been, was suspicion and something like disgust. She realised he was holding her arms firmly. Abigail tried to shrug him off, but his grip tightened.

"Over here, down the path," he suddenly yelled, "I have her."

Abigail was confused, and within a moment around the bend came Farmer Brooks, the Miller, the Watchman, and steps behind, the Puritan Reverend and Nathaniel.

She started to scream, and fought the Officer with all her strength. Her father's knife dropped from her hand to the ground.

The officer swiftly retrieved it and secreted it away into a pocket.

"There!" she pointed at Nathaniel, "Thou art the beast which has mutilated those girls and tried to kill me!" Abigail was hysterical and clawed her way around the officer to put him between herself and Nathaniel.

To her chagrin, he began to pray out loud with his father. Now clean and composed, in the clothing of the Puritans, his only mishap beguiling the night's events was a large bandage across his right shoulder.

Farmer Brooks crossed himself and began retreating back down the path.

The Reverend pushed Nathaniel behind him, and suddenly he withdrew a cross from his robes. Abigail watched incredulously, as he held it up and began reciting Latin.

The Petty officer now pulled out heavy manacles.

"Murdering Witch!" exploded the Miller. "You butchered my daughter, and those other poor souls, for what? A favour from Satan?" he spat at Abigail.

"We will run ahead and find the place of your Sabbath, the unholy place where you murdered those souls!" His eyes were wide and he was violently shaking.

The Miller with the Watchman ran back down the way Abigail had come.

"Hold yerself still," and she was roughly placed into the manacles. Comprehension washing over Abigail, she fought the constraints.

"Cease your foul accusations! What folly abounds that I who was dragged away from my home by that devil," she motioned to Nathaniel, "and witnessed horrors unbeknown to Earthly creatures, wears the manacles, wherefore the villain stands free?"

The Petty officer looked her up and down, and motioned to Nathaniel

"Forsooth, the Puritan's son has revealed all. He states he did try and stop thee from the Sabbath ritual, but Nathaniel could not prevent the murderous death of yet another young woman, and a stab wound he did also incur!" Abigail could not believe that these men were so fast to believe the words of Nathaniel, and completely disregard the obvious fact she had been abducted and almost butchered like the other woman her age.

"I know not why you accuse me of such abominable acts!" Abigail cried, "'Twas I who was locked in the hut, and murdered I would have been if I had not escaped!"

She was shivering in her thin garments, hair asunder, eyes wild and full of fear.

"By heaven, girl, look at yerself," the Officer shouted to Abigail, "standing aloof in naught but yer undergarments, stained by the blood of innocents and clutching the very knife which butchered them. As well, the wound young Nathaniel has at your hands," he motioned, "the stain of evil stands before me, and as God is my witness, death walks with you."

Abigail cowered, stunned by the accusations, and furious that the villainous creature stood by unencumbered.

The Reverend stopped his prayer and approached Abigail, "Tonight, Goody Barter bore a hideous monster, pulled forth dead from her womb." He eyed Abigail with fear and disdain. "Clearly, this abomination was unfavourable in God's eye, and in His Almighty wisdom, God chose to let the monster babe return to the depths of hell from which it was begot, but not without first killing its mother, the Good wife." He looked at Abigail with condemnation. "Satan, your paramour, was on blood lust last eve, as thy butchered one young innocent, Satan took two more souls himself."

Abigail fell to the ground in despair. Goody Barter had been well, and her babe kicking within. How could these terrible events all have occurred within a few hours of her being gone?

Where was Orla, oh God, what would she think? Would she see through the eyes of her jailers? Nay, Orla would stand by Abigail, suddenly, recalling that poor Orla once had stood accused of such atrocities.

Nathaniel's eyes glinted at her when no one was looking, and he went after the Miller.

Minutes later, they all returned, out of breath from running, the Miller looking pale and shaking.

"There is great evil done at the old trappers hut," stated the Watchman soberly. "There is no doubt of her heinous crimes." The Miller bent down and vomited.

"I shalt locate the Potter as his poor wretched daughter is laid out, butchered like the rest. I shall gather more men to bring her forth," the Petty officer added.

"But first we must silence this Witch."

"I swear it was not me!" Abigail screamed and struggled in the manacles. "It was Nathaniel, he is the Devil's spawn, not I!" And she was cut off as from behind the cold metal of the 'Brank' or *Scold's bridle*, an iron cage, was roughly pushed onto Abigail's head. It was a man's creation specifically to humiliate and punish women. It consisted of a hoop of iron, hinged on either side for fitting and latched in the back. A wide piece of iron also led from front to back over her head, splitting at where her nose was. The last piece of iron ran along her jaw across her mouth, where a cruel piece of iron held spikes. While it was being locked from behind, the Watchman drove the spiked plate into Abigail's mouth and over the tongue. Searing pain, like an electrical current, shot through her mouth as the spikes bit into her tongue. If Abigail tried to speak, the spikes would lodge deeper into the tongue, causing unspeakable pain. The weight of the device was heavy on her head, and Abigail struggled to keep her neck straight. This torture device was notoriously used to silence gossiping women, but the Watchman had decided to apply it in order to lead Abigail on a leash through the village in shame, and in silence. Tears of pain and injustice streamed down Abigail's face.

The Petty officer looked to the Watchman with grave concern. "Deliver this Witch to the town centre and stretch her neck in the pillory while we await the arrival of the Magistrate."

Abigail was dragged away, back towards the main road, with everyone, all but Nathaniel, following.

He chose to stay and await the others to remove the girl's body.

And there he stood laughing.

Orla was greeted by the bleating of her goats, and chickens complaining that they were still locked up from the night before.

She swung off her horse, stiff and tired, as she had risen early and rode hard to get home. The task had proven to be grisly, but she had confirmed that no doubt there was a murderer amongst them.

Irritability was replaced by vague concern, as Abigail's horse neighed in welcome, still tied in the small byre. Orla went to the door and listening, she did not hear stirrings from within. Abigail was always up early, often before Orla, and it was well into late morning.

"Abby, my lass? Blast, one night I am away, and trouble there is," she spoke opening the door.

The hearth was cool, and Abigail's working clothes still hung on the peg.

Now concerned, Orla started searching and calling out for her apprentice. There were little clues to tell of her whereabouts.

Thinking she might be attending Goody Barter and her babe, Orla decided she should go there and check on things. But as Orla reached for her birthing bag, she saw that Abigail's bag still hung next to her own.

Alarm hit her stomach like a rock, and Orla hastened out to saddle Abigail's horse, as hers was too fatigued to go any further.

Once again, she was heading back down the road, only in the opposite direction into the village.

Something was not right.

Mortified and stunned, Abigail was led to the town centre by the Watchman and jailers, where she could see the pillory awaiting her imprisonment.

Word travelled fast of the accusations that the Wise woman's apprentice had committed these horrific crimes. People were already crowding the streets gawking and jeering at Abigail, as she stumbled onto the scaffold of the pillory.

Abigail had seen many a wayward person in the 'stretch neck', a penal instrument used for an array of crimes, but never imagined it would be her neck within the device.

"They say she is a Witch," Abigail heard from one woman standing near the platform.

"Who saith that? The lass is a good girl, gentle with my little 'uns she was when they caught the fever last winter," another woman argued.

"Don't ye know the tidings?" the first replied. "The Reverend's own son didst catch her with knife in hand, butchering the Potter's daughter."

"Balderdash! That boy is a queer one, if anyone butchered that lass, 'twas him!"

And then a third person added, "Ye can't say the girl is right in the head—remember when she arrived out of nowhere, and the Wise woman took her in like an orphaned kitten." The people around nodded.

"'Twas not from nowhere," someone added, "she came from London on the plague road, untouched by the pestilence she was. They saith her whole family was taken by the plague, and that she did walk a blighted road all the way unscathed. Perchance Satan did protect her?" One nodded, and the women all made the sign of the cross.

Abigail made a sound in her throat and tried to make eye contact with the woman, but the scold's bridle did not allow any such movements. The argument in her defence helped lighten her heart, but when the conversation swiftly shifted to the notion of witchcraft, Abigail's stomach dropped.

Once on the platform, the scold bridle was clumsily removed, taking chunks of Abigail's tongue with it. Spittle and blood ran down her mouth and chin.

Choking from the blood, Abigail cried out, "'Twas the Reverend's son Nathaniel who stole me from the house and was going to kill me, only I escaped!" She struggled with her jailers, "Someone, I beg thee, find Mistress Flower, she will reveal the truth!"

"Silence Witch," the Watchman commanded. "Or back into the brank with you," he threatened.

"Did he say Witch?" someone in the crowd asked

"Yay, the girl hath done abominable acts, and only a servant of Satan could go forth and chop up innocents," replied a Puritan woman.

"And did thou know of poor Goody Barter?" the gossiper's voice was pitched loud enough for all to hear.

"Nay, know what?" asked another gossipmonger in the crowd.

"Her babe, the poor mite, was born a monster, and Goody Barter did die from the trial. They say 'twas this girl," pointing at Abigail, "who did curse the child, when she would go there and visit…likely because she is a Witch!"

A collective gasp was heard. Abigail turned to the accuser,

"How now! Vicious words and I am not a Witch!" Abigail was hysterical. "I would not hurt any creature, especially a babe!" Her mouth was thick with blood and she stumbled over the words.

Abigail's hands were seized and roughly pushed into the openings of the pillory, and her neck crammed into the head-hole.

Offenders generally had their ears nailed to the backboard to confine the head from moving from the public's scrutiny. Abigail prayed that the lawgivers would spare her this cruelty.

Orla was almost to the town's centre when a speeding horse and rider intercepted her. She recognised the young man as a neighbouring farmer. Orla and Abigail had nursed his ailing father through the winter and delivered them a healthy baby girl only months earlier.

"Mistress Flower!" he called out, looking anxious and slowing his steed. "'Twas on my way to find thee. Have thou heard the ill tidings of your apprentice, Abigail?"

"Nay," replied Orla, irritated to be stopped, "hence why I rush thitherward to find her."

The farmer looked concerned and replied, "She hath been arrested!"

"Abigail arrested?! Pray God for what?" Orla asked incredulous.

The young farmer averted his eyes. "She hath been accused of the unholy butchering of the Potter's girl, and likely for the murder of the other lass," he hastily said.

"The Potter's daughter? I thought it was only the Miller's girl?" Orla asked quickly.

"They found the Potter's girl this morning, with Abigail," replied the farmer. Orla frowned.

"That makes three, as I hath just returned from Chippenham and confirmed that the mutilated girl there was murdered by the hands of the same demon, who is not my apprentice!" Orla exclaimed.

"But Mistress, Abigail was found clutching a small blade, the very one they say has mangled those girls," he argued, and added, "the Reverend's son as well, stabbed by her!"

Orla stared at him, shocked by this news, but quickly recovered.

"This is misguided nonsense. Those lawgivers would not have had enough time to conclude these findings and accuse Abigail!" Despite her words, anxiety washed over Orla. "Only the feeble-minded would accuse her of anything but sweetness!"

"The Reverend's son bears witness, and he hath told the lawgivers under oath, that he discovered Abigail, covered in the blood of the girl, butchering her." The farmer was clearly shaken from the news.

"That menace!" Orla was trembling with anger. "If anyone has butchered these girls, 'tis Nathaniel!"

The farmer looked surprised by her outburst, as he was the Reverend's son after all, and avoiding her gaze continued, "But there is more, Mistress, Abigail hath been deemed a Witch."

Orla's heart skipped a beat. "Those superstitious fools, so quick to blame the strong, young woman." Orla said under her breath, and without another comment, hastened Abigail's horse into a gallop, leaving the young farmer behind.

Terrible memories of her own Witch trial flashed in her mind as she raced towards the town. Tears blurred her eyes with the memory of the trauma and loss she endured that day.

How could folk be so cruel? How could they be so blind?

The trees cleared, and she could see people hurrying over to the pillory platform.

Her eyes were not the best, but she could make out a figure in white confined in the device. The red of the hair identified her own Abigail. Riding closer, Orla could see she was in disarray. Dressed only in her nightdress, hair exposed and untied, Abigail looked a common harlot. But the bloodstains on her gown and around her mouth gave her a more fiendish and startling appearance. One could easily see how she looked the part of a Witch.

Already standing for hours, Abigail's neck and shoulders were aching. She was small for the pillory, and her feet barely touched the platform, causing her to mostly hang from the stocks rather than bend into it. But the humiliation and accusations stung worse than the discomfort and occasional pelting of rotting vegetables. Abigail kept her gaze fixed to the platform, refusing to look at anyone. But the sound of her horse neighing in agitation from all the people, made her look up.

"Orla!" Abigail screamed, relief washing over her. "Help me!" her hands flapping in agitation from within the device. Orla climbed down from her horse and hurriedly walked to the platform. Her face was impassive, which took

Abigail off guard. She imagined her Mistress running to the stock and embracing her.

The jailers had left Abigail to the mercy of the mob, and so Orla fought through the crowd to get closer to Abigail.

"Make way, and stand back!" the commanding voice of the Wise woman forced those closest to the platform to move away.

Orla did not know how long they would have to talk in private.

She jumped up and firstly helped Abigail drink some water, as the care of prisoners was not the duty of jailers.

"What sayeth you?" Orla asked emotionless.

"What doth thou mean?" Abigail answered between gulps, "What sayeth I? I am innocent! You know this! And it's Nathaniel, not I! Orla, he is a monster," Abigail cried.

"Shhhhh! Quiet thy voice girl," Orla scolded, looking around, "this is between us."

Abigail, lowering her voice, whispered, "You were right about Nathaniel, Orla, all of it. The Devil hath tainted his soul, and horrible things he didst to those girls…and he would have killed me if I had not escaped," she hurriedly explained.

Orla did not immediately reply, but then asked, "What were thee doing with Nathaniel at this place? 'Twas folly to venture into the night with him! Did I not tell thee to stay home?" She scolded, and then asked, "What would have happened if Goody Barter had gone into labour? What hath she done?"

Noting a new look of anguish on Abigail's face, Orla asked, "What Abby? What is it? Did mishap occur with the Goodwife as well?"

Abigail looked to the platform again. "Thou did not hear these terrible tidings? I didst hear the townswomen say that Goody Barter delivered a heinous child in the night…deformed, purple…and both died." Abigail swallowed. "They hast blamed me and added their misfortunate deaths to my charge of being a Witch." Fresh tears filled Abigail's eyes.

Orla was aghast and saddened to hear this news. Goody Barter had been well, her babe growing strong. But Orla knew more than anyone that growing babes were a mystery, and a myriad of things could go wrong. But worse, her concern for Abigail was escalating. Charges of infanticide by a newly accused Witch meant sure death.

Orla tried to ease Abigail's worry, "'Tis not thy fault the babe died, Abby, a great sadness this is, but I hath seen this years before. But dark times have fallen on this village, and tragically, thou art the scapegoat." Orla bit her lip and looked away from Abigail.

She then spotted the lawgivers hurriedly walking alongside the Reverend and someone else, who was likely the Justice of the Peace, also known as Magistrate, advancing towards the pillory platform.

The crowd became animated and excited, as many had never seen a Magistrate, and parted to allow their passage.

The Justice of the Peace was an appointed role by the King to dispense justice, enforce civil legislation and administer just punishment to those who broke the laws during these times of upheaval and restoration.

His appearance signalled the gravity of the circumstance and the crime.

Orla stepped back from the platform, as the men advanced, leaving Abigail to face them alone.

The Magistrate was easily identifiable by his linen lace collar, slashed doublet and ornate broad brimmed hat. He walked straight up to Abigail and appraised her.

"This girl, thou hath claim has butchered three young women who art the same age as her?" he asked the lawgivers flanking him.

"Yes, yesss, your Worship," the Watchman stammered, nervous in his presence, "the accused girl was caught in the act of murder by the local Puritan Reverend's son—a God-fearing boy himself."

"And this God-fearing boy, wherefore is he?" The Magistrate looked to the Reverend for an answer.

"Your Worship," the Reverend smiled nervously, "I hast not seen Nathaniel since we left him on the path near the hut and the deceased girl...my boy is often about....praying," he added.

"Is that so?" the Magistrate regarded the Reverend sceptically. Being a faithful Church of England parishioner, like so many of his class, he regarded members of the Separatist movement as boorish and zealots. He had little patience for their kind. "I suggest thou find him soon, praying or not, and bring him forthwith." He flicked his hand, dismissing the Puritan. The Magistrate then turned his attention back to Abigail.

"What is thy name, woman?"

"I am Abigail Midwinter-Flower, your Worship," she answered and kept her gaze lowered.

"Thou art aware of the severe charges?" he questioned.

"Yes, your Worship, sir."

"And they are?" he pressed.

Abigail stammered and looked at Orla who avoided eye contact.

"Murder, sir…and Witchcraft," yelled a voice from the crowd.

"She did hex a Goodwife and her babe, making it dead," hurried another gossipmonger.

The Magistrate frowned at the crowd as interruptions were not something he tolerated well.

"Is this so?" The educated Magistrate was a man of law, and dubious of the tall tales of bored wives.

His irritation growing, he chose to humour their superstitions and asked the Watchman, "Hath the girl hexed a Goodwife, as well as butcher women? What wickedness dost you host in this village, and pray is there more?"

The Watchman and Petty officer shuffled their feet awkwardly, as the Magistrate insinuated that the cause of sinful and potentially Satanic behaviour was somehow a reflection of bad policing.

The Watchman answered first, "Nay, your Worship, we believe that when the girl hath paid for her punishment and sins, then order shall prevail in our village."

"And the evidence?"

The Petty officer cleared his throat. "As prepared in the document, your Worship," he gestured to the rolled parchment given to the Magistrate earlier, "the girl was followed by the Reverend's son Nathaniel to the forest and to a remote hut. He then caught the girl with a knife, the very same knife she did use on the two other young women." The Magistrate frowned at the queerness of the story.

"Why pray tell wast this man, the Reverend's son, Nathaniel, out at night following a young woman?" the Magistrate asked, raising an eyebrow.

Before the lawgivers could answer, Abigail interjected, "Sir, Nathaniel didst come to my home and persuade me to go on an evening walk," she hurried. "He then dragged me to the hut, where I did see the mutilated Potter girl. Nathaniel locked me inside; after I stabbed him, I tried to escape." Abigail realised after she spoke, how incriminating her story sounded.

She looked to the faces in the crowd and saw disbelief and growing anger. Her eyes fell to Orla who stood staring at her, eyebrows furrowed and struggling to understand what Abigail was saying.

"Half naked you were, salacious Witch, what decent lass would go out in her nightdress," an old woman yelled from the crowd.

"Before which, she stole over to the Barter's home and cursed the Goodwife whilst she laboured with the babe," added another voice.

The Magistrate was growing impatient—feeling hot in the sun, he wanted to end the spectacle and return to his manor, and so he hurried the interrogation.

"Why girl, would you venture out at night, unchaperoned—a very distasteful act, I shall add—and then blame the same fellow for abducting and attempting to murder you?" The Magistrate held his hand up, indicating he did not want an answer.

He then unrolled the parchment, quickly scanned it, then addressed Abigail.

"Young Mistress Flower, these charges are very grave, and I have no choice but to recommend this matter be determined by the Justice of the Assize courts."

Orla and a few others who knew the court, gasped. The Assize courts were presided over by professional, travelling judges who heard the more serious trials in the district and summoned juries. The trials were lengthy, exhausting for the accused and usually ended in execution.

Abigail looked to Orla for an explanation, but she stood unmoving, and did not meet her eyes.

"However, as the judges have recently been to this district, they will not be returning till late winter," the Magistrate added.

A murmur went out in the crowd, and for a moment, Abigail thought she might be able to get through this unscathed. But then the Magistrate continued,

"And so I hast little choice but to issue punitive actions to the accused, in the form of corporal punishment," the Magistrate announced.

"Abigail Midwinter Flower, I sentence thee to thirty lashes of the cat-o-nine whip, thence to the gaol to await the arrival of the Assize court for further trial and subsequent sentencing."

The crowd erupted into shouting and rushed the platform.

Abigail had begun to wail, and Orla stood stunned, tears in her eyes.

Thirty lashes was deemed a cruel punishment for a brutish man, but Abigail was a diminutive-sized woman, thirty lashes would likely kill her.

The Magistrate immediately turned to leave, and hoped that his punishment would deter any further law breaking and misbehaving. He was in no hurry to return to this backward, superstitious village.

Abigail was desperate for Orla to be near her, to console her. But Orla just stood there being pushed and jostled by the crowd, staring at Abigail.

And then shockingly, Orla turned from Abigail and started walking away from the platform.

"Orla!" Abigail cried. "Where art thou going?" Orla kept walking, and some of the crowd quieted, and wondered if the Mistress healer was truly leaving her beloved apprentice to suffer the lashes alone.

"Orla?" Abigail's voice was plaintive. "Please do not leave me, I am scared! And you are all I have in this world! Come back Orla!" she pleaded. All were surprised as Orla walked expressionless, climbed on the horse and rode away, not looking back.

Abigail began to wail with grief. She was forsaken by the last person who ever loved her.

People eventually tired of standing in the sun and berating the accused, so slowly the crowd dwindled. By late afternoon, Abigail was left alone in the town centre.

She was mercifully released from the pillory at sunset, where Abigail collapsed, shaking with strained and torn muscles. The Watchman had doused her with a bucket of water to wash away the bodily waste pooled at her feet and clinging to her gown. Humiliation had peaked when Abigail was no longer able to control her functions. The Watchman had dragged Abigail from the pillory platform down to the stocks and locked her feet inside. At least she could now sit down. Moments after the Watchman left, a Goodwife for whom Abigail had successfully mended her child's bone, had crept out of the trees, and gave her water and bread. Though Abigail was deeply appreciative, the kind gesture only magnified the point that her own family, Orla, was not there to care for her.

Abigail leaned forward and cried piteously. She was terrified by the coming day and her awaited flogging. She had treated many souls after lashings, and if they did not die from infection, they were permanently maimed. Abigail trembled at the thought of her own back rendered to ribbons of flesh. But her heart ached more than the anticipated flagellation. It was broken a thousand fold from betrayal and abandonment.

Abigail dozed, exhausted from the torture of the day and her despair.

The fumbling of the bolt on the stock roused Abigail.

She opened her eyes, and there bathed in the moonlight was Orla. Holding her finger to her lips, she smiled and Abigail obeyed, stifling her exuberance.

Within a moment, Orla had released the lock with a key she held. Opening the stock, Abigail collapsed into her arms, sobbing with relief.

"Hugs and explanations will have to wait." Orla gently untangled Abigail, but without first kissing her head. "We hast only a short time to escape." Abigail nodded and tried to stand, but immediately her legs crumpled beneath her weight. She then began to crawl away from the stocks. Orla's heart skipped as she could see how broken and yet stoic this young woman was.

Bending down, Orla wrapped Abigail's arms around her neck and pulled her out of the town centre. Abigail stumbled alongside Orla, and soon they reached the trees and their awaiting horses. She instantly saw that the horses were packed with numerous bags and baskets.

Abigail looked at Orla questioningly. "We leave this accursed place tonight," she explained. Orla realised that Abigail would be unable to ride, so swiftly she tied her horse to her own, making adjustments to the weight of numerous bundles.

Orla then struggled to hoist Abigail upon the saddle of her horse and climbed behind her. Taking the reins, she drove her mare through the woods, and then once on the road, urged them into a gallop.

"Thou was correct about Nathaniel," Abigail broke the silence

"I hath a special skill in reading people, and that boy has a tainted soul— revealing itself to me, almost laughingly." Orla replied, "Now hush about that devil, we shall talk when resting."

The ride was hard, and though Orla slowed the horses often for rest, they did not stop. They chased the moon, travelling roughly southwest, and after some time, the small road fed into a larger road. After a few hours, Orla's horse was showing signs of exhaustion, so she slowed her to a walk, and then stopped.

Orla found Abigail some clothes and handed her a sweet cake. She watered and fed the horses a few apples. They soon continued southwest, slower, but still at a steady pace.

"How did you get the key for the lock?" Abigail asked.

"I traded the contents of our home and animals to the Lock smith," Orla answered.

Abigail was taken aback. "But what will happen when we return? You hath traded all your worldly possessions! All thine years of work gone!"

Orla replied flatly, "We shall not be returning thither. Firstly, that demon Nathaniel still lurks, unjailed, and likely will return to finish his sinister job of butchering you!" Orla could feel Abigail recoil and placed her hand on Abigail's leg for comfort and added, "But he won't as you are now safe. Second, our worldly possessions be strapped to the horses and besides," Orla squeezed Abigail, "thou is well worth the trade."

They rode a while longer in stillness, then Orla said, "It broke my heart leaving you strapped to that abominable device and to the abuse of those fools. But playing as if I was through with thee, 'twas the only way I could deceive them and free you from the lashings on the morrow." Abigail did not immediately reply, trying to give voice to her emotions.

"When I thought I hath lost you, Orla, the pain was greater than when I lost my own mother to the plague." And fresh tears fell, "Please do not ever leave me again." Orla hugged Abigail tight, but did not reply.

It was mid-morning as they reached the large market town of Blandford.

Orla rested the horses and examined Abigail. After determining there was no lasting damage, she told Abigail to wait with the horses while she went out to gather a few provisions.

Abigail dozed, and within a few hours, Orla returned with numerous packages. After making a herbal rinse for Abigail's tongue wounded from the Brank, they sat down together.

Orla handed Abigail a hot bun and asked, "Art thou now fit to ride?" She assured Orla that she was fine, but still required help to climb up.

As they rode, Abigail asked, "Where do we travel to, Orla?"

Orla looked around. "We ride to Dorchester, where we shall stay overnight, and then we ride south towards the sea," Orla answered, "our destination is Weymouth."

"Oh!" Abigail said, intrigue and excitement setting in, "I hath never seen the sea...and this shalt be our new home, yes?" Orla nodded, but did not speak.

Abigail could see that Orla was preoccupied and stayed quiet the rest of the journey.

By the time they arrived at the quaint town of Dorchester, riders and horses were exhausted.

Orla registered them into the first inn, tipping the stableboy to give extra care to her mounts.

After they ate their fill of a tasty meat pie, Orla brought out numerous books and one particularly worn ledger. They were an assortment of medicinal books, including those written by Culpepper and Galen. Abigail recognised them from the shelves at the house. Abigail was happy that her mother had insisted that she learn to read, and that Orla had continued her education.

"These art the Bibles to healing, lass, there are countless maladies and remedies written here," Orla said. "These volumes were my husband's joy, and the key to much of his healing," and Orla smelled one and hugged it. "This one," and she held up the ledger, "was the sickness journal myself and my sisters kept for many seasons. What remedies were used for which afflictions and injuries." Her eyes misting nostalgically as she ran her fingers over the words with, she whispered, "Our whole life is here."

Abigail nodded and knew the journal well, as Orla still referred to its entries, and continued on occasion to update it. Abigail was very proud the first time Orla added one of her own innovative formulations, and following that day, numerous more of Abigail's unique observations about healing. She frowned at Orla, slightly wondering why she was speaking of them now. Abigail wasn't aware that anyone needed healing. She was certainly acting queer. But before Abigail could question her Mistress, Orla announced, "Alas, 'tis late and we must be up before dawn, as the sea awaits us." She tried to smile, but it quickly left her face, and Orla returned the books to her leather saddlebags.

They climbed into the fresh bed, and immediately Abigail fell into a deep slumber. For Orla, sleep came later, as she lay there stroking Abigail's curls, tears slowly rolling down her face.

Weymouth

They could smell the sea before they saw it.

Neither Orla nor Abigail had ever seen the ocean, and they were dazzled by the beauty of the sun sparkling off the water. They hurried their horses as they were eager to see the water closer.

They rode into the port, where many small and great ships were tied to docks or moored in the harbour. Orla pulled her mare up and climbed down. "Stay with the horses, lass, I shan't be long." Though Abigail was keen to investigate this beautiful place with Orla, she obeyed and instead occupied herself with looking at the bright houses and the many people bustling around her. Weymouth reminded Abigail of a smaller, cleaner London. Abigail was eager to see where she and Orla would make their new home.

Sometime later, Orla returned, looking sweaty and hassled.

"Art thou sound?" Abigail asked, worried.

Orla waved her concern off, and instead said, "Let us walk the horses to the beach and gaze upon the beautiful water." They picked their way through the busy port, and soon they were wiggling their toes into the sand on a beach facing the English Channel.

They stood quietly appreciating the crashing of the waves and the many creaking and clanging sounds coming from the nearby ships.

"This channel meets up with the great Atlantic Ocean," Orla said. "I hath never been here, but Abraham and William would speak of their travels abroad and the vast beauty of the open seas." Pointing west, Orla continued, "And thither, is the New World...America, a place of great beauty and wonder, they say."

Abigail's exuberance over their new home faded, as she saw the look on Orla's face. Taking her hand, "Orla, pray tell me, what vexes thee? What is happening?"

"Why do you look so forlorn?" Abigail was becoming agitated, and she saw tears forming in Orla's eyes.

Turning to Abigail, Orla released a deep breath and said, "Lass, you make sail for the new world this very afternoon."

Abigail's grip tightened. "Do you not mean us?" she asked quietly.

"Nay, Abby, you, only you." And pulling Abigail towards her, Orla hugged her tight.

Abigail stepped back, now shaking, "Orla no! I cannot go hence without you…we wilt travel together, we are family. I do not wish to go without you…I can't go without you, we have only one another!" And she began to cry.

"There is no other choice, we don't have the money to buy passage for two!" Orla shook her gently. "You art a known murderer, a renegade…a Witch," and Orla stumbled over the word.

"Very soon, my girl, there shalt be a reward on thy head. Greedy and cruel men will let nothing stop them from obtaining this gold. They will return you to ultimately face your execution. Thou art better taking your chance in the New World than here with those superstitious fools!"

Abigail's mind was spinning, and she felt ill from knowing that she would never see Orla again. "But what of thee, Orla? Of course they shall hunt you as well! Where will you hide?" Abigail exclaimed.

"Nay, child. I am not worth the effort in their eyes…neither beautiful nor clever."

"You are precious to me," Abigail argued, "forever!"

Orla tightly embraced Abigail, and both women stood crying for the injustice of women in this world, and for the heartbreak that they knew they would never see one another again.

Orla gently untangled Abigail from her and bent to collect two wrapped packages. Handing them to Abigail, Orla said, "'Tis not the most beautiful items I have ever bought, but a necessity thou shalt need." Abigail unwrapped the first package and frowned at the brown flax. Unfolding it, the plain dress of a Puritan woman fell open, along with a knitted cap. The second contained a heavy woollen, fur-lined cape. Abigail gaped at Orla.

"What? Am I to wear these?" Abigail sniffed incredulously

Orla hurried, "And there are smalls, petticoats, a broad brimmed hat and a new muff as well. The winters are said to be icy and unforgiving."

Abigail frowned. Most of the Puritan Protestants were kind and temperate, but consumed with their Godliness and often fanatical in their criticism of those who were not. Abigail had not even read the Bible in its entirety.

"Why can I not be myself?" she questioned.

Orla explained. "Thou goes to the New World where many a Puritan resides. You must be one of them to live out a life…with a prayer, a good life. We do not have enough gold for thou to travel as a maidservant to the wealthy. You must naught be in the 'guise', but become a Puritan Midwife, and healer," Orla stated, deadly serious, and then, eyes softening: "Thou art no longer an apprentice, but a Mistress healer in your own right," Orla stated proudly.

Abigail was taken back by her words, but Orla could see a rebuttal coming and hurriedly said, "Please, Abby, let us spend our last hours celebrating your new status over tea and cakes," she said, trying to lighten the heavy mood.

After Abigail changed into the demure clothing of the Puritans, she and Orla found a teahouse nearby. There, Orla tried to keep them distracted from the impending departure. "And I have packed many pots of salves and jugs of syrups for lung distempers…oh, and all the dried Velvet dock and Woundwort we had. There are continuous plagues of smallpox I have heard, and so extra blood herbs have been added. I know not the herbal lore of America, but with hopes thou shalt fast discover a new herbal pharmacy," she tried to sound bright and positive, though her heart was shadowed by worry of this savage, unknown land.

"And all of these thou shalt take as well," and Orla pulled over the leather bags packed with books.

"But, Orla, these are all thou hast left of your bygone days! Bless me, but these should stay with you!"

"Nay, my girl, these are tools for a healer and Midwife. Thou journeys to a new and wild place. Thou shalt need these to heal and birth the many people of your new home." And Orla turned her face as she choked back tears.

The bell tower in the distance tolled three times.

"We should get thee to the ship," and she smiled weakly.

The women walked silently, leading the horses till they saw the sign for the *'Temperance Duty.'* In the background, an impressive square-rigger was being loaded with barrels, timber, and crates of chickens and pigs.

They stood in line behind numerous passengers, awaiting to pay the final cost of the passage.

Abigail's anxiety grew with each step closer to the ship, and Orla took her hand.

"Next," called the Steward, not looking up from his ledger.

Orla took a breath. "Mistress Abigail Flower," she announced. Abigail noticed that 'Midwinter' had been dropped and with pride, her new title added.

The man ran his quill down the thick book. "Yes," and finally looking up he said, "thou hast paid £4 sterling, and thou owes...oh yes, two horses." Without looking at the women, he assessed the horses behind them. Snapping his finger, two sailors appeared and began stripping the horses of their baggage and tack.

"Orla, you sold our horses? But how will thee travel?" Abigail was shocked and worried for the older woman, which added to her distress.

"They will pay thy way, Abby, all will be well." With a last pat and a quiet thank you, Orla watched the mares being led away.

All but one small bag, which Orla had kept for herself, was loaded onto a wagon under Abigail's name and taken to the ship.

Orla seemed to be looking for someone, and within a few moments, a heavily pregnant woman and young man saw her and waved. Both identified as Puritans by their dress and manner. "Mistress Flower," they acknowledged Orla with a small bow.

Orla smiled back, and turning said, "May I introduce my niece, Abigail, an accomplished healer and Midwife. Abigail, this is Master and Goody Hopkins."

"You shalt be staying in the same cabin as the Hopkins, to keep a close eye on the Goodwife in case her babe decides to arrive on the voyage." Orla had been lucky to make these arrangements to keep Abigail safe on the three-month voyage.

Abigail was surprised by the introduction but curtsied and replied demurely, "'Tis my pleasure and honour to be at your service." She noted the stern, unsmiling appraisal from the Master, but the Goodwife appeared warm and welcoming.

The whistle blew, startling Abigail, informing passengers to embark.

"Well," said the man, "we shall join the other ninety something passengers and await thee on the deck." And he touched his hat to Orla. The good wife waved.

Turning to Abigail, the dreaded moment had arrived.

Tears ran from Abigail's eyes unabated. Orla pulled Abigail into her arms.

"My lass, my Abby," and Orla choked, "how very blessed I hath been to have thee in my life. Thou brought so much sunshine and have healed my broken heart."

Abigail clung to her. "No, Orla, no, I don't want to go, I do not care if they find me, if only I am by your side, then I can face anything. I am afraid, and I am not brave," she sobbed.

"Oh, but thou are! Thou art the bravest person I have ever known...and you will go forth to this new land and make a wonderful new life. You will heal many souls and bring into this world many lives. One day, thou shalt fall in love and have babes of your own."

The whistle blew the second and final time.

"Now go, lass," Orla pushed Abigail out of the embrace. "You sail to a place called Boston in Massachusetts, and I will try and discover a way to get letters to thee." Orla was not certain a means existed, but she wanted Abigail to leave with some hope of future correspondence.

Orla took Abigail's hand and walked her to the gangway.

"I have this for thee," and like the one she gave to Abraham all those years past, she placed in Abigail's hand a ribbon with an oak carved pendant.

Looking closer, Abigail could see a tiny rising sun, and in the centre of the sun, a heart. It was fragranced in oils of rose and lavender. She placed it over her neck and hugged Orla one last time.

Abigail joined the Hopkins on the deck, and she waved to Orla until she could see her no more. The ocean was beautiful and the sky clear. Turning her back to the English shore, she looked forward into the open seas.

Facing Goody Hopkins, Abigail asked, "So, Boston will be your new home?"

"Oh nay," she smiled sweetly.

"Once we arrive in Boston, we shall journey on to a place known for its goodly Puritan community."

"Does this place have a name, Goodwife?" Abigail asked.

"Yes, my dear, 'tis a place called Salem."

"Salem," Abigail said out loud, "dost have a happy sound to it." She smiled at the Goodwife.

"I believe I shall go to Salem as well."

Epilogue

Orla watched the *Temperance Duty* disappear into the horizon.

She left the pier broken-hearted, and shook her head at how fast their lives had gone from peaceful and fulfilling to chaotic and destitute.

She had not thought past the time of assisting Abigail to escape a sure death. What would happen now?

Orla fingered her few remaining coins and hoped she could scratch out a new living as a healer. However, she was concerned, as Orla was now seen as an old woman, and establishing herself in a new community would be difficult.

Her mind cruelly flashed back on memories of herself and Abraham, sitting by the fire dreaming of days when grandchildren played at their feet, and they would spend their last days together.

Old wounds opened up, flooding Orla with new tears.

She felt so alone.

Walking up the hill towards the town centre, Orla noticed an Apothecary. It had been many years since she had frequented one, but remembering that she had given all of her herbs to Abigail, she decided to have a look.

The door creaked open, and the familiar scent of dried herbs, decoctions and other remedies brought a feeling of contentment. This was her world.

She noted a Goodwife at the counter pointing towards jars of herbal simples. Orla's eye was caught by the movement of a tall, hunched figure. His hair was white and he walked slowly with a shuffle. Without turning to the person at the counter, he said, "Apologies, Goodwife, but that simple has not been acquired this season," and he turned around and met Orla's gaze.

Her breath caught. She would recognise that melodious voice anywhere, and the deep sweetness of those brown eyes.

"Orla?" his voice quivered, and he lost a step.

Her breath caught. "Abraham…yes, 'tis I, your love and your rising sun!" She stumbled towards him.

And her heart was alive again.

CPSIA information can be obtained
at www.ICGtesting.com
Printed in the USA
LVHW081618300621
691572LV00008B/391